Praise for *What Grows i*

"A surreal and deftly crafted debut. Evans
and family through impossible forests, ma
character and truth in unsettling yet deeply satisfying ways.
Though readers might invoke writers such as Paul Tremblay and
Kelly Link (and perhaps even Joe Hill), Evans carves out a patch of
cursed soil all her own. This is the rare book that crawled under
my skin so deep that I wanted to re-read it again to see what I had
missed in the dream state Evans conjured."
    –Sequoia Nagamatsu, author of *How High We Go in the Dark*

"At once suspenseful and tender, *What Grows in the Dark* joins
the ranks of *Yellowjackets* as a queer horror masterpiece. It is so
many things: a spooky page-turner, an unflinching examination
of trauma, and a moving and brilliant exploration of all the things
that possess us and keep us trapped in the past–guilt, shame,
failure, and monsters, both real and of our own making. This is a
surprising, haunting, and necessary book."
    –Marisa Crane, author of *I Keep My Exoskeletons to Myself*

"Through mounting dread, with every turn of the page,
What Grows in the Dark explores–terrifyingly so–the notions of
family, indebtedness, and how the past never really lets us go."
    –Keith Rosson, author of *Fever House*

"Jaq Evans offers you a trip back home to unravel the mysteries
of a traumatic but half-forgotten past.... A smart, absorbing debut
novel with memorable characters and much to say about remorse,
friendship and sacrifice."
    –Christi Nogle, Bram Stoker Award-winning author of *Beulah*

"Atmospheric and haunting, *What Grows in the Dark* gripped me
from its first pages. The chilling imagery has stayed with me, but
so have the intricately crafted characters. It was hard to close
this book and part with Brigit and her found family. I could have
followed them forever."
    –Cole Nagamatsu, author of *We Were Restless Things*

"Jaq Evans's dazzling exploration of grief, identity, and the ties that
bind is a powerful and unflinching journey into the hidden corners
of the human heart. Compulsively readable and unfurling with the
seductive beauty of a night-blooming flower, *What Grows in the
Dark* is a thrill ride of a debut."
    –Robert Levy, author of *The Glittering World*

WHAT GROWS IN THE DARK

IN THE

DARK

JAQ EVANS

mira

Recycling programs
for this product may
not exist in your area.

ISBN-13: 978-0-7783-6968-4

What Grows in the Dark

Mira
22 Adelaide St. West, 41st Floor
Toronto, Ontario M5H 4E3, Canada
BookClubbish.com

Printed in U.S.A.

For my grandparents, who would probably not love this book,
but do love that I wrote it–and for everyone else
who's helped me keep going.

1: BRIGIT

Connecticut
October 2019
An Attic

Brigit Weylan slid her fingers across the vintage tape recorder in her lap, the plastic warm as living skin.

"Are you picking anything up?" Ian asked, snaking a hand beneath the camera on his shoulder to massage his trapezius. He caught her watching and she cut her eyes away, thumbed off her mic.

"Nothing but your breathing."

"It's ambience. And we're stalling because…"

She shifted on the pine floor. Pinkish clouds of insulation erupted from the walls on either side, and the ceiling sloped aggressively. It was a delicate maneuver to uncross and stretch out her legs in this tight space, but her foot was at risk of falling asleep. Brigit switched her mic back on.

"Sorry for the technical difficulties. We're getting a little interference, which is actually a good sign—"

At the far end of the attic, a cardboard box fell off its stack. Papers spilled across the plywood in a plume of dust that brought the moldering scent of dried mouse droppings. Ian coughed but kept the camera level. In the living room downstairs, the baby goth who'd hired them would have a perfect view.

"Hello?" Brigit asked calmly, holding in her own cough as her throat burned. "Logan, is that you?"

Logan Messer, struck down by a heart attack in 1998. Craggy of face and black of eye, he'd glared up from the obituary they'd found in the Woodbridge library like a nineteenth-century oil magnate. Definitely the most likely of several spirits that could be haunting Haletown House. At least, that's what Brigit and Ian had told its newest occupant.

A gust of wind ruffled the scattered papers in the corner, although the attic had no windows and the rest of the air sat thick and claustrophobic. Dust motes swirled through the wedges of light cast by the single hanging bulb. Brigit pushed her short hair back from her forehead and presented Ian's camera with an unobstructed slice of profile.

"Logan, my name is Brigit Weylan. My sister and I are here to help you find peace." She took a moment to steady her voice. "Is Emma with you now?"

From the corner came a sharp rap like knuckles on wood. At the same time Ian strangled another cough in the crook of his arm, nearly drowning out the knock. Brigit kept the tension from her face by digging her fingertips into her thighs. A small black hole had opened in her chest where her sister's name had passed.

"I know you don't want to leave, but I promise you'll be happier once you do. All you need to do is take Emma's hand and you'll be free."

The knocking came again, louder. Brigit had expected an echo, but the air seemed to catch the sound. The rest of the house was so chilly, all its warmth trapped up here like breath.

Whatever mice had left those droppings probably suffocated. Little mummies in the walls.

"Brigit," Ian murmured. "Can you see them?"

"I can't see anything." She licked her lips. Her tongue felt dry, chalky with dust. "But Logan is here. I can feel him in the room with us. I may need to move—don't lose me." Brigit raised her voice. "Emma, I'm with you. Let me help. Let me give you strength."

She stretched her hand toward the corner. The knocking was a drumbeat now, even faster than her pulse. Slowly, Brigit shifted to her knees and readied herself to crawl toward that wedge of darkness—and the drumming stopped. Ian let out his breath in a quiet whoosh. Brigit exhaled too, long and slow. Then she turned to face the camera and smiled.

"It's done," she told Haletown House's youngest resident. "This house is clean."

The boy who'd paid for their services was waiting on the couch when Brigit and Ian climbed down from the attic. Brigit went first, Ian following with the camera bag now stuffed with their equipment: the laptop and its associated Bluetooth speaker, the miniature fan she'd hidden underneath the boxes, the fishing line trap in the corner. There were a few other props around the outside of the house—such as the rotten eggs in the upstairs gutter, which had been carefully planted in an early-morning excursion that had nearly put Ian in the hospital—but those were all biodegradable and couldn't be traced back to them.

In and out, that was the modus. They were surgeons like that, implanting a psychic placebo effect. Honestly, most of these people? They just wanted to feel believed. The rest wanted to see themselves on YouTube.

Brigit hadn't needed that moral reassurance when she finally agreed to Ian's pitch for the series a year ago, but there was something about this kid today. A familiar sloppiness to the liner drawn below his pale blue eyes. He asked, "You think the old man's really gone?"

"I hope so," she said. Ian watched her from the doorway to the living room. Brigit could feel it on her neck as she dropped into a plush armchair. "You've got our contact info if he isn't."

The boy shrugged. "Guess I'll be on the show either way."

"Technically we need the waiver signed by someone over eighteen," Ian put in. The kid looked at him while Brigit looked at the kid. Dyed black hair, chapped lips. His sneakers weren't actually black, just Sharpied to a purplish gray. She sat forward.

"You'll be on the show. Your birthday's what, next year? This wouldn't go online for a few months anyway. We can hold the episode."

Why had she said that? It didn't matter how old he was. Their first season hadn't gotten picked up despite all attempts to woo a real television network, and neither would the second. Ian was fooling himself if he thought this thing was going to happen for real.

The kid smiled, and his eyeliner cracked. Discomfort fisted in Brigit's chest. "Cool," he said. "Thanks."

"I do need something in exchange. If things keep happening around here, stuff only you can hear, smell, whatever? Tell your parents. Call us too, but you have to tell your folks."

"Why? They'd lose their minds if they knew about this."

"Because you're a minor, and this isn't exactly a hard science. If it turns out I screwed up in there and it comes back on you, I need to know you've got someone in this house who can get you out."

Or if he was in real trouble, the kind that could hit kids at around his age, that he would confide in someone other than a fake psychic out to pocket his summer cash. It was a moment of weakness, wanting this promise she'd never be able to confirm, but Brigit couldn't stop herself.

The kid chewed at the inside of his lip. Something turned behind his eyes, a decision being weighed as Brigit held her ground. Then he grimaced. "What if I lied to you just now?"

"About what?"

"They wouldn't lose their minds. They wouldn't care at all," he said. "My dad doesn't even live here. The house was a bribe to keep my mom from making his life more difficult, and she hates that she took it, so she just works all the time. I tried telling her before, about the old man, and she said I needed more friends. That was *before* the wine."

The spike of decade-old commiseration at this was so sharp and startling that Brigit almost laughed. Behind the kid, Ian looked faintly stricken.

"Got it," she said briskly, and relief eased the kid's shoulders. "How about a neighbor? Someone at school?"

"Ms. Brower, maybe. My English teacher?"

"Classic choice." Brigit calibrated a wry smile and won half of one in return. "Okay. More weird stuff goes down, you tell Ms. Brower and then you call me. Deal?" She stretched her hand across the coffee table.

The kid hesitated. Behind her, Ian's breathing was louder than anything else. Then a slim, chilly hand smacked into hers, and for a moment, Brigit wasn't in this stranger's living room at all. She was in the woods, the Dell, in the cold dark night, her sister's icy fingers clamped around her own.

You want to be the wild child, Wild Child?

"Deal," said the kid. Brigit didn't blink. The room came back to her, his grub-white face, cold palm against her own. Vanilla candles on the mantel. Nothing of Emma or their game but the bitter tinge of earth beneath her tongue.

★ ★ ★

"Cheers," Ian said thirty minutes later. They clinked pints of beer over a table featuring a menu permanently sealed beneath a layer of gluey resin. "To a job well done."

"I'm so proud."

"I don't love lying to a teenager, but I do love taking money from his douchebag parents behind their backs."

"Mmm," Brigit agreed, though what she wanted to say was, *You don't have to sell it to me.* If Ian needed to sell it to himself, the least she could do was let him.

"We should be good on gas and board for another week or so. Want to drop down to Florida and see the gators? It could make for some cool B-roll."

Brigit picked at a scab of ketchup that had hardened near her coaster. She wondered if he could smell it on her, the pit in her chest, but no, of course not. That wasn't the world in which Ian lived. She took a drink. "Florida's never been at the top of my list."

"Really? I figured you'd be all over the Everglades. They have airboat tours and stuff."

"Please. Like you would risk that fancy camera in a swamp."

She'd meant to say it flippantly, but her tone fell flat. Ian's smile faltered, and guilt squeezed her ribs. He'd only been trying to change the subject. Get her to engage. Brigit swiped a fry from his plate and forced lightness into her voice. "What about the Northeast? They've got islands, evergreens, ambience for days. Imagine the savings on mood lighting alone."

She managed to keep the conversation rolling for the rest of the meal and the drive back to their motel, but by the time they pulled into the parking lot Brigit was ready to drop face-first into bed. That cold, clammy hand on hers—the kid's, not the kid's, the kid's—wouldn't quite leave her mind.

Just as Brigit was about to close herself into the room across from Ian's, he clapped one palm on his door and swiveled back toward her. His black hair curled across his forehead, sprinkled with attic fiber she hadn't noticed in the bar.

"I'm going to grab some water," he said. "Want anything?"

"I'm good." She needed a shower. They both did.

"They've got almond Snickers. My treat?"

Brigit waved him off and ducked inside her room before her smile grew too forced. She brushed her teeth in the shower, then gargled mouthwash for good measure. It tasted like rubbing alcohol garnished with spearmint, and was almost strong enough to sear away the taste of dirt.

No dreams that night, or none she could remember. Just darkness and the wind outside, thin glass letting in the cold. Brigit woke after dawn in a tangle of blankets, one pale thigh rashed with gooseflesh, but her mood had improved and she wanted waffles. There was a strong chance Ian had already eaten; maybe she could win him over with the promise of some scenic roadside diner. Brigit went for her phone, hopping one-legged into her jeans, and her appetite bled out.

A single missed call stared up from the otherwise empty notifications screen. No message. Brigit didn't recognize the number, but she didn't need to. The area code was enough.

Brigit waited to return the call from her hometown until after she had dressed, brushed her teeth, and flossed for the first time in several weeks. She considered not calling back at all, but whoever it was might try her again while she was trapped in the car with Ian.

The obvious solution was to block the number and pretend she'd never seen it. Except when she flumped onto her mattress and held her thumb above the red Block Caller button, she couldn't bring herself to touch the screen. Nobody important still lived in Ellis Creek. Who would have her number?

Maybe this was for some kind of retrospective, an article for the local paper. Interest did seem to rise and fall like a reliable crop. Brigit's mother might have sold her remaining child's contact information for a little sympathy.

Brigit groaned aloud. The only thing worse than knowing was not knowing, and if she didn't do something soon, Ian would come looking for her. Probably armed with coffee and a disgusting amount of cheer. She pressed the phone against her ear.

It rang once, twice. Above her, cracks spiderwebbed across the pocked white ceiling where the paint had gone a sickly yellow. One of the cracks looked like something alive, a creature from Emma's stories, and Brigit was tracing its misshapen spine when a low female voice picked up the line.

"Brigit? Brigit Weylan?"

Startled to hear her first name on a stranger's tongue, Brigit didn't answer right away. The caller inhaled one audible breath before continuing.

"This is Alicia Nguyen. I was a friend of your sister's." Good voice. Unfamiliar but striking, both smoky and reserved. The name rang no bells either, although that wasn't saying much. Most of the people Emma had brought around the house had faded into blurry amalgamations of features, laughter, snippets of overheard conversation.

"Ah," Brigit said, racking her brain for a distinct memory of someone named Alicia.

"Sorry to call so early. I hope I didn't wake you."

Wake you. The words jarred something loose, a distant piece of information that slipped and slid until suddenly Brigit had it: Emma sneaking back to the house after midnight, not alone, a confusing rush of feet and hushed giggles. Creaking up the stairs, past Brigit's room, pausing at the opened door to peer inside and whisper, "Sorry, B! Alicia's the loudest human in the world." Behind her another girl, dark and slender, one hand on Emma's waist. This girl murmured in a low, hoarse voice, "I hope we didn't wake you." Both of them smiling but not really at Brigit, only at each other, like Brigit could have been anyone or no one at all.

That had been…the summer before Emma's death. Must have been, because Emma had only gotten her license that final July, and her newfound freedom of movement had made her bold. Brigit thought she'd seen Alicia a few times after that night, but she and Emma must not have lasted beyond puppy love. Now that Brigit could picture the girl she'd been, she was pretty sure Alicia hadn't even come to the funeral.

"I hear you're a spiritualist now," adult Alicia said. "If that's the right term."

"Who told you that?"

"I'm still in Ellis Creek. Word gets around."

"I didn't know anybody back home was keeping tabs on me."

"We have a lot of time for gossip. If it's true, I have a job for you. It's local."

Brigit rolled onto her stomach. She was curious, sure, but the rest of her was already starting to withdraw. There was a sweet spot for the jobs she and Ian would take, and anything that necessitated a 5:00 a.m. phone call to someone you think is psychic did not slot in.

Sorry, B.

"What's going on?" Brigit asked, tracing the argyle ridges of her duvet.

I hope we didn't—

"It's sensitive. I don't think I can get into it on the phone. But I can pay you for your time if you'll come to Ellis Creek and hear me out in person."

Rejection climbed up Brigit's throat, and she sank her teeth into her tongue to hold it back. Her heart was fucked up. She could feel it knocking at her ribs, trying to get out. *Sensitive.* Few situations were sensitive enough to drive someone to make this kind of call but refuse to discuss any details over the phone.

"I don't get involved with wrongful death," Brigit said. "That's not negotiable. I'm sorry you've wasted your time."

"There is no death. Not yet."

"Not yet?"

"Come to Ellis Creek. Let me tell you what's going on. If you don't want to take the job once you've got the full story, I'll drop it and delete your number."

This persistence. Brigit wasn't sure what to make of it. On the one hand, she didn't want to know why anyone would make that offer to the kid sibling of a dead girlfriend. On the other hand…

"A hundred dollars for the consultation." Her senses sharpened, nostrils flaring with the smell of rug cleaner. "After that it's sixty an hour each for my partner and I."

"You work with a partner?"

"Is that a problem?"

A brief hesitation. Interesting. "No. A hundred dollars each for the meeting, and one twenty an hour after that. We'll call it a thousand dollars base fee, even if it takes less time for you to resolve. How soon can you be here?"

It was Brigit's turn to pause. Two hundred dollars just to talk? A thousand dollars no matter how long it took them to pull off the scene? The curiosity clamped down on her nape and gave her a little shake. "This job. It's not dangerous, is it? I won't put myself or my partner at risk, friend of the family or not."

"The only dangers are ones I'd imagine you're familiar with in your line of work." Brigit couldn't tell if she'd heard a sneer hiding somewhere underneath those words, or if she'd only wanted to hear it. "And remember," Alicia continued, "all I'm asking for is a conversation in person. Then you'll understand why it had to be this way."

A conversation in person. In the town where she'd spent the first eighteen years of her life and not a minute more. But five hundred dollars equaled two months of student loan payments for the film studies degree she'd never finished, and while Brigit had picked up a couple under-the-table barista shifts between their last few gigs—bless Starbucks' total commitment to efficiency—she wouldn't mind skipping that hustle while Ian sourced their next job. And he would get a major kick out of seeing her home turf. Southern temperatures could be nice, too, with winter clawing at the door.

Liar, a quiet voice scoffed. *You don't care about any of that.*

Pain stung her hand. Brigit unstuck the corner of her forefinger nail from her thumb. She hadn't even realized she was digging.

"Brigit? Are you there?"

She inspected the nail. No blood. Her heart pounded, dread and something wilder rising in her chest. No death. Not yet. Just a woman who'd loved Emma once. Or at the very least, one who could say her name and picture a living person, a girl she had touched. How long had it been since Brigit had seen that wound on someone else?

And that kid yesterday with his pathetic shoes and cracked eyeliner, his insistence that a ghost was keeping him awake. That he could pay them, that he wanted to pay them because he'd seen the show and he loved the hook, the drama of the living sibling and the dead one. Talking to him had been like a vise closing around her heart, and god, she hated that. Her insides were her own. Nobody else should be able to touch them with their fish-belly fingers and needy eyes, or their expectant voices on the phone. She couldn't be manipulated so easily, or if she could, it would be her own goddamn doing.

Besides, Ellis Creek was just a town. Sad things happened everywhere. Far worse things than one dead teenager. If anything, going back now would prove to Brigit that was true, and maybe she needed a little proof. A little proof with a fat check.

Closer. Still bullshit. But closer.

Once she'd said her farewells and hung up the phone, Brigit placed her forefinger nail into the shallow groove above the joint of her thumb. Pressed down until her breath caught. Then she went to tell Ian they were heading south after all.

INTERLUDE: 2003

Nelson County Police Department
Supplemental/Continuation Report

1. Date/Time Received: 10/20/2003 / 23:17
2. Page: 1 of 1
3. Supplemental [X] Continuation [ ]
4. Station Complaint No. 06-55747
5. Offense/Incident: Attempted arson (third degree)
6. Victim/Complainant: Sophia Mulroy
7. Address: 717 Russet Road

The following is a transcription of the report of an alleged arson attempt on the Ellis Creek Ruritan and outlying properties on 20 October 2003.

Dispatch: (23:17:29) Ellis Creek Dispatch, what is your emergency?

Caller: (23:17:34) Yes, hi, we're doing a lock-in at the Ruritan on 20 and a girl is trying to set the Dell on fire.

Dispatch: (23:17:46) Is there a fire now?

Caller: (23:17:51) [Heavy breathing] Uh...

Dispatch: (23:18:03) Ma'am?

Caller: (23:18:06) She's—wait. Emma? Emma, is that— Boys! Get back inside! Listen, the cops are on their way. You don't want to do that.

Unidentified Female #1: (23:18:08) [Laughter] Trust me on this.

Caller: (23:18:10) What's on your face? What— Hey, stay back from her. I'm on the phone with the police right now!

Unidentified Female #2: (23:18:12) Stop it! Please stop it!

Unidentified Female #1: (23:18:14) Fuck you. Fuck you for coming after me.

Caller: (23:18:16) Send someone. Now!

Dispatch: (23:18:17) Ma'am, please stay on the line. Ma'am. Hello?

[Caller hangs up]

2: IAN

Elkton, Maryland, was the kind of town that boasted multiple nature preserves also named after elk. It was probably full of quaint cafés filled with creepy family artifacts, or so Ian Perez imagined. This truck stop was all right too.

"I don't know why we haven't done Virginia before," he said as they stood in line for sandwiches. "We should do a whole pre and post for Ellis Creek. We need a better intro video for you anyway, for promotion."

At least the morning showers had cleared up, leaving blue skies and petrichor from the freshly laid interstate. There it was, the bright side of a truck stop lunch. Just like he'd found the bright side of their visiting Brigit's hometown with neither warning nor explanation. Yet she remained quiet as they found a rickety picnic table and tucked into their food.

"What about local legends?" Ian offered, swirling his lemonade to dislodge the raft of ice. "Any folklore I should google? You guys are near the mountains—you've got to have a regional Sasquatch."

"None that I can think of," Brigit said. Her attention flicked to a pigeon as it edged closer from the trash cans, and Ian wished for his camera. He'd get the light glancing off her cropped hair, turning it a thousand shades of honey and amber, and that tiny furrow between her brows as she watched the pigeon sidle closer—but she wasn't watching the pigeon. Her hazel eyes were blank, unfocused. Like she wasn't here at all.

An eighteen-wheeler pulled in behind their table with a squeal of metal and exhaust. Brigit's gaze returned to Ian, and her lips quirked. "You've got ketchup."

He swiped at the side of his mouth. "All right," Ian said. "Guess we should hit the road. Another five hours to go. I already want a nap."

Usually that would have been a glaringly unsubtle hint. Brigit might have knocked him with her elbow before holding out her hand for the keys. Not today. She only nodded, and was already waiting at the car by the time he gave up looking for a recycling can.

Virginia brought rush hour. It took them almost fifty minutes to get through the deadfall of Washington. Eventually, though, the scenery on either side of the road changed from concrete and glass to pocket neighborhoods so well-groomed Ian could practically smell the grass cuttings and the sweat of the men who looked like him, strangers who would arrive at dawn in their dirt-encrusted trucks and who, once the heat of the day had passed, would disappear once more. Men his father called *your ma's cousins*.

"So this is NoVa?" Ian asked over the low thrum of indie rock. "Lives down to expectations."

Brigit didn't reply. Ian glanced over; she had her head against the window, eyes closed. Their empty plastic cups sat in her lap, jouncing slightly with the rhythm of the road. Ian turned the radio off and focused on the taillights ahead.

It wasn't unlike Brigit to make seemingly snap decisions that impacted other people—the midnight break-in of 2013

WHAT GROWS IN THE DARK   23

came to mind, when she'd dragged him out of his college apartment in order to attend a secret rave—but she generally followed up with a reason. That time, their famously strict film professor was in attendance, and both of them got better grades than they deserved on the final. Ian tried not to let her evasiveness now annoy him. At least not while she was asleep and couldn't defend herself.

As late afternoon blurred into evening, Ian's map app directed him off the interstate. A series of smaller roads snaked toward the Blue Ridge Mountains, though autumn had turned them against their name. Furious sheets of red and orange swept down toward the lowlands like fire.

Brigit woke around the time Ian's ears popped. "Where are we?" she asked on a yawn.

"Last sign I saw was for Montebello." Ian tapped his phone in its dashboard holster, lighting up the map and Brigit's face. It wasn't black outside, not yet, but they had wended their way so deep into the mountains that blanketed slopes blocked out the sunset. The road was a curl of iron, a needle threading this massive tapestry together, and their car was a tiny, lonesome insect on that needle.

"We'll be there soon," Brigit said, her voice raspy. Ian couldn't tell if she sounded relieved or resigned or just tired. "Sorry I slept so long."

"I had these pretty hills for company."

"Mountains."

"That's cute." Ian switched the radio back on, filling the car with static.

"Yeah," Brigit said, "our hills block signal."

"I'll give them points for effort." Ian reached for the radio again, then nearly ran them off the road as a car with its brights on careened around the curve. "Shit!"

Ian corrected back into his lane, heart hammering against

his ribs. There was no shoulder on this road, only a wall of what could have been granite or limestone or shale; he couldn't tell—he wasn't good at rocks—and it didn't goddamn matter, did it? But Ian couldn't stop the names from running through his head like images in a stop-action film.

"Hey," Brigit said, possibly not for the first time. "We're okay. Slow down more if you want, turn the hazards on. It's all right."

Her hand hovered over his arm. He could feel the heat from her palm, or maybe just the brush of skin on fine hairs. Ian swallowed. Thankfully no cars were behind them, no one to honk or flash their brights as he cut his speed from forty to twenty-five. Breathed.

"Want to pull over?"

"Nope." Ian eased back up to the speed limit. Brigit removed her hand.

For a few long minutes, there was only low static above the air rushing past the windows like dark water. Then they came around a curve and several pressures released at once: Ian's ears popped again, the radio hissed into coherence, and Brigit let out a hitched sigh. Off to their left, framed by the ancient black lines of the mountaintops, glimmered a perfect spoonful of lights.

His phone put Ellis Creek at fifteen minutes away, but the darkness and Ian's unsettled pulse cast an illusory quality over the valley. As if when they finally made it out of the mountains, they'd find nothing but a canvas wall.

Ian cleared his throat. "I just put in the town for the destination, so you'll have to point me to wherever we're staying."

Brigit directed him off the mountain highway and onto a four-lane road that quickly went from abyssal to lit with streetlamps and the neon glow of gas stations. Cars began to bunch up at intersections, clusters of people appeared on the sidewalks, and soon the speed limit dropped below thirty.

"Was that you?" Ian asked at a red light, nodding past Brigit toward three kids climbing on a copper sculpture of a triceratops beside a small park.

She smiled and tapped her knuckles on the window. "I'll have you know Steggy and I were brilliant military tacticians in our day."

"Steggy?"

"I don't know why we called it that. Emma used to help me get on top." Brigit huffed a laugh. "I remember sending her on recon missions to the ice-cream shop on Mill Street. It was easier then. That whole strip mall was trees."

Brigit lapsed into contemplative silence, and Ian risked a glance. She had her eyes on the triceratops too, back of her hand against the glass, scraping at her thumb with her forefinger nail. A bright bead of blood seeped into the grooves of her knuckle. The light turned green. Ian returned his attention to the road.

They wound up at a Super 8 motel a mile or so north of downtown Ellis Creek, where the white man behind the counter eyed them coolly before handing out room keys. Once they'd deposited their things, Ian excused himself to the bathroom while Brigit fiddled with her phone on his bed. He washed his face with complimentary soap that smelled both floral and capable of disinfecting a wound. Summer lingered in the darker-than-usual brown of his skin, as the clerk downstairs had noticed. When Brigit asked for separate rooms, had the man's shoulders eased a fraction?

"Don't do that," Ian whispered to the mirror.

"You hungry?" Brigit called through the bathroom door.

"Starving!"

"Well, hurry up. My favorite dumpling place is open for

fifteen more minutes. Dinner's on me for sleeping the whole way here."

He gave his reflection one last stern glance, then headed out to enjoy the cheerful side of Brigit's nostalgia.

As usual, Ian woke with the sun. He cracked his back—the Super 8 mattress had done what it could—and flopped back down, blocking out the light with a groan. Brigit wouldn't wake for at least another hour.

Except no. This could be a good thing. A chance to get a feel for Ellis Creek without her directing his focus. Being here was an opportunity to add depth and backstory, to strengthen emotional bonds with their viewers. This could be what finally got them a streaming contract, made the series something Ian could keep.

He dressed in his usual nondescript outfit. Ian felt best in grays and blacks, less visible. His father had always hated that impulse. Found it weak. But his father had a Scottish face to match his Scottish name. Armed with his favorite lightweight camera, a Canon XF-100 with high definition and a grip he'd rewound in soft faux leather, Ian set out into the cool morning air.

Ellis Creek today was all crisp leaves and roasting coffee beans. Ian followed the lure of caffeine to a small café at the end of the block, filming the short walk past historically designated benches and flower-lined sidewalks. He panned up toward the coffee shop's entrance and nearly smashed his lens into someone's elbow. A dark-haired man about Ian's age dodged the impact, barely saving a stack of papers from cascading into the street.

"Whoops, sorry," Ian said.

"No worries." The man gave him a tight smile. He slapped

a hand on the curling poster he'd been gluing to the wall, hiked the rest beneath his free arm, and strode away.

Ian scanned the poster through his viewfinder. A white teenager peered out from beneath a bolded *MISSING* headline, his handsome features grainy, the photo clearly ripped from social media. Ian zoomed in on the boy's blurry eyes, his nape tingling with a mean but unmistakable thrill: the ambience practically crafted itself. He turned off the camera and shouldered it, feeling vaguely unclean, then entered the coffee shop and joined the line of patrons. Tacked to the message board above the cream station was an identical *MISSING* poster. A few more faded faces peeked out from older posters pinned beneath tutoring and pet care ads, but the line moved quickly past them all.

"Making a movie?" asked the barista when Ian reached her, a young Black woman with a cloud of hair held back from her face by a black-and-yellow bandana.

"A show. Don't worry, I'm not filming now." Ian nodded toward the fresh poster as she rang up his drip coffee. "What's his story?"

The barista rolled her eyes conspiratorially. "I guess someone thinks he's in trouble. But my sister has dance class with his girlfriend, and my god, the drama that girl causes. I'd bet you a million dollars they're clubbing in Myrtle Beach. Do I know your show?"

"Not yet," Ian said. "And no promises you ever will. But if you do catch us streaming someday, remember me as optimistic."

"Trust me, any episode you air will become part of our local lore. Assuming you manage to leave." She smiled and slid his to-go cup across the counter. "Ellis Creek is sticky that way."

"Not for him," Ian said, glancing again at the missing boy. The barista's smile slipped.

"Yeah, well. Some of us have more ways out than others."

Part of him wanted to ask her to repeat this exchange on camera, but that was rude, would take coaching, and there were people behind him—and of course, Ian still had no idea what else he should ask locals about. He fought off a hint of irritation as he left the café, focusing instead on how different Ellis Creek felt by day. The low bridge that had crossed a void by night was now a charming arch over a brown and glittery creek. Birds twittered from dogwoods not yet entirely gone to gold. As Ian started filming, he tried to imagine Brigit as a child, playing here. Running ahead of her parents on this same sidewalk, racing her sister to the dinosaur sculpture a few blocks down the road.

The images shifted, invaded by memories he preferred not to touch: there'd been a similar type of sculpture at Ian's elementary school. A plastic lion. His chest constricted as he recalled clambering up its side while a new nun addressed him in Spanish. He hadn't even realized she was speaking to him until she yelled his name.

A harsh laugh snapped Ian back to the present. His lens drifted up to catch a pale brunette halfway down the block, a taller white woman leaning against the brick wall beside her, platinum hair woven into a braid.

"Please," the blond said loudly. Ian drifted closer. "Gabi has a whole-ass life ahead of her, and whatever shit she's stirring now, I guarantee her future is a lot brighter than ours. That girl is just fine."

"You're probably right," said the brunette. She flipped a cigarette between quick and nervous fingers. Something clenched in Ian's gut, watching her, like cramps from spoiled meat. "I just keep thinking, I was so *mean* to her. I'm not a mean person! She just wouldn't stop pushing, you know? And what if I—" Her voice cut off abruptly, and she swallowed, seemed to change tack. "What if she got sick of it, and did something stupid?"

"Still not your problem. You can't make someone else's choices." Teeth flashed in Ian's viewfinder. "As you know." The blond pushed off the wall, but froze when the brunette flinched. When she spoke again, Ian had to strain to hear. "Look, just…next time you walk into my bar, at least pretend to care about your job. If you can't do that, stay home."

A faint nod. The shorter woman dropped her cigarette and stepped on it once, the movement almost delicate; then she reconsidered, retrieved it in a rush. Ian lowered the camera as she pocketed the crumpled cigarette and started down the street. His stomach still felt strangely gnarled. Conflict hangover from the café, no doubt, intensified by guilt at capturing this unexpectedly intimate moment—but he couldn't help himself. He noted the time stamp on his phone, in case they might want to track these people down later. You did this kind of thing enough, you got a feel for when some accidental footage might turn into a narrative cornerstone.

"Hey," came a sharp voice. "Should we sign a waiver?"

Ian looked up. The taller stranger stood inches away. Her eyes were gray and hard as river stones.

"I'm so sorry," he said, his heart suddenly drumming through his solar plexus. "I didn't mean to get you in that shot. There's no audio."

Ian tilted the camera toward her as if she'd be able to tell by looking at it. The woman shifted her weight, one hand at her hip, accentuating long lines of vine tattoos that snaked from wrist to elbow.

"Right," she said. "You should know that around here, we ask permission to get up in a person's grill."

"Yeah, absolutely. My bad. Just taking in the ambience."

She snorted. "Oh, for sure. Enjoy that." Then turned on her heel and left.

Ian went the opposite direction and dropped onto a metal bench, thrums of anxiety smudging the eavesdropped conversation. That could have been very bad. Brigit would be pissed if she knew; Ian wasn't usually so sloppy in his scouting. But again, if she'd told him anything about why they were in Ellis Creek, anything at all, he'd have been able to use this hour to do some targeted research. Start building a list of people to speak with on purpose, and topical locations that could benefit from a cheerful morning frame-up. That would have been a useful way to kill time... Although, he reminded himself, Brigit's sister had died here. This place was more than a marketing opportunity.

For Ian, Emma existed in the few stories Brigit had shared about her, which were nearly identical to their client pitch. That was the shiny version. Ellis Creek contained another girl, a private Emma whom Brigit worked hard to protect, or maybe hide from. Ian understood. Frankly, he envied either. There were times he would have killed for those versions of his mother instead of what he had. Whatever had drawn Brigit back here, it must be big.

The buzz of a call against his hip bone was a welcome jolt. "Where are you?" Brigit asked when he picked up. "I knocked."

"Coffee run," Ian said, summoning lightness. "I'm pleased to report I've been in Ellis Creek for five minutes and it's already delivered on the small-town drama."

"Ah, yeah, we bottle that here." She sounded tired. "Meet back at the motel when you're done? Or I can come to you."

"No," Ian said, already turning back toward the bridge. "I'll grab breakfast. See you soon."

When he knocked on her door twenty minutes later with

coffee and a bag of pastries, Brigit opened before the second rap. The sight of her stopped his greeting in his throat. Dark circles plunged her hazel eyes even deeper in her face. One side of her hair stuck up in violent spikes while the other was pressed flat against her skull. At least that was a sign she'd slept.

Brigit grabbed the coffee and crossed to one of the double beds. Her weight creased the coverlet, which retained every tuck and line from the turn-down service between tenants. The other bed looked equally untouched. It smelled like lemon cleaner in here, as his own room did, but Ian had also contributed a wet towel over the bathroom door. Brigit hadn't even unzipped her bag. She still wore the wrinkled blue button-up and jeans of the day before.

If he'd said something as soon as she opened the door, maybe it would have been fine. Maybe she would have smiled wryly and said, *I should have known I'd sleep like shit back here after all this time.* Maybe he would have said he knew what she meant, that every time he considered going back to his hometown, he thought of bruises and dead teeth and had to swallow a panic attack.

Instead, Ian sat on the free bed and opened the pastry bag. Brigit hadn't sipped her coffee yet. She was simply sitting with it, breathing in the scent. "Croissant or Danish?" he asked, as if all of this was normal.

Brigit stretched out her hand for a pastry. An ugly scab crusted the gouge in her thumb.

"Danish, please. Eat fast. We've got a date."

3: BRIGIT

After forcing down a few bites of pastry, Brigit directed Ian onto the highway leading north. He concentrated on the road, and she concentrated on keeping her shit together. She'd spent a few years in South Carolina, dreadful summers in New York. Mountains and concrete and sparkling lakes, the Atlantic Ocean slapping beaches into dust. None of those places could hurt her like this one.

The smell of it, for one. Grass and kudzu and bark and leaves, the sunlight thick and molten, sliding down the windshield in sheets. Ian's car had an elderly ventilation system that couldn't keep the outside out. Half-delirious from lack of sleep, the coffee not yet active in her veins, Brigit was all too vulnerable to the memories this air brought back.

Sitting next to Emma in their parents' sedan, heading home after the latest in Emma's endless stream of school plays, Emma pinching her arm and pretending it hadn't been her.

Driving north for one holiday or another, Brigit now in high school and alone, rolling down the window so she couldn't hear her parents' mutual contempt.

Groomed neighborhoods quickly gave way to forest, first thin and neat, then less kempt. Houses dotted either side of the road, but fewer and fewer as it narrowed. They were following the Dell as it clawed out from the quiet valley it was named for. In another ten miles, the woods would relax into rolling green hills and, off in their permanent gloaming, the Blue Ridge Mountains—but soon they'd enter the nowhere-land where the Dell ran wild. Recognition of this stretch of road tugged at her, cold-handed, dreadful. They rounded another bend in the highway and Brigit's heart dropped.

"Shit," she said.

"What's up?" Ian asked, slowing the car as they approached the two houses that stood around thirty feet from the highway, right at the edge of the trees. Saw grass and late-blooming wildflowers had turned them into islands. A small Caterpillar excavator was parked out front like a bridge to the road.

"My dad built those," Brigit said, because she had to say something. Sickness rose up her throat and she swallowed, forcing a laugh. "We called them the Dollhouses because nobody ever lived there. There's no potable water for miles. I can't believe they haven't been torn down."

"Looks like someone's trying," Ian said, easing his foot back onto the pedal. In the side mirror, a flash of white darted behind the houses. Vertigo slammed Brigit back in time.

The crisp, rich scent of rotting leaves. Emma flanked by trees, grinning in her white puff jacket, her sharp teeth glinting in the moonlight.

You want to be the wild child, Wild Child?

Brigit shivered, blinked, refocused on the mirror. Just a birch tree nestled in oaks. That memory had come from somewhere deep, like a splinter in her brain, making her see things. But it made sense. They'd spent so much time here as children. As the houses receded in the mirror, Brigit recalled the first time she and Emma had sneaked inside. A grackle had flown down the chimney and gotten stuck in the empty living room. They'd stripped off their shirts—Emma in her plain cotton bra, Brigit naked, screaming—and used them to usher the bird through an open window. She could still see the sticks in Emma's hair, could feel the dried mud cracking against her skin as she shrieked and laughed. They'd been playing Wild Men. Brigit pressed the heel of her palm against her sternum, suddenly dizzy. She rolled down the window and tilted her face into the wind.

The café, when they found it, was tiny. Another toy dropped here by accident, infringed upon by trees. If not for a dirt-spattered Ford Focus and a stack of old tires, the place could have been deserted. Brigit paused at the front door. Something smelled like gasoline.

"Hey," Ian said beside her. "You good?"

"Just gearing up the ol' razzle-dazzle." She pinned on a smile, but he wasn't looking at her face, and Brigit followed his gaze down to the scrape on her thumb. The scab hung open like an oyster shell. Dark blood clung to the top of her nail. She sucked it clean, copper bursting on her tongue. In her peripheral vision, Ian looked away.

Inside the café was more charming than out. The tiny kitchenette at the back emitted a solid wave of butter and sugar. A young barista in a flower-print dress completed the ambience, alone save for a woman in a bright red cap who sat with her back to the door. She held a mug in one hand and a cell phone in the other. A dark angled bob sliced across her nape below the cap.

Brigit breathed in slowly, exhaled. Then she and Ian approached the woman in red.

Alicia Nguyen set down her mug as Brigit slid into the tall-backed chair across from her. Ian followed suit, placing his camcorder on the table, and for a moment all three of them were silent. Emma's old girlfriend had brown eyes, darker than Ian's, the color of freshly watered soil. Light brown skin, black hair, unpainted lips. Her gaze on Brigit was steady as a forest pond.

Another flash of memory: Emma and Alicia sharing a pizza on the front porch, trying to stick pepperonis to each other's arms. Stealing kisses in between. Regret pierced Brigit now, familiar and aching and so fucking pointless. Emma would never know her sibling was nonbinary, or—rare as romantic interest was for Brigit—that she sometimes dated women. There could have been some future where that mattered.

"Alicia? Hi." These were useless thoughts. "I'm Brigit." Mostly useless. "She/her is okay when pronouns are necessary."

"Good morning. She/her all the time." Alicia took her hand, gave it one firm shake, and smiled thinly. "What's it been? Twelve years?"

"Probably longer. You were at school when I left. This is Ian Perez."

Ian leaned across the table to shake Alicia's hand, and Brigit had the urge to yank him back, out of reach. She clenched her fingers into fists below the table.

"He/him for me. Nice to meet you," Ian said. "Bridge, you want coffee?"

"Yes, please."

"Be right back."

Both Brigit and Alicia watched him walk toward the coffee bar. Then Alicia fixed Brigit with a stare that struck her as toothy. Assessing.

"Does Ian see ghosts too?"

"He's the filmmaker. And he handles all the technical equipment. The EMF reader, that kind of thing."

Alicia took her time with a nod. "So. Brigit Weylan, all grown up and licensed to investigate the paranormal."

"Not exactly." Brigit managed an easier smile for Alicia

than the one she'd given Ian, but only just. She'd thought it would be uncomfortable to sit with someone who'd met her while Emma was alive, but that nausea was nothing compared to the real thing. "I like to be up front with my clients. This isn't formal investigatory work, and I don't have any kind of blessing from any religious leaders. No degree in parapsychology either. Just a gift I want to use to help, when I can."

"And when the beneficiary has deep pockets."

"The meeting fee paid for our travel and lodging," Brigit pointed out. "You're the one who set the price if we decide to stay. I assure you, we've worked for free in the past."

Usually this lie came easy. There was something about Alicia's posture, though, a cool confidence that fractured Brigit's own. The teenager she remembered had been shy compared to Emma's brashness, but this woman looked accustomed to outlasting others. Some of these thoughts must have played across Brigit's face because Alicia's smile took on a sharper edge.

"I'd love to hear your origin story sometime. I don't remember any ghost-busting when you lived here. But I'm glad you took my call."

Ian returned with two ceramic mugs filled to the brim, and his efforts to angle himself into his seat without spilling spared Brigit having to respond. Once situated, Ian produced a slim tape recorder from his coat pocket and set it beside the camera, followed by a sheet of paper and a pen. "We won't use this without your consent," he said. "A record of our conversations will help piece together the details of your situation, and the more Brigit knows about what's going on, the stronger the connection will be." Ian slid the waiver toward Alicia. "If you're willing to be recorded now, please sign where I've circled. We will need you on camera for the actual cleansing, so there's a second line—"

"No recordings, please." Alicia looked briefly at Ian, who remained frozen for a moment before sitting back with the pen still in his hand. Then she returned the full weight of her gaze to Brigit's face. "Do you remember Elaine Markham?" Brigit shook her head. "She was a few years older than Emma, so I suppose you might never have met her in person."

Alicia's expression seemed to harden when she said Emma's name, or maybe that was only Brigit reading into the subtle knitting of her brows. It was impossible not to take a scalpel to Alicia's every move, this stranger who owned memories of her sister that Brigit didn't share.

"She lives downtown," Alicia continued, "with her husband and their daughter. Gabrielle. I was a senior when she was born. Last week Gabrielle disappeared. So did a boy she'd been seeing, James Mulroy. They've been gone two days now."

Ian set the pen on the table beside his camera, his enthusiasm visibly diminished. Missing kids meant there was a chance they could be found—and if they turned up dead, the people who needed someone to blame would look at Brigit and Ian first. A thousand dollars wasn't nearly enough. The news should have felt like an out, but Brigit's tension only rose.

"Oh," she said, "listen. I'm sorry if you got the wrong idea about what we do, but missing people aren't really in our repertoire. If you think you have some information that might help locate those kids, you need to bring it to the police, not a psychic."

"I thought you might say that." Alicia crossed one leg over the other, revealing sturdy black boots with mud-caked treads. "The police know there's a connection between Gabrielle and James, but they don't care about the part I find most interesting. That's why I called you."

"Again—" Brigit started, already shaking her head, but Alicia cut her off.

"Gabrielle was having dreams in the weeks before she disappeared. I think those dreams are why she and James went missing. I say dreams, but it seems like only one. A recurring nightmare." She focused her gaze on Brigit, and the hairs along Brigit's forearms rose. "Starring your sister."

"I don't want any part of this," Brigit murmured, her arms folded tight across her chest. She lowered them to her sides with conscious effort. She and Ian stood by the far end of the café while Alicia Nguyen sat sipping her coffee. Brigit wasn't fooled. If she broke for the door right now, she'd bet good money that Alicia would beat her to Ian's car.

"We're not hard up," Ian said quietly. "We can leave." He glanced toward Alicia, then dropped his voice further. "Those kids probably don't even need help. I saw some missing posters this morning, but the locals seem pretty sure it's just teens being teens. What if they invented this nightmare story to throw people off?" Ian gestured at Alicia with the camcorder. "Besides, how would she even know about the dreams? Maybe she's the one making things up."

Brigit nodded but she couldn't stop a shiver that drew her arms back up. *Starring your sister.* "You're right. Though that'd be pretty fucking easy to debunk."

"Do you want to just go?"

She did. And she didn't. Despite her gulps of sugary air, Brigit tasted ash on her tongue. *Starring your sister.* She shook her head and led him back to Alicia.

"Okay," Brigit said as they retook their seats. "We're listening."

Alicia considered them for a moment, then sat forward. "This stays between us. I need to know you understand that."

Ian nodded. "Go ahead."

"Gabrielle is a party girl. James is sheltered. Therefore, the running assumption, including by local authorities, is that she lured him away and they'll be back when they run out of money. I disagree. If I'm right, what I'm about to tell you relates to an investigation that's about to become a lot more serious, and nobody knows this but me. So if it were to get out somehow, show up in the papers, I would know exactly who to blame."

"We wouldn't sell your theory to the press," Brigit said shortly. "Say what you called me here to say."

Alicia inclined her head, rested her elbows on the table with her fingers laced in front of her chin, and did as Brigit had asked.

When she finished several minutes later, there was a prolonged beat of silence. Brigit stared at Alicia, but her mind was out of reach. Brigit had slipped further down the years with every word.

White grinning teeth and the smell of dead leaves. Heart pound-pound all the way to her toes before the ready-set-go that means run.

Brigit's hip throbbed where her body weight had pressed a curve of bone into the thin carpet of the Super 8, where she'd woken that morning with one arm completely dead.

You want to be the wild child, Wild Child?

She swallowed and tasted loam.

"Well?" Alicia asked. "Can you help me or not?"

Brigit refocused her attention on the older woman's face. "No." She pushed away from the table and stood. "We can't. Ian, let's go."

Alicia let them leave without argument. Brigit registered that she wasn't getting up to follow, but mostly focused on getting outside into the cool October air. She didn't stop until she reached Ian's car, where she rested both hands on the hood, dropped her head, breathed in. Out. In again.

Footsteps approached. A shadow fell over the hood, erasing her silhouette in the metal. "You okay?" Ian asked.

"Is she coming after us?"

"No." Ian's shadow slid away as he moved around the front of the car. He rummaged for a moment before returning with an open water bottle. Brigit took it and downed half.

Slowly the panic in her chest began to settle. She turned to lean against the car, pressing the plastic against her face. Her palm told her it was cool, not cold, but it felt like ice against her flushed cheek. "Thanks," Brigit said. "I don't think I should have come here."

"Then let's go. You said the Northeast? I've got an email from Maine. A haunted inn. It sounds scenic as hell."

Dreams. Just the one. Brigit swallowed phantom grit. The café door swung open. Alicia's red hat caught the sun, burning crimson across the tarmac, and Brigit shoved off the car.

"Yeah. Yeah, okay. Maine it is."

Only once they were back on the road and heading toward Ellis Creek proper did Brigit take another swig of water and speak. "You know about my sister."

"I do."

"So…" Brigit stopped, gathered herself. It was just a story. She told stories every day. "We had this game, kind of like hide-and-seek meets tag. We called it Wild Men." Her voice faltered again, not a momentary break this time but a full stop as she recalled what Alicia had said: *Gabrielle saw a girl with blond hair stuck with twigs.* "Our parents made us wear bright colors even in the offseason, so first you needed camouflage. Dirt, sticks, things like that." *Her face so muddy it was like a mask.* "One person hides, and the Wild Man seeks." *Chas-*

ing her through the woods. "If they find you, you have to run to wherever's safe. You have five minutes to either get there, get caught, or everyone forfeits."

"What happens if you get caught?"

"You decide before each round." She smiled, reflexive. "Anything from giving up your allowance to following orders for a day. Anyway, we played that game the night Emma died. Out in the Dell. I never told anyone, after, but it was all… It was like that girl said she saw."

"That dream might not have been real."

"Ian…" Brigit trailed off as her gaze drifted across the windshield into the blurring fractal of trees. Her fingernails itched with phantom mud. Ian hesitated, seeming to measure out his words, then shifted in his seat.

"All right. So this woman knew your sister when you were playing that game. They dated, right? But she never tried to talk to you after what happened, and then you don't hear from her for over a decade. Now suddenly she calls you up with this story about nightmares that match this traumatic night from your past, one that—in theory—no one knows about but you?" He shook his head. "I don't know. Still feels weird. Those missing kids are pretty convenient."

"Yeah, well," Brigit said. "Whatever game she's playing, it can't follow us to Maine." Cold fall air filled the car through the vents, tinged with woodsmoke from some backcountry chimney. To her right, Dollhouse windows caught the sun and winked with vicious, blinding light. "In fact, let me find the fastest route."

Brigit pulled out her phone. Three numbers into her passcode, Ian shouted, jerked the wheel, and sent them careening off the road.

4: IAN

Ian stopped the car inches from a massive red oak, his head snapping forward and back. The seat belt cut a band of fire across his chest. Everything was loud, too bright—sunlight through the windshield, a mechanical ticking from somewhere beyond the dashboard. Ahead, the oak trunk broke the foreground at a strange angle. Ian couldn't remember braking. Procedural memory to the rescue: a defense mechanism he'd hoped never to need again.

A low groan cut through the ticking. Pain and panic flared down Ian's spine as he twisted toward Brigit. Her head lolled, eyes closed. Ian reached for her across the center console, but she lifted a hand to the back of her neck and said, "Ow." Brigit turned to him, grimacing. "Are you hurt?"

"Not badly," he said. Then Ian remembered the girl.

He got himself out of the car and up the grassy ditch at a pace his back did not want to support. The girl who'd lurched out of the forest lay in the center of the two-lane highway. Mud streaked her sweater and spattered her jeans from sneakers to knee. She was breathing—he could see her chest rising faintly, could hear the rasp of oxygen entering lungs.

Ian swallowed dryly. There was an odd smell in the air,

a cold, peaty scent he couldn't quite place. Carefully, heart jackknifing against his ribs, he reached out and turned her head his way. Young. Fifteen or sixteen. Tan skin, dark lashes, dark matted hair. A fresh scrape on her cheekbone, tiny bits of gravel embedded in the flesh, but other than that no blood gleamed in the sun. He'd swerved in time. So something else was wrong.

"We have to get her out of the road."

Ian started at Brigit's voice, jerking his fingers away. With a faint popping sound from her knees, Brigit sank down to her haunches beside him and gripped the girl's ankles. Ian took her armpits, and together they heaved her up between them and staggered back to the car. Once they'd lowered the kid to the grass beside his back wheels, Ian pulled out his phone to call 911.

"Hi there," he said when the responder picked up, and nearly lost his train of thought at the sheer inanity of that greeting. "I need an ambulance to… Brigit, what road is this?" She didn't answer.

"Where are you coming from, sir?"

Ian turned to find Brigit on her knees. She wasn't touching the kid, just staring down at her with one hand up to block her nostrils. Then, slowly, her gaze lifted to the forest on the other side of the road.

"Uh," Ian said. A line of tension split Brigit's brows like a fingernail pressed into her skin. "We're on whatever highway runs north, about—I don't know, five miles out of downtown? There's a café, some old houses right nearby."

"Route 20," Brigit said roughly, getting to her feet. "Sorry. It's Route 20. Tell them we're a couple miles south of the Ruritan intersection."

Once the responder confirmed an ambulance was on its way, Ian pocketed his phone and winced. He lifted the hem of his shirt. The seat belt had practically fused the waistband of his jeans with the top front arch of his hip. He could feel his pulse down there, throbbing away too close to the surface.

"You okay?" Brigit asked, leaning against his bumper.

"Yeah. I mean, no. I almost hit her." Ian joined Brigit against the car, not wanting to let the girl out of his sight but unable to stay too close to her. That smell, like compost. "She ran out of the trees and I almost fucking killed her, Bridge."

"But you didn't." She sidestepped closer to him so their shoulders almost touched. "You handled that shit like a pro. I would have put us into the tree."

He smiled, helpless to stop it entirely. Brigit hadn't dropped her gaze from the woods, but now she crossed her arms over her chest. Her knuckles brushed, then pressed, against his upper arm. Firm contact. Deliberate.

Something turned behind Ian's ribs. He wanted to put his arm around her shoulders. He wanted to take her hand and hold it hard enough to hurt. Instead he stood beside her, agonizingly focused on the warm impressions in his arm, until sirens sliced the air to ribbons.

The EMT giving him a cursory check had a nose stud shaped like a tiny silver rose. It stood out against her dark skin. Ian did his best to pour his attention into that gleam while behind them, two more EMTs lifted a stretcher into the back of the ambulance. The girl's foot slipped off and one of them caught it, placed it gently back on.

"Hey," the EMT said, and Ian refocused on the foreground. "Y'all should come with to the hospital. Get yourselves checked. They'll tell you how she is if you wait."

She looked from Ian to Brigit with an expression like pity before joining the others. The police who'd arrived with the ambulance had only spent a few minutes with them, but Ian had to swallow a shudder at the look on the EMT's face. What if they decided he *had* hit the kid? No. They couldn't. There were no impact wounds.

On the way to rescue his car from the ditch, Ian caught sight of the padded duffel buckled into the back seat and wished with sudden urgency that he'd captured the girl on film. Hell, it would have been enough to use his phone. Distracted, he nearly clipped his own foot with the door. Jitters: no good. Brigit slid into the passenger seat, and as Ian eased them back onto the road, he felt her gaze like a light touch on the side of his jaw. But when he cheated a glance, she had her head against the seat back, eyes closed, her posture stiff as his own.

"Are we going to the hospital?" Ian asked. His hands clenched in a reflexive spasm. "I think we should go to the hospital."

"Then let's go to the hospital."

"We don't have to. I'm not that banged up. Are you banged up?"

"We can go."

"They probably won't even tell us anything. I bet they have rules about that."

"Ian," Brigit said. Her hazel eyes shone like gold-veined stones in water. "It's okay. Let's go to the hospital."

The ambulance turned its siren back on. He and Brigit both jumped. It peeled around them in the direction of Ellis Creek, and Ian sank his foot onto the gas.

There was no university in Ellis Creek, no mine or other node of infrastructure large enough to justify a proper hospital. The ambulance led them to a long, low building more like a high school than a medical facility. Ian parked in the visitor lot. Climbing out hurt more than climbing in, and he and Brigit took their time crossing to the front doors. It was just as well. He hadn't been inside a hospital in seven years, but the minute they entered, he was twenty-one again.

Fluorescent lights clashed with pastel walls. The smell was a cocktail of disinfectant and artificial lavender. Recycled air sent a wave of gooseflesh down his arms, and the upper right side of his mouth throbbed. The false incisor couldn't feel pain, but his gums remembered. So did his tongue. The taste of rot.

Ian focused on breathing. He had good reason to be here. And this time, he wasn't alone. As he and Brigit filled out their paperwork from plastic chairs, Ian took particular pleasure in writing his last name, the graceful *P*, the *z*'s satisfying tail. Here was the other side of that memory: the emergency extraction was the first time he'd ever used his mother's surname on an official document, a much shakier *Perez* written less than two months after the name change went through.

They called Brigit in first. She knocked her shoulder lightly against Ian's before disappearing to the left of the nurse's station. With the waiting room to himself, he mentally cycled through the footage he'd recorded that morning. Red leaves tumbling across the bridge: keep. Platinum hair and an angry smile: discard. Although—shit. Overheard words clicked abruptly back into focus.

Gabi has a whole-ass life ahead of her, and whatever shit she's stirring now—

What if she got sick of it, and did something—

"Ian Perez?"

Ian followed the nurse into a small examination room. No more lavender in here. As the man took his vitals, a familiar antiseptic smell snuck into Ian's mouth, the little spaces between his teeth. He pushed his tongue against their backs. The acrylic incisor tasted of nothing. God, he hated hospitals.

When the nurse stepped out and an older white woman in

a doctor's coat entered, Ian did his best to hide his discomfort. By the wry smile on her face, it wasn't working.

"So," she said, glancing down at her clipboard. "You're the one who found her."

Queasy rills churned in his stomach. "Sort of." He winced as the doctor placed her hands at either side of his jaw, tilting his head gently to either side. "We were driving and she ran out of the woods. Is she going to be okay?"

She released him and peered directly into his eyes. Ian froze. "That may leave a mark, but I think we'll make do with a butterfly." Ian's bafflement must have shown on his face because the doctor smiled and touched the skin above his brow. "You've cut yourself." She lowered her hand. "Shock is a hell of a drug."

"I don't know how that happened." Ian touched his forehead and stared down at his fingers: tacky red. "What about the girl, though?"

Gabi has a whole-ass life—

"She's alive," said the doctor, retrieving a butterfly bandage and gauze. "I'm afraid that's all I can tell you."

After declining an MRI for his whiplash in favor of daily stretches—he could afford the scan, but Ian knew what Brigit would say to that offer for herself, and he didn't want either of them to be here any longer than necessary—Ian returned to the nurses' station and paid with his debit card. He would have tried to cover Brigit's bill, but she was nowhere to be seen. Nerves pounded in Ian's joints. Had she been hurt worse than him, maybe a concussion? Ian recalled how she'd kneeled by the girl, still as a captive image.

"Excuse me," he said, attempting to regain the attention of the man behind the plastic panel. "Has—"

"Hello," a soft voice interrupted Ian from behind. He turned to see a woman six or seven years his senior, with dark hair and tired, deep-set eyes. Beside her stood a man around the same age who looked equally exhausted. "Are you the driver?"

His heart tripped, but Ian nodded. The woman stepped forward and pulled him into a hug. Uncertain how to escape without causing offense, Ian circled his arms loosely around the stranger's back. He inhaled the scent of her unwashed hair as she murmured something unintelligible into his shoulder, then said it again. This time he heard "Thank you." A cliff collapsed inside his chest, and Ian's hug turned real.

After another moment they released one another, and she stepped away. "I'm Elaine Markham. Gabrielle's mom." She reached a hand back and the man took it. "This is my husband, Todd. Thank you for saving our daughter."

"I didn't save her," Ian said through the new lump in his throat. "We just…" He trailed off. Didn't hit her? Followed her here to be useless?

Gabrielle's father shook his head. "Thank you," he echoed, voice hoarse. "We knew it was bullshit, what people said. We could feel it. When she wakes up, I'll make sure she knows your name."

No, Ian wanted to say, the impulse sudden and shockingly intense. *Don't tell her. Don't tell anyone.* They hadn't meant to find anyone's daughter. They'd meant to—oh, who even cared? Ian knew how to make an old man feel supported by his dead mother. He could reassure some exhausted young parents that their kid was not, in fact, about to disappear into the television; there were problems with the wiring, that was all, and Ian could fix the cable, no charge, tips more than welcome. That was his speed, what made him feel like he'd made someone happy and earned a little cash at the same time. This…

The doors behind Gabrielle's parents swung outward, and

Brigit strode into the waiting room. Her expression stayed blank as she sidestepped the Markhams and grabbed Ian by the elbow, pulling him toward the exit. He protested, but Alicia appeared through the swinging doors behind Brigit, and Ian's voice failed him. A badge now gleamed from a chain around her neck. At her hip, a holstered gun.

She didn't try to stop them leaving, but fresh panic spiked as Ian and Brigit spilled into the parking lot. "Alicia's a cop?"

"Try the fucking lead detective."

"What did she say?"

Brigit shook her head, face grim. "I'll tell you in the car. Better yet, I'll tell you over drinks. Strong ones. Right now."

INTERLUDES: 1941, 1978, 2009

Ellis Creek Tribune
September 12, 1941

$500 REWARD!

$500 will be paid by the Nelson County Citizens' Service Club for information resulting in the safe return of ELEANOR TEMPLE, who disappeared in Ellis Creek, VA, September 9, 1941.

ONE HALF THE REWARD MONEY will be paid for information resulting in the recovery of her body. This reward expires March 9, 1942.

Description of ELEANOR TEMPLE

Age 12 (Twelve) Years. Caucasian. Blue Eyes. Long Straight Brown Hair. Wearing Black Coat, Blue Dress and White Patent Leather Shoes. Last Seen Picnicking Near Local Forest.

Ellis Creek Library Bulletin Board
September 29, 1978

MISSING
SHANA LEVITT

DATE MISSING: 9/23/78
FROM: Ellis Creek, VA
DOB: 3/2/65
AFRICAN AMERICAN FEMALE
EYES: Brown
HEIGHT: 5'2"
WEIGHT: 117
HAIR: Black

Photo is current. Shana was last seen wearing a gray hooded sweat-shirt and blue jeans, riding a black Schwinn bike. She was going to meet a friend at the Stone Ridge Ruritan at 8:00 p.m. on September 23 to discuss the annual Halloween event.

Dana Levitt, mother, states: "Shana is a smart girl, always exploring. Huge imagination. She loves nature. She loves people. She loves her family. She didn't just run away. If you know anything, if you've seen her, please help us get her home."

Contact Ellis Creek Police Department if you have seen this or any other missing child.

Facebook.com
Post in "Virginia Missing People" group
May 15, 2009

PLEASE SHARE:
HELP BRING MICHAEL PATTERSON HOME

Last seen on May 12, 2009, in Ellis Creek, VA, wearing a white shirt and blue jeans.

Age 15 / Caucasian / Brown eyes / Red hair / 5'10" / 167 pounds

Please contact his family with any information that can help us find him

(434) 555-0782

#HelpFindMichael
#MissingHikers
#DnDVA

5: BRIGIT

They stopped at the first open bar. As Brigit and Ian crossed the threshold of Tim's Tavern, silence fell as heavy as the smell of beer batter. She looked down at herself, abruptly certain there was blood on her shirt, but no. The short hair, then, and her outfit today: urban gender neutral? Suddenly it was ten years ago, the summer Brigit discovered chest binders, a crush of terror and pride as she dared people to stare—but when she lifted her gaze, normal bar sounds seeped back in: clinking dishware, a soccer game playing on the television. None of the few patrons were looking at them. Ian wasn't even standing beside her anymore. He'd found them a booth in the back and was hovering there, watching her with a faint frown pulling at the butterfly stitch above his brow.

Which she hadn't asked him about.

She'd noticed the cut by the side of the road, but his eyebrow caught the blood and it had coagulated by the time the paramedic had finished checking him over, and she'd just… forgotten.

"Is your face okay?" Brigit asked as they settled into the booth. One side of Ian's mouth tugged up. Warmth kindled at the sight, confirmation that he was all right and she still held the power to draw out that unintentional smile.

"Yes," he said. "My face is okay."

A server approached, a white brunette with a high ponytail who looked barely old enough to serve drinks. "What can I get you?"

Brigit asked for a pale ale and a whiskey, something cheap enough for her limited cash reserves but not so poisonous she couldn't drink it neat.

"Make that two," Ian said, squinting up at the girl. "Or four, I guess."

The server's greenish eyes glanced off his face, gaze skittering toward the door even as she jotted down their order. "Coming right up." She pivoted on her heel and left.

Once the girl was out of earshot, Ian raised his brows as if about to speak, then winced and lifted a hand to his forehead. "Ah." His fingertips hovered just above the bandage. "I take it back. That's going to get annoying fast."

"Just picture the scar," Brigit said, and rubbed at her eyes. She could feel a headache building. When she lowered her hands, the server was approaching with their drinks on a small round platter. Ian snagged his rocks glass just in time to save it from sliding onto the table.

"Shit," said the server, and jumped as an impatient voice called, "Lacey!"

Over Ian's head, Brigit glimpsed a woman with platinum blond hair leaning over the bar. "Order's up."

"Sorry," the server—Lacey—said. "I'll be right back for your food." She spun and hurried toward the bartender.

Ian set his elbows on the table and lowered his voice. "There's something I forgot to tell you. That girl knows Gabrielle."

"How do you know?" Brigit stopped, shook her head. "We'll come back to that."

"Right. The lead detective," he said. "Does she know what we really do?"

"Not yet, but how hard is it going to be for her to figure it out? She told me her call was off the books, so at least the rest of the cops don't know. Only, now that we found one teenager…"

"How about the other."

Brigit nodded and knocked back half her whiskey. "Do you know what kind of jail time you get for fraud? That wasn't rhetorical. I can't remember."

"Maybe it'll just be damages," Ian said. "My father would love that." She looked at him, worried by the reference, but his eyes were still on his pint, so dark in the bar's dim lighting they seemed more black than brown. Brigit thought of Alicia's obsidian gaze on her in the hospital, when she'd walked into the examination room and asked the doctor to step out. How the detective had waited, patient as a folded blade, as Brigit argued that they'd had nothing to do with Gabrielle running out of the Dell at just the right time in just the right place.

Brigit held a sip of beer on her tongue until the fizz turned into fire. Ellis Creek was starting to feel less like a town and more like a fence. Today she and Ian could stand on their tippy-toes and peer over the top, spitting distance of the world they'd driven out of the day before, but there was someone on the other side of that fence. Building it up. Walling them in.

"The funny thing is," she said without really meaning to, "I do need that money now. I didn't budget for a trip to the ER."

"I was going to cover you."

"I don't want you to cover me." This forced his gaze to hers and if there was something greedy in her, pleased by that, Brigit ignored it. "Your mom left you that money so no one else could waste it—not your dad, and not me."

"Brigit…"

"Stop." He did. They drank.

She'd wanted his attention, but Ian's soft expression made her skin itch. At least her knees still hurt where they'd bounced off the dash, and her hip ached from waking up on the floor that morning. Those pains helped a little, but no physical discomfort in the world would stop her chest feeling tiny and wrong.

"We can't help her," Brigit said.

"Alicia?"

"Gabrielle," she clarified. "Or James. Or Alicia, for that matter. I can't do anything for any of them."

Lacey returned just long enough to drop off two food menus. Ian picked one up and scanned it. "She really was missing, though," he said. "So presumably James is too. And you have to admit the timing is weird." Brigit waited him out. It didn't take long. "Should we talk about the dreams?"

She picked up her menu and read it without retaining any of the words aside from the giant **Special!!! Fries with Garlic** at the top.

"Maybe they happened. Maybe they didn't. What more is there to say?"

Bullshit, she would say if he tried that on her. *Stop deflecting.* Ian hummed a noncommittal noise, and Brigit had a sudden image of herself sweeping her glass to the floor. Could practically hear the crash. She rubbed her temples and readied herself to do better, but before she could speak, her phone buzzed with an incoming call. Pathetically grateful, Brigit checked the screen.

Everything stopped. The bar noise. The vibrating phone. Everything except the slow, sick thudding of her pulse.

She knew that number by heart. It was the first she'd ever memorized.

Dimly, from miles or galaxies away, Brigit's palm buzzed

as the phone rang again. Her thumb moved to the Accept Call button without her permission. She held the phone to her ear, her eyes locking on Ian's. He looked confused, not scared, and that helped her speak calmly. "Hello?"

"You have to come back," Emma said from their childhood landline. "You promised."

Brigit couldn't reply. Something stung at her eyes, not the tear glands but farther back, a piercing pain from all the way inside her skull.

Her sister's voice wasn't familiar like the voice of a real person you know and love. It had the quality, rather, of a commercial or a childhood cartoon. An illusion boring into Brigit's neurons like those tropical insects that tunnel through your ears to your brain.

She swallowed. Her throat was sandpaper. Everything hurt.

"Emma." Had she said the name or only thought it? Ian was frowning. Brigit couldn't look away from him, couldn't move at all. One layer of her mind focused so intensely on his face that she could count the dark freckles—the only good things his Scottish side had given him, he joked once—dusting his olive cheekbones. The rest of her knew nothing but the voice in her ear.

"What I say goes." Emma sounded thin and cold as January wind. "You promised, Wild Child."

"You—" The words cracked against her tongue, crumbling before they left her mouth. Brigit licked her lips and tried again. "Don't call me that."

No response. Another sound came over the line, something harsh, almost like static but with more substance. Like dirt being scraped across the mouthpiece, or as though the phone were being dragged along the ground. Brigit strained to hear.

"Bridge. Brigit. Who is that? What's wrong?" Ian had transitioned from worry to alarm, and this volume spike broke her focus. Without thinking, Brigit hung up, then dropped the phone like it was something dead.

"Excuse me. I'm sorry." The whiskey and beer had hit her harder than she expected. When she stood, she stumbled against the side of the booth. She pushed away, ignoring Ian's stream of questions. Dark waves threatened her periphery as Brigit strode from the tavern proper and down a short, narrow hallway marked with a neon bathroom sign. Halfway there, she struck wood with her palm; she hadn't even felt herself stagger. One breath. Two. The world brightened. Brigit leaned heavily against the door frame of a small office, the door ajar to reveal a desk stacked with paperbacks: William Gibson, J. G. Ballard. She focused on the glaring orange text that spelled out *The Dispossessed* until she could trust her feet to carry her the rest of the way down the hall.

The tavern bathroom was all graffiti and crumpled paper towels, but the toilet was clean. Automatically Brigit unzipped her pants and sat, then covered her eyes with the heels of her palms. Black and red spots overtook her vision as she pressed down. "Get your shit together. Get your shit together right now." She pulled her hands away, smearing wetness from her eyes, and clenched her fists atop her thighs.

That didn't happen. Any of it. Not the scent memory of a cold dark place that had grabbed her by the throat when she'd first leaned over Gabrielle. Not the accusatory quiet of the bar when they'd walked in. And sure as hell not the phone call from a girl sixteen years in the ground. But if it didn't happen…

There had been voices in the hallways of her high school. More in the dark of her head.

You know why she did it, right?

Why does any eighteen-year-old kill herself?

Because she was crazy. Emma was crazy and so are you.

But the dreams. The dreams. Gabrielle was connected to those woods, to Emma, to Brigit herself. And there was what she hadn't yet told Ian about her conversation with Alicia: *Something is wrong with this town*, Detective Nguyen had said in that sterile hospital hallway. *Disappearances, deaths. You know. Kids who vanish, or don't.*

At the time, Brigit had wanted to shove her into the wall and run. Now she clung to those words, nails digging into the bare meat of her thighs.

Nightmares.

Starring your sister.

There were fries and another whiskey waiting for her when Brigit returned to the booth. Her phone sat beside the drink, its screen black and locked. She took a sip. Coughed. Drew a ragged breath and pulled up her call history before the burn dissipated. The latest incoming call was from Alicia, yesterday morning.

"Fuck," Brigit said. Then again, loudly enough that the bartender shot them a wary look.

A fresh bout of tears pricked her eyes. She dashed them away with her free hand, refreshing her call list as though her family's old phone number would suddenly appear.

"Brigit," Ian said, "please. I have been freaked out over quota today. What's going on? Who was that?"

"No one. Just some asshole playing a joke." The answer came too fast, a protective reflex Brigit couldn't control. A laugh burbled up. "You know what they say about going back."

"What?"

"I think it's Thomas Wolfe? You can't go home again. Except he was talking about capitalism and Nazis, which, fair, here we are." She wasn't making any sense. She hated not making any sense. She hated everything about all of this. "Let's go," Brigit said. "You and me, right now. I would like to evacuate this fucking town."

Ian frowned. The bandage tugged at his skin. "You're really not going to tell me what happened there?"

Her lungs compressed. He was looking at her like she'd slapped him, and now Brigit wanted to do it for real. Anything to make him stop watching her like this, stop digging, stop expecting things from her while she was busy falling back through the years into a pitch-black bog. She should have broken the pint glass.

"Just did," she said.

Frustration and hurt spilled across his face. Brigit could imagine his voice going dark, that jagged tone she'd heard him use once in regard to organized religion, and once on his birthday when he reached the childhood reminiscence stage of drunkenness. She could even picture the words: *What the fuck, Brigit?*

A muscle jumped in his jaw. Then Ian pulled his wallet out and dropped a handful of bills on the table. "All right," he said, his tone giving nothing away. "Let's go back to the motel. I think we could both use a shower, and then we can order a pizza or something."

Brigit left her whiskey half-drunk and followed Ian to the car, her chest still hot but her mouth full of ash. She was being unfair, but it was impossible to stop. Food would have been smart. And yes, a shower might help. It might erase the queasy vertigo of the Dollhouses, or the stench of dark, loamy mud on that girl's jeans.

They closed doors, buckled seat belts, and pulled onto the highway in silence that felt as present as a back seat passenger. Then Ian said, "Hey."

She tensed. "Yeah?"

"I shouldn't have pushed you. This day is getting to me."

Suddenly, horribly, more tears. Brigit bit her tongue hard before answering. "You didn't push. I was an asshole. Of the two of us, I'm always the asshole."

He smiled a little. "I'm not going to argue with that."

"Listen," Brigit said over the balloon rising in her throat. "I…" *I'm scared. I don't know what's going on. I'm glad you're here.* "It's getting to me too. All of this. Sorry for being the asshole."

"Thanks. That felt very mature. Are we adults?"

"Look at us go."

The air between them lightened with a palpable shift. Five minutes later, though, when Ian turned into the parking lot of the Super 8, Brigit's stomach dropped. Waiting for them by the entrance was a bright red, dirt-spattered Ford Focus.

Inside the motel lobby, Alicia Nguyen leaned against the reception counter and chatted with the clerk. When they entered, she gave the counter a light slap and pivoted smoothly toward the door. "Brigit. Ian. I'm sure you're exhausted so I thought I'd save you a trip to the station."

"We are." It took everything Brigit had to smooth the edges from her tone. "Is there something you needed right now or can it wait? I was hoping for a shower. You know. Clean off that hospital smell."

"I'll be quick," Alicia said, her expression pleasant but implacable. "Mind if we take it out of the lobby?"

Ian shifted beside Brigit, enough to brush her elbow with his. "Sure. Come on up."

Ian led them into his motel room without apology for the open backpack spilling clothes onto the floor or the half-eaten bag of chips on the bed. It was a talent of his, this ability to come into any space for even the smallest amount of time and make it feel lived in. If they left right now, Brigit's room would require nothing of the maid service at all.

As the door clicked shut behind Detective Nguyen, Brigit and Ian formed rank against the desk. Brigit's headache hadn't dissipated, the pain a constant grinding hum since they left Tim's Tavern, but at least she'd lost all tipsiness.

"I should tell you, first of all, that this conversation is off the public record." Alicia looked from one to the other, expression serious despite the fact that she was standing awfully close to a pair of Ian's boxers. "I trust you understand what I'm saying."

"That won't be an issue," Brigit said. "We have nothing to discuss. I hope Gabrielle wakes up and tells you where she was. I hope you find James without a scratch on him, and I hope he's not the one who hurt her."

"I'll give you two."

"What?"

"Two thousand dollars," Alicia clarified. "Each." Her hands were in the pockets of her slacks, her long coat brushed back, the brown leather of her holster visible at her ribs. Brigit had never been so close to a gun. "If you help me stop this."

Four grand. She could fund another month on the road without needing to pick up any side jobs. Ian's savings would last that much longer before he was inevitably forced to give up and go back to the real world, whatever that looked like for him now. Whatever it looked like for either of them.

"Stop *what*?" Brigit asked. "What do you think is going on here?"

"Look, none of us wants another kid to get hurt. We both know Emma is part of this." Alicia reached for the doorknob. "I'll let you sleep on it. Any information you provide that leads to us finding James Mulroy, alive or otherwise, gets you paid in full. Call me tomorrow if you decide to stick around." She stepped into the hall and pulled the door halfway shut behind her, then paused without turning back. "I

missed her every day, by the way. Every day for a long time."
Then Alicia was gone.

Brigit rested her hip against the desk as Ian threw the dead
bolt, then turned and leaned against the door. He folded
his arms, an odd expression passing over his face—not quite
anger, not quite concern—and spoke before she could head
him off. "We need to talk about this."

She climbed onto the bed beside the chip bag. Stretching
out on her back with her legs dangling off the end, Brigit
reached for a pillow and placed it over her face. "Give me a
minute."

The pillowcase smelled like his shampoo, some generic
drugstore brand that evoked dish soap and lambs a-frolicking.
Her body dipped as Ian lay down next to her, a whuff of air
ghosting her cheek as he grabbed the second pillow. The
quiet that followed was anything but soothing. Ian's desire
to speak radiated off him like static electricity. Even without
seeing him, Brigit could picture the line of worry between
his brows, the quirk of his mouth as he worked to hold his
tongue. She wasn't much better. Brigit tried to focus on the
uneven hitching of the air conditioner instead of the pressure
on her ribs, the one that made her want to confide everything just to relieve it.

She could start with the phone call. That would be easi-
est to articulate. Move into the taste of earth in her mouth,
caking her tongue, these layers of sediment that built higher
the longer they stayed in Ellis Creek. Or maybe she could
tell him how she'd woken that morning fully clothed, face
pressed into the carpet, with no memory of falling asleep
at all. Hard to choose between so many exciting options.

"Okay," Ian said. "Here's how I see it." He rolled to face
her on a squeal of mattress springs. Brigit slid the pillow halfway off her face and pinned him with a single, squinting eye.

"I don't want to ask you to do anything that makes you un-comfortable," he started—slowly but gaining speed. "And of course this place does that. But we have an opportunity to try and help these people, and you, for real. I think… I think maybe we should take it."

"I don't need help," Brigit said, but it was performative. His brown eyes searched hers, open and patient, and she couldn't look away. The pressure on her chest was getting worse.

"Okay," he agreed. "You don't need help. But Gabrielle does. James does. They need actual, tangible help."

"And you think a pair of liars with a camera can give that to them?"

"We could ask around."

"The cops are asking around."

Ian eased onto his back. Brigit mirrored him. Her heart thudded, light and quick. "Sure," he said, "but how many times has that story been told? Small town, missing kids, cops no one can trust. You don't really believe there's anything supernatural going on here, do you? They're hiding something that got that girl hurt."

"Who's 'they'?"

"Alicia knows more than she's saying. I'm five hundred per-cent sure of that. The people at that bar, too, the server and the bartender. They know something about Gabrielle that's stressing them out—they just need someone to push them on it. And people *want* to tell you stuff, Bridge. Remember that kid spilling his lonely little guts out in Connecticut? Get enough people talking and maybe you could find out what's going on behind the scenes. If all this really does have some-thing to do with what happened to Emma…" He stopped, realizing, perhaps, how thin his ice had grown. She stared up at the ceiling, heat stinging at the corners of her eyes, but no tears welling high enough to fall.

Dead leaves and cold. The deep wood. Running, running, Emma's arms closing around her from behind like jaws—

You want to be the wild child, Wild Child?

Again, the memory fell away. If it was a true memory. If it wasn't just her mind stabbing itself over and over, breaking a dozen real experiences into random shards and conflating them with the night Emma died.

But Gabrielle's story. The phone call. Her sister's voice, and not from sixteen years ago—her sister's voice right now. *You have to come back. You promised.*

"What if I can't?" she asked, barely audible even to her own ears.

The air conditioner was too loud. Crumbs stuck to Brigit's forearm where she'd lain on the chips, suddenly impossible to ignore. Ian took a breath, let it out slow.

"Maybe we could just try?"

They opted for a vending machine spread after that, jerky and chips consumed mostly in silence before Ian sent her off with three of his ibuprofen. As she stepped into the hallway, he lingered in the door frame, tugging at his curls, and Brigit's heart twanged an odd note. "We'll leave tomorrow if you change your mind," Ian said. "No questions asked."

Possible responses filtered through her mind like raindrops, there and gone in an instant. Brigit raised her pill hand. "Bottoms up."

A blur of motion followed, rote movements tipping into one another: door lock, bathroom, toothbrush, clothes on the floor. Then there was only her stuttering brain and eventually silence until, hours later, something stirred her out of sleep. A shift in the air, or her shoulder protesting at being pinned too long beneath her weight, or just her lips cracking painfully.

Brigit opened her eyes with her brain still sluggish, mired in a dream of damp squirming things. Her water bottle sat on the floor beside her bed. She felt for it in the dark and chugged a few sips. Set it back down, rolled onto her back, and froze as something cool and sharp collided with her cheek. The world narrowed into that prick against her skin, the icy sweat suddenly gathering under her armpits, the hum of the air conditioner, and, above it, barely audible, the sound of breathing from her left.

Her eyes weren't adjusted. The darkness loomed, thick as tar poured down her throat as her lungs froze and her mind sped into overdrive, trying to think of how to knock away the knife—but no. Not a knife. The tip was sharp but not metal, and as Brigit lay paralyzed on her back, white lines eased into view above her face.

There was a birch tree in her room.

A single branch arced over her mattress, bony fingers indenting her cheek. Pale arrows of wood dragged toward the corner of her mouth, but it wasn't the tree that was moving. Something hid behind the birch, leaning heavily against the trunk.

Another noise then, irregular and secretive: laughter, half-swallowed. That broke her shock, and Brigit tried to brace her hands so she could shove herself upright, but her fingers wouldn't work. Her arms lay heavy and useless. All the hairs on the back of her forearms rose as a low rasp filtered up from the floor. Feet shifting on the cheap motel carpet? She couldn't turn her head, couldn't even wrench her eyes to the left so she could see—

But she didn't want to see.

She wouldn't scream. She couldn't. Her tongue lay stiff inside her mouth. The air tasted staler than it should, and peaty, like the black mud inside the Dell. Like Gabrielle had smelled. In the very leftmost corner of Brigit's field of vision, a flash of red. Crimson gloved fingers on a dappled trunk, barely visible, like four fat beads of blood seeping out from behind the birch. Pain flashed inside her skull as if some great insect had slipped its forelegs through her tear ducts to her brain, forcing her head still and her eyes wide. Gravity lurched and swooped. For a moment, the bed wasn't on the floor anymore. There was no floor. She and the tree and the thing behind the tree hung together in unstructured space as reality sloughed like dead skin. The tree couldn't be, the gloves couldn't be, and so Brigit couldn't be.

Red fingers twitched in her periphery. There came another muffled snicker, and the hand jerked out of sight.

Salt stung her sclera. One tear caught in her lashes and tickled her eye, and finally, finally reflex kicked in. Brigit blinked. When she opened her eyes, the tree—and whatever had tucked itself behind it—was gone. Brigit lay alone in the quiet motel room, left with nothing but her sweaty sheets and shuddering breaths and the rising light of dawn.

It took a few minutes, but she got herself out of bed by crouching at the edge and jumping, like she'd done as a little kid, as though over a moat. Brigit locked herself into the bathroom and turned the shower on lukewarm. Heat would fog the mirror. She needed to be able to see. Once under the spray she slicked her short hair back from her forehead, then slammed a fist against the plastic-lined wall of the shower. Pain rippled from hips to shoulder blades.

"Fuck!" Brigit slumped against the wall. Her floor-bruised thigh pressed into the tile. She bit the inside of her lower lip until her mouth became like white noise.

She couldn't hold the gloves in her mind, could not allow herself to consider them for more than fragments at a time, but the branches overhead cut deeper than her ability to block them out. Those arcing shadows reached some chilly part of her that lived below memory, a visceral sense of recognition that wasn't from fear, exactly, and that fact scared her more than red fingers on bark. *You have to come back*, her sister had demanded. Emma, or something else. Poor little dead girl, sick of being used? Something worse, playing games? Or just Brigit's own mind, finally turning on her the way Emma's had?

She'd wondered if that would happen. There had been… moments. Lapses in time. But she hadn't had an episode since high school. Her first therapist blamed puberty more than PTSD. Her second therapist explained how traumatic events caused a neurochemical shift that could impact your ability to form memories. It would pass, she'd said, and it had.

Brigit shut off the shower and dressed with her hair still wet and clammy against her temples. Then she knocked on Ian's door. When he opened it, appallingly awake for the hour, she shouldered past him. There were bees under her skin, a buzzing energy that drove her past the desk until she stood in front of the pulled drapes.

"Good morning to you too," Ian said as she flung the drapes open, needing sunlight, warmth.

"We need to talk to the friends," she said. The parking lot outside his window gleamed with early-morning rain. Cold water beaded on her collarbones.

"The friends?"

"Gabrielle's and James's friends. Whoever they were closest to. We need to talk to anyone who might know about the dreams."

6: BRIGIT

"We've been doing this for a long time, Detective. You don't need to worry about that." Ian was using his filmmaker voice, the one that mixed earnestness with a dollop of arrogance. He was better at it on the phone, when he didn't have to look people in the eye. "Thanks. I'll give you a call when we have something."

Ian hung up and turned to Brigit, gaze bright and eager.

"We have more leads."

He smiled, the crooked one that invited conspiracy, but Brigit couldn't quite make herself return it. Today she had to gain the trust of strangers. She'd have to ask pointed questions that, with Gabrielle in a coma and James still missing, would inspire both guilt and defensiveness. Normally this tightrope walk was her favorite part, but Brigit could still feel branches scraping her cheek.

"In that case," she said, "let's get breakfast. I'm starving."

"Perfect." Ian ran a hand over his chin, which would soon need a shave. "How do you feel about dive bar brunch?"

Tim's Tavern on a Saturday morning was significantly more inhabited than it had been the previous afternoon. This time

they had to wait for several minutes by the door before a har-
ried server waved them toward two bar stools, and Brigit sank
into the human noise as though it were a warm bath.

"Is Lacey working today?" she asked when the bartender
plunked a sweating water glass by her elbow and spun away to
fill a second glass for Ian. "And we would love some coffee."

"You got it," said the woman, already turning to the coffee carafe behind her after setting Ian's glass down. Brigit
watched her pour, admiring the floral tattoos that snaked
up her arms, the platinum braids piled atop her head. "And
Lacey's not exactly working, but if you're willing to wait,
maybe your buddy can talk her into a sound bite."

The bartender swung back around and placed two mugs
on the bar, finally piercing Brigit with a pale blue gaze. Her
brows knitted with recognition—and on seeing her face
clearly for the first time, Brigit's palms went cold with dis-
may. But there was nothing for it.

"Hi, Max," she said.

"Brigit. Of all the gin joints, et cetera. I can't say I ever
thought I'd see you back here."

"It wasn't high on my list," Brigit admitted. This had been
a known risk, practically an inevitability, but god, what a time
to run into someone who actually remembered her. She felt
Ian's curiosity burning into the side of her face, and swiveled a
bit to include him. "Max and I went to high school together.
Max, this is my friend Ian."

"And what *does* bring you and your camera to town?"
Max's eyes traveled past Brigit, across the bar. "You friends
of Lacey's?"

"Not exactly," Ian said. He cleared his throat, evidently
feeling the tension. "Could we grab some food menus?"

"Sure." Max unearthed a familiar pair of laminated menus
from below the bar and handed them over. "Well. If there's

one thing I remember about you," she said as Brigit accepted hers, "it's that I probably shouldn't bother asking anyway. I'll be back in a minute for your orders."

She strode off down the bar without looking back. The pit in Brigit's stomach was shrinking now that the initial shock had faded, and as she took a sip of drip coffee, it settled into a nice, manageable ball. Max had barely known her then, and she certainly didn't know her now; she'd have no reason to dig into Brigit's business beyond whatever involved her directly. This was fine.

"What was that about?" Ian asked. Brigit shrugged.

"Guess I wasn't known for my open nature in high school either. Your turn. What was up with the sound bite dig?"

"I may have stalked her a tiny bit yesterday. It was an accident."

He twisted on his stool, searching the bar in the direction Max had looked earlier, and Brigit did the same, doing her best to keep her spine aligned as she moved. She'd completely forgotten to do the stretches. There'd be time for them later.

"There," Ian said. The young woman who'd served them the afternoon before sat in a booth, perched on the lap of a man who looked to be a few years older than Brigit and Ian. She had an arm around his shoulders, her face in profile, head tossed back in laughter.

"Okay," Brigit said. "Let's get some food and keep an eye on her. If she goes on break, we can try to talk to her then, or just find her again when we pay the check."

"Do you recognize the guy?"

"Can't see his face." Brigit eased back around with a wince. Max returned just as a huge group entered the tavern and collected around the far end of the bar. She disappeared to deal with the crowd as soon as she'd taken their orders, which suited Brigit just fine.

They listened to the other patrons as they ate. Two men argued over fishing spots. A young family reviewed the local pumpkin patch. Whatever Ian was or wasn't thinking, he kept it to himself. And she still hadn't told him whose voice she'd heard on that phone call. Or about the visitation— hallucination? Would that actually be better?—that morning. It was easy to say she should wait until she could prove that what she'd seen and heard was real, but in truth, her silence was a fault line running through her. A cowardly vein of rot. The tree could not be voiced. Certainly not the gloves, red fingers twitching like infected grubs. Brigit slipped off her stool.

"I'm going to the bathroom. If you see Lacey, ask if she has a minute to talk?"

This time the back office was closed. So was the bathroom door. Max leaned outside it with a dog-eared copy of Butler's *Parable of the Sower.* When Brigit approached, she glanced up without lifting her head, pale eyes piercing through mascara-coated lashes.

"So," Max said. "Not doing the goth thing anymore, I see."

"I feel like we traded," Brigit said, trying for a smile. "I like the hair. And the ink."

Max lifted her book arm and turned it from side to side, inspecting the spray of orchids past her elbow. "Thanks. I started right after graduation. My mom was thrilled. No, for real—she was scared I would be a nerd forever."

"Clearly you showed her."

"Oh, yeah," Max said. "Max Temple, chief bartender at the same place the Little League comes to celebrate. Feels awesome."

Brigit snorted, and Max smiled faintly back. The bleak haze pressing into Brigit's chest relaxed for a moment, just enough for her brain to kick back in.

"Well, it's convenient for me, anyway," she said. Max did live here, after all. This connection could be an advantage.

"Yeah?"

"Ian and I are consultants," Brigit said. "We're here about Gabrielle Markham and James Mulroy, to help figure out what happened. I assume you know what's going on?"

Max nodded slowly. "Hence Lacey."

"Right. We heard she and Gabrielle are close."

"Mmm." Max smiled again, but there was something new and hard around her eyes. "To a point."

Before Brigit could tug on this thread, the bathroom door cracked and Lacey slid into the hall. She paused, regarding Max and Brigit, then rushed back toward the bustle of the tavern. Max caught Brigit's eye and gave her head the tiniest shake. After another moment, the man Lacey had been sitting with pushed the bathroom door fully open.

Brigit blinked. She flashed between turning back to the bar or pretending to get a phone call, anything to buy herself some grace, but it was too late.

"Shit," Lacey's boyfriend said with a grin. "Beth? I almost didn't recognize you without the makeup. Looking very, ah, professional."

"It's Brigit," she said coolly, scanning his face. "And you are… Pete."

Scion of the local construction company Brigit's dad had once contracted—RIP, Dollhouses—and debate club champion; frequent special guest on the morning announcements, which Brigit had helped produce when she was a sophomore and he was a senior. He'd been one of those popular boys who didn't use queer slurs to her face, but laughed when others did. His smile faded ever so slightly when she said nothing more.

"This is fun," Max said, "but some of us are on the clock."

Her words were light, but they had an edge. It drew Pete's eyes to hers, fast and cold above those white teeth.

"Apologies," he said. "Nice to see you, Brigit."

"Yeah," she said.

Pete tipped an invisible hat and followed Lacey back to the bar. Without another word, Max entered the bathroom and slammed the door behind her. When she came out, she side-stepped past Brigit on her way back to the bar without speaking. Brigit let it slide. One thing at a time. She shut herself inside the bathroom, and at the click of the latch, a dizzying wave of black spots swept across her vision. Brigit staggered forward, barely finding the rim of the sink with one hand. Cold porcelain bit her palm.

Freezing ground against her knees. Pain in her hand where Emma grips it, pain from being dragged all this way through the trees. Pale trunks rise around them like bars, a prison filthy with mud and leaves and nothing else. No birds, no deer. No sounds at all except for shallow breathing and a sharp, metallic SNICK—

Brigit jerked a hand in front of her face, but there was only her reflection, graffiti-covered walls closing in. Her skin had lost all color, lips chalky and chapped. Sweat turned her short hair from honey brown to soil.

Real. Not real. Getting worse either way, and certainly not helped by the jarring intrusion of her actual past. But that floating, half-there person wasn't Brigit anymore. She knew who she was, knew her own damage. Could trust in her brain because at least she understood it.

Right?

A splash of cold water felt good. Sleep would too. Christ, imagine twelve good hours.

Back at the bar, Ian was speaking quietly with Lacey, who backed off as Brigit approached. "I'll be outside," she told

Ian, her eyes slipping back toward Pete's booth before she walked away.

"I told her who we are," Ian said, curving his shoulders as if he could conceal their conversation with bad posture alone. It must have hurt, if he was in the same shape as she was. "And why we want to talk. She's afraid we'll blame her for not believing Gabrielle."

"She said that?"

"She didn't have to."

Brigit dug her nail into her thumb, just once. "Right. I'll be careful with her."

They paid for their breakfasts and headed out. Max leaned against the counter with her arms crossed, tracking them all the way to the door.

Around the corner, Lacey waited by a set of industrial trash bins. She refused to be filmed, didn't want them to record at all until Brigit told her it was for legal reasons—having the interview on tape would help them prove they hadn't interfered with the official investigation. Amazing what people would believe if you said it with confidence.

Brigit was glad to hold the camera's focus, though. That made it easy to be someone else.

"You don't have to tell us anything that feels private or uncomfortable," she said as Ian adjusted the viewfinder. "We're not the police. If you want to stop at any point, just say the word."

Lacey tapped an unlit cigarette against her forearm. "You think you can find James?"

"We're going to try."

"Everyone's trying. They say Gabi's in a coma?"

"Sounds like. Does that surprise you?"

That drew Lacey's eyes up for the first time. "I thought she was making it up." She switched to flipping the cigarette between two fingers like a pen. "Or not making it up, exactly, but—making the dreams into a bigger deal than they were. She likes to be the one people talk about, you know? Not that she's selfish," she added with a quick, pained smile, "just… she likes being the main character. I guess we all do. I'm not explaining this well. Gabi would do it better."

"It's okay," Brigit said. "I know what you mean. She's a storyteller?"

Lacey nodded rapidly. Her gaze kept sliding over Brigit's face and away, unsettled and unsettling. That burst of words seemed to have tired her. Time to shift away from generalities and toward questions with simple, definitive answers.

"Did she talk about the nightmares more in the days leading up to her disappearance?"

"No." Lacey answered so quickly that Brigit recalculated. Maybe she did want to talk. She just hadn't known how to start. "She actually brought them up less. To me, anyway." There was a complex note in Lacey's tone, fondness cut with something messy. Brigit nodded for her to continue.

"Gabi…has a hard time when people don't take her seriously. She's younger, obviously, and that's a big thing. We actually met in a club. She snuck in with some older girls who ditched her, and—it wasn't a great night for me either. So I was crying in the bathroom, and she came in all furious, and we made each other feel better. She didn't tell me she was still in high school for months. One time Max called her out for trying to buy beer here and she almost threw up after. God, she was embarrassed." Lacey's smile bloomed, then died on the vine. "But the dreams… You have to understand, that was just the latest thing, and by then we weren't—it was weird, between us."

"Weird how?" Brigit asked when the pause grew tangible.

Lacey sighed, looking as though she regretted the caveat.

"Well…because of my boyfriend. At first, Gabi was all *Pete, Pete, he's gorgeous, you're so lucky.* We'd go out to the woods to smoke and one time she even carved our initials into a tree—not mine and hers; his and mine—like we were this big love story she was in charge of. Except when I moved in with Pete, I guess she got jealous. She completely turned on us last summer after—well, some things that aren't important. They had nothing to do with Gabi at all, but you would not believe what she called me. She said I was Ellis Creek's fucking—what's her name? Patty Hearst. Who name-drops Patty Hearst?" Lacey asked, and suddenly her eyes were bright with angry tears. "So at first, I figured the nightmares were just the next thing, a way for Gabi to make me feel like *she* needed me more than *he* did, but then—I don't know. She realized it wasn't working and went to James instead? And a few weeks after that, she was gone."

The fury drained from Lacey's expression, leaving only exhausted sorrow. Nearby garbage bins had staked their claim on the alley, perfuming the air with decay. Brigit let that stench fill her nose and mouth as Lacey collected herself with a few hard breaths.

"Take your time. There's no rush."

"I'm sorry. I don't like talking about her like this when she's not here. Filming it."

"I understand," Brigit said. "It feels ugly, like a betrayal— but you're helping us look for James. I'm sure she'd prefer that. We can come back to the dreams. Can you tell us anything more about Gabi's relationship with him?"

"They were dating. That's what people say, anyway."

"That's what people say?"

Lacey rubbed at the back of her neck, the sound of it dry and chitinous. "James's family is religious. Like, missionary-style-after-marriage religious. Gabi isn't into that. If she was in love with him, it would have been a big deal, loads of sneaking around. Epic stuff. She would have talked my ear off. Anyway, my break is almost over. So." Lacey slipped her unlit cigarette back in the pack. "You should talk to Sam Levy," she added, looking away. "He was bothering me too, after Gabi and James went missing. He asked if I'd seen—"

Lacey stopped again, smoothing her hair down over her neck with quick, fastidious movements.

"If you'd seen who?" Brigit prompted. "Gabrielle?"

"No." Lacey was already retreating toward the tavern. "He asked if I'd seen the birch trees."

7: IAN

The blood dropped out of Brigit's face as Lacey rounded the tavern corner, and something turned in Ian's stomach.

"I take it you know this Levy guy?"

Brigit shook her head. Then she huffed a short, humorless laugh, color returning to her cheeks. "Although you know what, who knows? I knew Max. I knew Pete. Fifty bucks says I find him with at least five more shared connections I haven't spoken to in ten years."

Brigit pulled out her phone, and Ian turned his camera off. Crows had collected on the power lines strung along the road. He didn't like the way they watched him and Brigit. Didn't like the scene she made with that phone, gripping it tightly, staring again at something he couldn't see.

"Let's get out of the alley," he said. She nodded without looking up.

Ian stayed behind Brigit as she turned onto the sidewalk, attention still on her screen. Tension ran through his shoulders and down to his hands. He wasn't sure exactly what he was ready to do—grab her if she walked into the street?—but this adrenaline felt different than what had filled him as they'd followed Lacey out of the tavern. It buzzed and spat, a queasy awareness of his body and of Brigit's.

Something is wrong with her.

This thought had grown beneath his skin like a cancer ever since they'd arrived in Ellis Creek. Now he couldn't unravel the words and tuck them back out of sight.

"Hell yeah, got him on Facebook. How's this?" Brigit asked when she stopped by the passenger side of the car. "'Hi, Sam, this is Brigit Weylan. I'm in town looking into a few things surrounding Gabrielle Markham's situation and I hear you might have some insights. Can we meet up to talk?'"

"Yeah," he said, focusing as hard as he could on the precise insertion of his car keys instead of the memory of the untouched beds, her disquieting energy when she burst into his room that morning. "Sounds good."

By the time he folded his camera and himself into place, Brigit had slid into the passenger seat and was pressing her thumb against the phone screen with the air of a student submitting a final. "And, sent." She flashed him a wobbly smile that knocked the breath from Ian's chest. "I know I've been kind of…off. Thanks for putting up with me."

His palms were cold, clammy on the wheel. Guilt crawled down his neck like sweat. "It's okay. Like we said, this is a lot."

Brigit cleared her throat and slapped her palms against her thighs. "Yeah. So. James Mulroy's parents."

"We can take a little time in between, if you want. Get some transition footage."

Brigit tensed, and Ian felt like kicking himself in the stomach. Transition footage? For the Very Special Episode they'd make about the missing kids who'd dropped Brigit headfirst into her worst childhood trauma?

She thought he didn't know how much it hurt her, using her sister the way they did, but god, it was obvious. He just couldn't bring himself to talk about it. Didn't want to risk whatever comfort and ease she'd grown to feel around him over the years, or push her into saying something cutting. And now here they were, where it seemed like the whole damn town wanted to ensure she thought about it every second of every day, and he'd nearly bit her head off over a prank call. Of course something was wrong with her.

Easy to see why someone might fuck with Brigit, also. They'd gotten to the hospital at the same time as Gabrielle, and Ellis Creek didn't exactly have a bustling ER. Anyone could have recognized her and drawn the connection between Gabrielle Markham and Emma Weylan. Two young girls. One stretch of woods. One other person in common. Those were the kind of dots that might come together ugly.

"Hey," he said. "Are you sure you want to keep going? We can still leave. I'm okay with it. You're probably right, anyway. I don't know why I thought you and I could find something the real police either can't or won't because they're part of the whole thing."

"No." She picked at her finger. "I want to keep going."

The Mulroys lived in a sleepy cul-de-sac twenty minutes from the Super 8. This side of Ellis Creek had yet to see the kind of hipster-lite development that characterized the downtown drag, and instead clung to an air of Americana that made Ian's scalp itch. Every lawn was square and neatly trimmed, and the fact that all the doors were painted different primary colors only served to accentuate their sameness.

"Wow," Brigit said as they eased up to the curb. "I think I got kicked out of this neighborhood when I was a senior."

"Kicked out?"

"Kindly asked to leave," she amended while Ian checked the charge of his tape recorder. "Real Town Watch vibe. I used to drive places where I didn't know anyone and just walk around in the evenings; they probably thought I was going to sacrifice one of their corgis."

They climbed out of the car, Brigit armed with a ballpoint pen and a folded waiver. She waited for him to come around to the end of the slate path leading up to the Mulroys' bright blue door, and Ian steeled himself.

"Maybe you should knock," he said, hating himself for it. "The detective said they were...traditional."

It took Brigit a moment to respond, but then her shoulders stiffened and she shot him a look of exasperated understanding. He despised having to suggest it might be smarter to lead with the person who looked like a standard-issue white girl. The only consolation was that Brigit did too, for his sake and her own.

"I guess Alicia would know," she said, and started up the path.

A partially deflated soccer ball sat by the carefully sectioned flower beds that lined this square of yard. Brigit knocked firmly as Ian stood behind her and did his best to look non-threatening. He'd left his jacket in the car and had rolled the sleeves of his shirt up to his elbows after the stuffy warmth of the ride. Now he wondered if this made him seem unprofessional. It rarely mattered when he was just the hands behind the camera, but those flower beds were kempt as hell.

Rapid footsteps sounded inside the house, and the door swung open. A woman faced them, lips parted, eyes wide beneath her wispy ashen hair. Her gaze darted from Brigit to Ian and back to Brigit. The air left her in a rush that Ian felt against his throat.

"I said no reporters." She stepped backward and began to close the door. Ian quashed the wild and dangerous urge to stop it with his palm. If he got himself shot by someone he wasn't even attempting to scam, his father would laugh his goddamn—

Another thought he crushed so completely he could almost hear the crunch.

"Mrs. Mulroy," he said quickly, "wait. We're not reporters. Detective Nguyen sent us."

James's mother paused with the door halfway shut. She looked him over once again, lingering on the voice recorder. Her eyes were the color of bluebells, bright despite the lines that spidered out from their corners. "She sent you? Why?" Suspicion threaded her voice, but so did something raw that appeared to prevent her from closing the door. "Do you know something about my son?"

"No," Brigit said before Ian could reply. "We're here to help the police with their investigation. My name is Brigit Weylan."

Mrs. Mulroy stared at her, and then those clear blue eyes narrowed. "Weylan," she said. "You're not Carrie and Evan's younger daughter?"

Ian glanced at Brigit, whose face went momentarily blank before she smiled.

"Those are my parents, yes," she said. "I'm impressed. They haven't lived here in ages. Do you keep in touch?"

"Oh, no," Mrs. Mulroy said, as if the idea was ludicrous. "I just remember— Well." She squinted more closely at Brigit. "You look quite a bit like your sister, you know. If you just grew that hair out."

"Mmm." Brigit's smile took on a slightly frozen quality that Ian was pretty sure only he could discern. He didn't love the way James's mother was looking at them now, or more accurately, at Brigit. There was a calculation to it. Judgment whirring into shape.

"I don't remember seeing much of you after what happened," Mrs. Mulroy said, crossing her arms to cup her elbows, "at church, or with the Girl Scouts, although I offered to take you into our troop, if I recall. Some people find comfort in community after a tragedy like that. I suppose your parents must have gone the other way, closed ranks around you, as they say."

Her words were neutral enough, but the tightness of her mouth told Ian that Mrs. Mulroy didn't approve.

"It was hard," Brigit said. "For all of us. I don't mean to equate what my family experienced with what you're going through now, but there's nothing like losing a child. Ian and I—" she smoothly brought him back in "—are here to help the search for James."

Mrs. Mulroy's fingers tightened on her elbows. "I've already spoken with the police. I told them Gabrielle Markham was trouble for James, and not just her parents' kind—you know what I mean better than anyone, I suppose. There are children born in this town who—who break with their homes in one way or another, and Gabrielle Markham was the sort. Nobody believed me until last night. Is that why you're here? Did she wake up? Did she say something?"

Every question came out quicker than the one before. Ian tightened his hold on the recorder, letting the plastic ridges bite into his palm until his heartbeat fluttered in the depressions. *You know what I mean better than anyone.* He felt that for Brigit like a slap.

"Gabrielle's not awake," Brigit said quietly, as if Mrs. Mulroy's comment had meant nothing to her. "But Detective Nguyen thinks I might be able to do something her officers can't with certain information you and your husband passed along. Information you might feel uncomfortable sharing publicly."

Mrs. Mulroy's eyes glittered, something new and wary

in the blue. Ian forced himself not to shift on his feet as she studied them for an agonizing minute. Then James's mother stepped back and opened the door the rest of the way, allowing first Brigit, then Ian, to enter her home.

The warm, rich scent of chocolate chip cookies permeated the Mulroy house. Every room they passed through on their way to the kitchen contained a crucifix, which Ian tried not to notice.

"Andrew calls it stress baking," Mrs. Mulroy said as she popped the oven and removed a tray of cookies, "but I just want to make sure James has something warm ready for him when he walks through that door."

She placed the tray on the spotless stovetop and reached for a spatula. Brigit sat at the kitchen table. Ian took the chair nearest the door. On the opposite wall, a square of fabric had been stretched over a thin wooden frame: embroidered roses, yellow and red, and a cursive quote he couldn't make out. Not that he needed the words to recognize a Bible verse.

Ian took a deep breath of cookies and placed his recorder on the table. It was a Sony device, thin and covered in buttons that made it resemble a dated television remote. When he'd first bought the voice recorder he'd been excited by the lightweight design and the professional grade microphone, but he'd learned there was a class of people who found it even more unnerving than a video camera would have been. He turned it on.

"Do you mind if we tape this conversation?" Ian asked, and when Mrs. Mulroy glanced over her shoulder he tipped the recorder to show her the speaker face. "This is not for public consumption, it's a private record of what you share with us today. I just need your consent on tape."

"If it'll help." Mrs. Mulroy began to shove the metal lip of the spatula around a cookie's edges with sharp, violent stabs. "I'm willing to do just about anything if it'll mean somebody listens. Well. Somebody that can help us." She pried the cookie off the pan with a faint crack, slid it onto the cooling rack, and turned to appraise them. "So, please. Tell me. What do you think you can do for my boy?"

For a moment, Brigit said nothing. Her short hair was neatly pushed to one side, accentuating her large hazel eyes. She appeared to be staring into the middle distance between Mrs. Mulroy and the stove, no sign of life—and then those eyes flicked up to meet the older woman's and Ian saw the shift. He *saw* it. How one moment she was lost inside her head, and the next, every piece of her was pouring into this room, this time, this person and her needs.

"Detective Nguyen mentioned that Gabrielle was having a recurring nightmare. She might have told James about it. It would have been a big part of their lives in the last few weeks, something he might have tried to help her with. I'm not going to tell you that's got anything to do with why he's not here, but if there's any chance that it does, I'd like to find out."

Mrs. Mulroy listened to this speech with the same measured attention as that with which Brigit gave it. Then she tugged a small glinting pendant from beneath her shirt, pressed it to her lips, and nodded. "All right. Have a cookie and we'll talk."

While Ian tried to eat a soft-centered cookie quietly enough that he wouldn't turn up on the recording, and Brigit waved off Mrs. Mulroy's insistence with a disarming firmness, James's mother told them about her son.

James was a bright boy, a track star, and a good student. A reader, not a fan of video games, always home in time for dinner with his loving parents. Not as involved with the church these days as in childhood, Mrs. Mulroy admitted, but never once had he shown signs of straying from grace. Until Gabrielle Markham.

"I won't speak ill of her," Mrs. Mulroy said, and nodded her chin at the recorder, "and I wouldn't even if you hadn't brought that. But I will say that my son changed after he met Gabi. He's still kind and thoughtful, but he started coming home later and later, and it was when they grew close that he stopped coming to services. He claimed it was for a study group that could only meet on Sundays, and I didn't want to accuse or doubt. But I worried about those two. Which honestly, God forgive me, but it seemed like a blessing at first, a sign that he—"

She pressed her fingertips to her mouth, attention slipping off beyond the wall. Ian was unable to form a prompt. Her words had struck him somewhere unexpected, not needles but stones against his breast. His father had said similar things about him when Ian graduated high school and shed any semblance of Catholicism. At least in public. At home, there was only silence and dread, the clock ticking for both of them until Ian turned twenty-one and claimed the insurance money his mother had left in his name.

The room stilled aside from the gentle whir of a ceiling fan in another room, and then one of the oven racks popped as the metal cooled. Mrs. Mulroy flinched and grabbed a cookie, eyes traveling quickly over Brigit. That judgment flashed again.

"Well, I wouldn't want to offend. She's a beautiful girl, that's all. But he'd been sleeping poorly. It was obvious. There were circles underneath his eyes, he wasn't eating breakfast, and two or three times in the weeks before he disappeared, he left after dinner to go climbing at the rock wall. I thought he shouldn't be exercising so close to bed if he'd been having trouble falling asleep, and we—fought," she said, obviously struggling to say the word aloud. Her throat jumped. "He told me it wasn't the exercise. He was doing research. He wouldn't tell me anything else, so that night when he went to the bathroom, I… I checked his computer. I saw what he was looking up."

She took a large bite of cookie. Ian held himself very still as Mrs. Mulroy chewed and swallowed. Set her unfinished cookie on the table.

"I'm not sure it will do James any good to share this with you. Of all people. What folks already think is horrible enough. There are devils in these mountains—I do believe that. Literal or not, I don't want my son's name anywhere near them."

"You're scared for him," Brigit said. The words were obvious, but her empathetic tone was a trap. Mrs. Mulroy didn't move. Of course she didn't. She was already caught. "Gabrielle might have gotten James involved in something dangerous, and the police can't help because it's not their jurisdiction anymore. Maybe it never was."

Slowly, Mrs. Mulroy nodded. Brigit placed a hand on top of hers and she allowed the contact, eyes shining, thin mouth pressed tight.

"When I was a kid," Brigit said, "my sister was the most exciting mystery in the world." She smiled faintly. "If you knew her, you know she was a handful. But Emma asked questions too, maybe the same kinds of questions as James, and she had so many secrets I wanted to learn. But I was too young. I couldn't keep up." Brigit didn't look away from Mrs. Mulroy even for a heartbeat. Ian felt his own pulse picking up as unease turned round and round in his gut. "Alicia Nguyen called me because of Emma. Because of a connection between her and Gabrielle, which I think maybe you know. James did get caught up in something he didn't understand. It wasn't his fault, or yours."

Brigit sat back and let the silence well. Mrs. Mulroy's hand twitched when she moved away but the older woman didn't speak. She watched Brigit hungrily, no longer glancing toward the voice recorder with every other sentence. Just before the quiet dragged for longer than Ian could take, Brigit filled it.

"And I think if you accept the possibility that I'm right, and help me understand what he and Gabrielle believed was happening to her, you and I might be able to give James a chance my sister never got."

8: BRIGIT

Sophia Mulroy told them everything in the end. Gabrielle's dreams. Her son's growing obsession with the Dell, with monsters, with the missing and the dead. And, of course, with Emma.

Mrs. Mulroy's story confirmed what Alicia had alluded to, or at least that Ellis Creek had a worse problem with runaways than it liked to admit. But it was how James's mother spoke that Brigit had really needed to hear. The careful way she described James and Gabrielle's friendship, her obvious fear that Gabrielle had cursed her boy. Brigit had walked into that house desperate to believe Gabrielle's nightmare was real—because if it *was* just a teenager's manipulation, Brigit had lost her mind. So Mrs. Mulroy's genuine terror, her confidence that James and Gabrielle were telling the truth? Relief like that should cost money.

But whatever this squirming, anxious feeling was as she and Ian climbed into his car, relief was not it. For one, Brigit couldn't quite scrape off Mrs. Mulroy's obvious disdain for her short hair and lack of makeup and whatever other aspects of her appearance screamed *other*, whether Brigit confirmed it—*younger daughter*—or not. If they hadn't been in Ellis Creek, would she have said something to that? It wouldn't have helped them get through the door—probably the opposite. But the question still gnawed at her stomach like a parasite. Then there were those references to Emma, tossed off like they meant nothing—and for reasons Brigit couldn't fathom, another cut that felt equally deep: *Your parents must have closed ranks around you.*

It was the natural assumption for someone like Sophia Mulroy. She would never guess that, after the death of their eldest, the Weylans didn't go to the church potluck or send their kid to summer camp because they simply forgot their younger child might want noise and friends and a home-cooked meal that didn't require a microwave. This wasn't something Brigit thought much about these days, or it hadn't been—the emptiness of her childhood home even before the divorce, family members creeping from room to room like they were haunting the place.

Worse, one thing Mrs. Mulroy had not mentioned was hallucinations. Yet that birch tree in Brigit's room hadn't been a dream. She buckled her seat belt with numb fingers. Two things could be true at once: something not yet explained had happened to James and Gabrielle, and the second Weylan sibling was finally starting to crack.

For a moment, while Ian checked his mirrors, Brigit considered asking him what he thought. Only she couldn't think of how to frame it, because he didn't actually know anything, and abruptly Brigit realized Ian hadn't said a word since they'd gotten in the car. Which was strange. Before she could land on how to break the silence, Brigit's phone jangled with an unfamiliar alarm. She checked the screen, not realizing she'd stopped breathing until the exhale.

"Shit." Brigit tapped her phone. The bottom half of a sharp-jawed face filled the screen.

"Sorry," Sam Levy said. "Can't type right now but I wanted to catch you early."

"No worries," Brigit said, trying to place the features she could see. "Thanks for getting back to me."

"You want to help James?" The lower half of Sam's face jounced like a faulty cable show from Brigit's childhood. He was clearly walking fast. "Meet me at that old barn on Stone Ridge and Russet. Eight o'clock. Bring a flashlight."

"Why?"

"Because I think those kids found something, and if you're for real, you're going to want to hear about it in person. See you there, Brigit Weylan. Or not."

With a downward chime, the call ended. Brigit stared at her screen for a moment, then lowered the phone to her lap. "All right, then." She looked to Ian, willing him to engage.

"If we show up," he said, "we're getting murdered. Right?"

Her whole body eased. "Oh, most definitely. Are you up for it?"

Ian pushed out a heavy breath. "Yeah. But not before I pick us up some mace."

They spent the rest of the afternoon in the Ellis Creek public library, reading everything from the last week about the missing teens. There wasn't much. Alicia had been right. Until this morning, the town hadn't felt strongly about Gabrielle Markham and James Mulroy vanishing, with the exception of their immediate families and, apparently, Lacey Rollins and Sam Levy. Their initial disappearances hadn't made it into any local news that Brigit could find; even now, twenty-four hours since she and Ian found Gabrielle in the road, Ellis Creek was not on fire. The *Ellis Creek Tribune* only reported that she was expected to wake and recover fully. Comments on that article expressed goodwill toward her parents and accusations toward James, but surprisingly few of either—anyone with an account on the *Tribune* website appeared to care more that Gabrielle was found near a paused construction site, a fact which quickly derailed the comment section into a heated argument over an upcoming shopping mall expansion downtown.

But where Ellis Creek's digital community failed them, the state and county missing persons databases did not. When Brigit tried to follow James's search path based on their conversation with his mother, several older reports popped up, almost all of them children or teenagers last seen near the Dell. She pointed these out to Ian and he nodded.

"The friendly local coffee shop collects missing person posters. I didn't get a close look, but some of them were practically antique."

Alicia's hospital visit came back to her. *Disappearances. Deaths.* How fast does a community get used to things like that? How fast does a person?

Well. Not every person. A few more clicks led Brigit to a Facebook page dedicated to one Michael Patterson—a memorial of sorts. He'd vanished in 2009, but the latest post here was only four months old: Holy shit, man. We literally just wrapped the final chapter of the final sequel to your Labyrinth of Souls campaign. My daughter's gonna be old enough to play pretty soon. She's got real Dungeon Master energy. Good thing nerds are in now.

Brigit smiled despite herself, but it fell away quick.

Too soon, dusk edged into the library and ushered all patrons outside. The temperature had dropped with the light, leaving Brigit shivering in her loose sweater. When they reached the car, she dug her scarf out of her duffel bag and wrapped it twice around her neck.

"Let's get something hot," Ian said. "And wholesome. Like soup."

She cut him a glance, suddenly too aware of the scarf fibers scratching at her clavicle, but Ian had his eyes on the parking lot as he guided them out of their spot. They found a Whole Foods that hadn't been there when Brigit lived in town and raided the hot bar for chili, then retreated to the sticky-floored café to wait until it was time to meet Sam Levy.

"Do you think we should tell someone where we're going?" Brigit asked as they sat.

"You mean Alicia."

"I mean someone."

"Maybe you should tell Max."

"Max doesn't have a cavalry." She tried the chili. Cacao in the spice blend, a surprising touch.

"I guess," Ian said. Then he wiped at his mouth with a napkin, not meeting her eyes. "I don't think we should tell Alicia everything we do, that's all. She's a cop. And she lied about it. Explain any way that we can trust her."

"We don't." Brigit stirred her food. "Doesn't mean we can't use her. More people know we're here now, and that she asked us to come. That's enough insurance for me."

"Okay, but… You really don't think she's part of this? Way deeper in it than she's letting on?"

For a moment, it was all Brigit could do not to laugh. She waited to reply until she was certain her voice would hold.

"Of course I think she's part of this. I also think the Dell—you know, that forest we're about to walk into, at night, with a stranger who might have hurt those kids too—is part of this. Pretty sure Gabrielle and James knew that. Pretty sure my sister did."

Her voice thickened as she spoke, until her last words were gravel on mud. Whatever Sam wanted to show them at the

Dell, Brigit suddenly understood she did not want to see it. Perhaps could not afford to. Lacey's voice dug into her like uncut fingernails: *He asked if I'd seen the birch trees.*

Brigit's eyes stung with the tears she hadn't managed to cry alone in the shower. Here in this brightly lit grocery store café, surrounded by shoppers and cashiers and one woman with a mop, several spilled down her cheeks and seamed her lips with salt.

"Bridge," Ian said, his voice soft as a bruise. She couldn't let him continue.

"No." The chili had gone to ashes and dirt in her mouth. All Brigit smelled was peaty soil, dry leaves in the dark. Her head ached. "I'm fine."

She dashed her napkin against her face, scrubbing the tears away with rough brown paper. Her eyes would be bloodshot on camera. Maybe that wouldn't show up with the night vision lens. Brigit crumpled her napkin into a tiny damp ball. As she reached for a fresh one, Ian did the kindest thing. Instead of saying another word, he tugged his compostable hot bar container to the edge of the table, picked up his fork, and began to eat.

At 7:40, Brigit scraped her chair across the floor and stood. She carried their empty containers to a nearby compost unit, but Ian didn't stay beside her. He jogged to catch up at the sliding glass doors and handed her a paper bag. Brigit held it up to her nose and inhaled butter and sugar and chocolate chips. When she raised her face, brows quirked, Ian showed off his too-white right incisor. "You didn't get one from Mrs. Mulroy."

She smiled back, the best she could offer.

While they drove toward the building where Sam had asked to meet, Brigit explained through a mouthful of cookie what exactly he'd meant by "old barn."

"It's a Ruritan. A community center, for voting and other stuff out in the country. We used to hold a Boo House there on Halloween," she said as they turned onto the curvy two-lane highway that cut north along the Dell.

"I'm sorry, a what?"

"You didn't have those? Haunted houses with themed rooms people had to walk through. Trauma for decades."

"I'm pretty sure you're making up that name, but I'm the one who wanted to film ghost-busting. Obviously I know the Boo House life."

"What did you call them in Vermont?"

"Spook Factories." She snuck a glance to gauge his profile, caught the twitch of lip just before Ian broke into a grin. "We called them haunted houses, because we have no imagination."

"Thank god you're my showrunner."

"I know," Ian said, and turned on his brights as the road around them narrowed. "We're both very lucky."

Another car whipped around a bend ahead, headlights slapping the night. Ian dimmed his, but the other car didn't bother, and in that flash of blindness Brigit slipped out of her skin. One breath she was in the car, smiling, living in the tired muscles of her cheeks and shoulders and the aching twinge deep in her spine, and the next, she was not.

The taste of sugar dissolved off her tongue. She could no longer feel the seat beneath her thighs. Everything went light, or black, or some explosive blur of colors her brain couldn't parse until there, straight ahead, a line of white that split at the top and bottom of her vision, branching out into a dozen crawling veins—

You've seen this before.

"Jackass," Ian muttered beneath his breath, and the world returned.

"Oh," Brigit said, blinking. Everything inside her had gone to seed, but she lifted a hand and pointed, and her finger did not shake. "There's the turn."

The Ruritan parking lot was deserted, the building dark. It was unlovely in daylight too, just a one-story block of brown wall and flat red roof that could be transformed into any number of things with the right amount of cloth and fake fog. By night the barn looked like a coffin waiting to be filled.

"So this is a community center?" Ian asked, unbuckling his seat belt. "Looks more like one of our sets."

She wanted to dig at her thumb, but he'd notice that. Brigit adjusted her scarf instead, wrapping it tighter around her throat so she could feel every place where the fibers chafed against her skin. "Believe it or not, they also host barbecues in the summer." She climbed out of the car before Ian, stealing a moment to suck in several deep breaths of clear, chilly air. Out here the evening smelled like bark and tree sap and—yes—woodsmoke again, carried on the breeze from one of the pinpricks of light that shone from the foothills to their left.

"Wait." Brigit turned to see Ian brace a hand on the hood. She couldn't make out his expression past the glare of headlights he hadn't yet turned off, but his voice sounded strange. "This is where we found her."

"It's not," she said, because of course he was right, or almost. "That was miles away." *At the Dollhouses*, Brigit thought but didn't add.

Ian ducked into the car without a reply, resurfacing with his camera bag just as the headlights ticked off. In the moments before her eyes adjusted to the cloudy gibbous moonlight, Ian became a hulking Quasimodo against the open road, cast in sharper relief thanks to the miles of rolling farmland on the other side of the highway.

"Hi," a new voice said from behind Brigit's back. She whirled and threw a hand up to block the glare of a flashlight aimed directly at her face. "Oh, sorry."

The light lowered, revealing a young man with a shock of straight brown hair, a nose that had been broken at least once, and pale, sharp cheekbones that caught every shadow. The rest of him blended into the night, all black turtleneck and dark jeans. His slender, lanky frame gave the impression of height, though he couldn't have had more than two inches on Brigit.

"Hi," he said again, and held out the hand that wasn't holding a heavy-duty task force flashlight. "Sam. You're Brigit? You look different. I remember a lot more eye makeup."

She squinted, trying to fill the hollow lines of his cheeks and form the teenager she must have known. How much could have changed in a decade? Brigit shook his hand. Thin fingers, but the grip was strong. Gravel crunched as Ian stepped into the pool of light from Sam's flashlight, widening it with his own.

"Hey." Ian lifted his light in a makeshift shrug. "I'm Ian. I think I nearly knocked you over the other day. Nice to meet you, and sorry again about that."

"Ah, right," Sam said. "Ten out of ten collision, actually. I didn't even drop a poster."

"Ian's my colleague," Brigit said. "He's here to help. And apparently cause strife."

"Not at all." Sam smiled, quick and nervous. "Documentation. Cool. Film away. I'm glad you came. Wasn't sure you would. Don't get me wrong, I'm not one to judge," he said to Brigit, "but you never struck me as a team player in school."

She didn't like the way he said this, as if they were old friends reuniting. There was something familiar about his face, the quick, sharp smile—but not enough for her to place. Behind him, the Ruritan building loomed in front of woods that hung like rough-cut sheets from an ashen sky. The cool air had been a relief when she'd first stepped out of the car, but now Brigit was chilly again, her toes curling in her canvas sneakers. She was too aware of her body, all the delicate machinery at work beneath her skin.

Nodding at Ian to switch on the camera, Brigit shoved her hands into her pockets and forced her voice to betray nothing but brisk curiosity. "You had something to share about James?"

"Yeah." Sam nodded several times, rocking back and forth on the balls of his feet. "Yeah. Officially okay to film me saying this. So, James and me are tight. I taught him how to climb. We're both regulars at Rocks On Top, and we got close. He doesn't have a great time at home. Kind of a big-brother situation, you know?"

"Sure."

"He asked if I would spot him for a session the night before he went missing. James was there a lot, evenings, weekends. He liked to talk and climb. Think it was one of the only places he didn't feel, you know... Observed." Sam turned and started walking back toward the darkened Ruritan. Brigit fell into step beside him while Ian turned off his flashlight and followed, their footsteps grinding along beneath the creaks of trees. "Except that night he didn't want to climb. He talked about Gabrielle. She had dreams. He was worried. He wanted help looking into the Dell, its history. Some images that might turn up."

They passed the corner of the Ruritan and their footsteps changed from noisy to soft, padding over dead grass as they rounded the side of the building. Beyond it the forest stretched out black and seamless. The air had begun to smell more like oak leaves and yellow pine than grass.

"I asked what images and he said, 'Trees. A circle of white birch trees.' I said I'd have a look, he said thanks, and the next day he was gone."

Sam stopped a few paces out from the woods and turned around with his thumbs hooked into the pockets of his jeans. Brigit stopped too. Her throat was very dry.

"What then?" Ian asked, sidestepping to the left and angling his camera to catch them both in the shot. "He goes missing and you…"

"Kept my promise. Everybody thought he ran off with her, but that was a crock."

"Was it?" Brigit asked.

"James and Gabrielle weren't together."

"Their families say—"

"People know what they wanted them to know," Sam cut her off. "That doesn't matter now. What matters is what he said about the trees. It was weird. I wasn't sure what he meant. Literal trees? A painting of trees? Could have been anything."

"So you went looking for more intel." Ian returned to his place beside Brigit and she couldn't help herself, she leaned toward him, just a little. White trees. Red gloves.

"I did," Sam confirmed. "Which you'd think would be hard, given…" He waved an arm behind him at the blanket of forest that rolled out toward Ellis Creek and beyond. Backlit by his own flashlight, his eyes glinted like mica. "Except, and not to put you on the spot," he continued, that dark glitter landing on Brigit, "but James and Gabrielle weren't the first kids to disappear from this town. Just because no one makes a fuss when it's not the son of two white pillars of the community doesn't mean it isn't true."

It took Brigit a moment to respond. Deep down, something whispered to be careful. Gabi dreaming about Emma. Emma's voice on a dead line. Real. Not real. Real and not real. She swallowed the dry taste of earth. "We were no pillars, but I assure you, when my sister died, there was a fuss."

"Not what there could have been. Maybe should have been. Did you know she got arrested the week before?"

Brigit's intake of breath betrayed her. Sam lowered his voice, closing the distance until the three of them stood in a tight triangle. The camera angle had to be terrible, but Ian didn't move.

"For trespassing. Out here in the Dell. There was a church group using the Ruritan for a lock-in and they found her sneaking around with a gas tank's worth of kerosene. Kind of wild connection, actually—James's mom called it in. Don't worry," Sam added quickly. "I made sure the place was free tonight. But yeah. Your folks came and bailed her out and, well, with what happened… Guess nobody wanted to make a scene. Including your parents. The whole thing just went away. Er. Not for you, obviously."

Sam finally looked uncomfortable in the uneven light of his torch and the cloud-skimmed moon. Ice spidered out along Brigit's bones. She licked her lips, but now she tasted nothing at all.

"And how the fuck do you know that?"

"The internet," Sam said. "And work. It's kind of what I do."

"Collect family secrets about dead girls?"

"Look things up." He cleared his throat and ran a hand through his hair so it stood up in points. "I'm a reference librarian. I—listen, I'm sorry. I shouldn't have said it like that. Or at all. I don't know. Sometimes when I find something interesting, I forget how to be a human being." He paused, but his whole body swayed toward her and the camera. Brigit took a breath, concentrating on her sore neck to keep herself calm, and sure enough, Sam kept going. "So anyway, the Dell has always been pretty off-limits, you know? No parks or anything. My parents told me never to go in there alone, which didn't seem odd, people get lost. But it turns out there are other stories like Emma's. Other kids who've gotten in trouble out here."

"Of course there are," Brigit said, although those missing posters needled through the cloud of self-doubt. Poor Michael Patterson's D&D friends. "It's a forest with no development. Perfect for parties and drug deals."

"Not that kind of trouble. More like runaways, or arson, or—" Sam stopped, twisting his mouth in an apologetic grimace. "Suicide. Seven cases in the last century, all involving the Dell. Probably more that were misreported or not documented at all."

Ian said, "Seven cases in a hundred years doesn't seem like much."

"Doesn't it? That's basically two per generation. It's not a big place. And like I said, I bet there's a lot that never made it onto the record, or not in so many words. Plenty of people wouldn't tell the cops if their kid had problems. Especially if those problems involved local secrets or things someone's ashamed of, like kids who are, you know, *different* in some way, which tends to be a local secret of its own—"

"What do you think happened?" Brigit cut in. "James and Gabrielle. You think they went into the Dell. Why? For what?"

"I don't know," Sam said. "But I'm pretty sure James meant real trees, so, yeah. I think they found something out there." Past him, the forest leaned closer. Oaks and maples pushed through the undulating dark. "Or maybe something found them."

9: IAN

In the ensuing silence, Ian shrugged up his camera shoulder to adjust the collar of his shirt. He was suddenly aware of an itch on his right heel, and the fact that his fingers were getting cold, and that he didn't want to go into the woods. He wanted to go back to his car, which would be warm from the drive and would smell like cookies and Brigit's hair and Ian himself, the deodorant he favored, which wasn't an amazing scent but was definitely nicer than October trees at night.

Ian thought of the very first episode he and Brigit had filmed. A year ago now, after ages of strategically pitching the concept to Brigit when she quit the Home Depot job in Maryland (boredom), and got fired from the bartending gig in Rhode Island (altercation with a handsy supervisor), and both quit and got fired from the cold caller agency in upstate New York (a mix of boredom and providing over-the-phone therapy on the company's dime). He'd believed in this idea. More than that, he'd believed it could be something Brigit might actually enjoy, a job that let her roam, let her dig into people and places and leave *before* they got mad at their exposed vulnerability, or before she simply lost interest and skipped town. For a while, that seemed like the aspect Brigit resisted more than anything else—the idea that maybe, just maybe, Ian actually kind of knew her. When she said yes, he felt vindicated. Then she suggested Emma as her fake spirit guide, and a crack opened up in Ian's certainty that this was a good idea.

But that first night he'd braced himself anyway, so excited he could barely speak. As a kid, he'd devoured ghost-hunting shows in secret. Studied them for projects at school. They were still his comfort food of choice. And no, his mother wasn't out there, but those shows took place in a world where she *could* be. A world Brigit spun up so convincingly she'd left their first client in tears. It had amazed Ian, surpassed his wildest expectations. He could occasionally summon that feeling as if no time had passed at all.

Not now. The only thing Ian could summon out here was the same thought that had circled him all day: he'd been the one to tell Brigit they should stay. That he wanted to try and help James. She had wanted to leave, but she'd rallied because of him, and now look where it had gotten them. Brigit staring at the woods with tight shoulders. A terrible distance in her eyes, visible even in the dark.

"That's why we're here," Ian said, a reminder to himself as much as her, though it came out more like a question. Sam and Brigit turned his way, Sam expectant, Brigit unreadable. He swallowed. "Brigit and I have done this before. Well, not *this*, but—it's why we're in Ellis Creek. To find what they found. Right?" Even as the words left his mouth, Ian felt like he was watching the film version of himself recite lines someone else had written. *What are you doing?* the theater would scream. *Get out of there!* "And the longer we stand out here, the less we're going to want to go in there."

Brigit nodded. She took a breath, audibly exhaling in one short push. "So let's get moving."

"Just like that?" Sam asked.

"You were going to go alone."

"I was going to think about going alone. Then we said all this aloud. What if we came back at dawn?"

"No," Brigit said. "Ian's right. We came here to go inside the Dell. There've been search parties since Gabrielle was found, and they didn't stumble over anything in broad daylight. I don't think they will tomorrow either."

Because Alicia and Lacey and maybe this whole town were in on it, covering up some kind of American Wicker Man situation that went back all the way to Brigit's childhood? Or because Brigit really believed there was something out there that could hide, if it chose, in the light? Ian could only think of one admittedly great reason to head into these woods here, now, in the dark, and that was for the ratings. Hell of a show if they actually found the boy. But somehow, he doubted Brigit cared about that.

"It's already been four days," she continued. "If we're doing this, we need to do it now." Brigit reached out and touched his arm, so lightly it could almost have been the wind. "Ian, don't lose me."

She meant with the camera. Meant for him to stay behind her and keep the angle close. Brigit started toward the trees, Sam falling in beside her, and Ian forced himself to follow.

The woods descended quickly. Moonlight splashed between each tree in shrinking pools as Brigit led them deeper, picking around brambles and sunken patches of earth. The air shifted as they walked, from bark and sky to something denser, older, a vegetable musk. Ian checked his viewfinder to confirm that the infrared camera was picking up enough light from the moon and Sam's flashlight. The tiny screen rendered Brigit and Sam as ghosts weaving through charcoal trunks and fungal clouds of undergrowth.

"What do you think we're looking for?" Sam asked, and Ian tripped over a fallen log. He caught his balance against an oak, the bark rough and cool under his palm. Brigit, a pace or two ahead, didn't reply. Maybe she hadn't heard.

"I think we'll know it when we see it," Ian said. Above their heads, the canopy thickened as trees clumped closer together. Sounds were muted now. Ian sensed their pace slowing too, the way forward growing less obvious. Did Brigit know where she was going? Would it be better or worse if she did?

They all moved carefully now, placing their feet deliberately so as not to make too much noise. The woods lay in near silence otherwise. Ian pictured the three of them as small creatures, ground dwellers hoping to move about unnoticed, and immediately felt eyes on his back. As if the forest were one massive organism they'd invaded with their cameras and flashlights, and now they'd drawn its attention in the dark.

"What?" Brigit said, stopping. Ian and Sam halted too.

"What?" Sam asked, glancing between Ian and Brigit.

"I didn't say anything," Ian said. "What did you hear?"

Brigit hesitated, head slightly cocked, looking off somewhere in the middle distance. Then she shook her head. "Nothing."

"Don't do that," Ian said, surprising himself. "Don't shrug it off. Not in here."

"It's just the dark playing tricks. It's fine." She turned back to the woods. Ian hadn't realized they were all standing that close to one another. Huddling: a prey instinct. They kept moving.

He'd been chilly by the Ruritan, but it was colder in the woods. The trees blocked the wind, but they also blocked any residual warmth from the blackening sky as overlapping branches sliced the moonlight into ribbons. Ian's fingers would hurt when they made it back to the car.

Brigit continued more or less north from the parking lot, in as straight a line as the terrain would allow. Soon the ground began to dip, sloping downward gently at first before forcing them to angle diagonally to the right and zigzag back when they reached the bottom of the ravine. A creek cut through here once, Ian thought as he filmed the snaking base of the gully. Now it held only a river of leaves.

Something hurtled past as they began to climb back up the other side, but no one was speedy enough to catch what it was. "Raccoon?" Ian asked, breathing harder. The camera wasn't as heavy as some of the others they used in static jobs, but he could definitely feel it. They'd been walking for at least half an hour.

"Could be," Sam said. "Maybe badger."

"Be grateful we haven't heard a bobcat yet," Brigit said, grabbing a maple sapling to help hoist herself up the slope. "They sound like someone being gutted."

Ian puffed a laugh. "So if we do hear a scream, ignore it?"

"Right. In the summer, we came out here at dusk." Brigit held the maple taut so he could reach it while Sam pushed on ahead. "Best time for Wild Men. I remember one night Emma climbed a tree so I couldn't find her. She let me wander around for maybe twenty minutes in the dark, and then there was this awful shrieking. I thought something was eating her. I didn't talk to her for two days after that, even though she came for me as soon as she heard the bobcat."

At the top of the ravine, Brigit turned to help Ian up the final steps. Sam hadn't stopped to wait. When Ian crested the hill, he was nothing but a bobbing shape and the sweeping arc of his light moving quickly away.

"Hey," Ian called. "Hold up!"

He and Brigit picked up their pace as the ground plateaued. Sam's flashlight was visible, but the trees were thicker here,

trunks combining into great twisted masses of shadow cut
with shocks of white where birches grew.

"Sam," Brigit hissed, clearly trying not to shout. "Sam!
Wait for us!"

Sam didn't stop. If anything, the sounds of shuffling leaves
and snapping twigs picked up speed, blurring together as
though Sam were trotting now, nearly running. Brigit looked
back at Ian, her eyes gigantic and worried, then broke into
a jog.

"Brigit!" Ian tried to run as well, but the camera was cum-
bersome and he kept scuffing his feet against piles of leaves
or moldering branches. Its weight skewed his shoulder, his
balance all wrong from the way he held the machine, and
soon there were only the crashing noises ahead—the distant
play of light—

10: BRIGIT

"I'm just going to catch him," Brigit called back to Ian, not slowing. Her flashlight swung up and down as she ran, dodging bushes and ducking under low-hanging branches that loomed suddenly out of the night. Sam's light was fainter and farther away than it should be.

Brigit's right foot hit something solid enough to spike tears into her eyes and she fell, knees sinking into the soft undergrowth, her free hand splaying flat on the ground. Cold bit into her palm, traveling up her wrist beneath her jacket. She opened her mouth in a wordless gasp. Damp chill. Dark mud. Her sister bloody on the ground. She hadn't seen that, though. Nobody had, nobody except the people who found Emma and brought her out of the cold.

"Emma?" Her own voice sounded choked and strange, quickly swallowed by the night before her flashlight went out.

Brigit froze. The dark became physical almost at once, thousands of fingers that pressed into her cheeks. Her eyes had adjusted to the specific visibility enabled by her flashlight combined with Ian's camera, but now he was gone too, somewhere off behind her; she could hear the crashing footsteps, but the only remaining source of light was that distant, muffled moon. No sign of Sam. No noise ahead, no flashes of light through the breaks in the trunks. Her breath quickened. Brigit tried to quiet herself, but each inhale rasped, shockingly loud, a beacon for every invisible thing that moved with her in this forest because now there were no footsteps either. The silence was thick. Fear grasped at her lungs, tugged oxygen from her brain, and made her dizzy, but when she blinked there was only more dark and more malicious quiet. She wanted to scream Ian's name or even Sam's, but she held her tongue, clamped her teeth down on the tip and held it tight because there *was* something out there in the woods and it wasn't a bobcat and if she screamed, if she screamed—

You're wrong, she told herself. *You're wrong, or you've lost it, and either way you're wrong.* She wasn't. They'd been walking, the three of them, in silence. Something had giggled out of sight.

Behind her, the sounds of movement grew fainter. Ian should have caught up by now. She'd told him to stay close, ordered him not to lose her, but now he was traveling steadily away. Unless he didn't know where she was. Unless they'd gone into different woods entirely, Brigit and Ian and Sam, drifting off the map into three places that were near but couldn't touch. Like Emma in the tree that night, before the screaming cat: there but not there, and nowhere Brigit could see.

"That was cruel, big sis," Brigit whispered. Her voice was oddly steady, and in the desperately brief wake of that steadiness, she closed her eyes. Forced an image to the top of her mind: Ian in the car, hands yellow-knuckled on the wheel, hyperventilating until she talked him down. In. Out. In.

Brigit opened her eyes. Shapes grew distinct around her. No white birches glowing in the final traces of moonlight. Only the oaks and maples and gangly Virginia pines she'd climbed a thousand times as a kid, first with Emma's help and then alone, proving to no one that she could. Brigit breathed in deep again, and this time tasted the cold, rich evergreens, the tang of sap. She knew that flavor to her bones. It had been over a decade, but these were her woods too.

A rustle to her left. She turned her head and the noise stopped at once. Brigit held her breath, head tilted, ears straining— and it came again. Something moving toward her, one step at a time. Her hands sank into the soft, cold earth as she pushed herself back on her haunches. Her left pinky finger grazed metal and Brigit grabbed her flashlight, holding it with both hands.

"Hello?"

The night shifted. More shadows coalesced as her eyes continued to adjust, the forest taking on new depth, but all she could see in the direction of the sound was a snarling jumble of brambles. Brigit shifted into a crouch. As her heels crunched into leaves, the thing in the forest moved too. Matched her small noises with its own, nearly perfectly, just a second off.

The cold ate through her jacket, her scarf, her skin. Ate through everything until it reached her core, trying its hardest to eat that too, but something rose to meet it. The same dark heat that had gripped her when Mrs. Mulroy or Sam spoke about her family. The grim and pounding fury that plagued her dreams and filled her mouth with ash. *Emma. Emma. Emma.* What happened to her sister, happened out here. If Brigit was hallucinating, it was in her blood, and if she wasn't, that was too.

She stood in one harsh movement, both knees popping loudly, and sank into a ready stance with the flashlight up above her right shoulder like a cudgel. A large, spindly shape lunged at her from behind a towering oak and Brigit swung the flashlight as hard as she could. She hit something soft but giving, the impact horrible, a hammer on meat.

"Ow! It's me!"

Light flared from her flashlight, sudden and blinding. Brigit stumbled backward and blinked until the swimming shadows resolved themselves into Sam. He held his shoulder with one hand, his own flashlight nowhere to be seen.

"What the hell?" Her voice was low, jagged, her muscles still twitching and ready to react. "Where did you go? Where's Ian?"

"I don't know! I lost you guys! One second we were all coming up the ridge and then I turned around and you were gone." He straightened, and Brigit saw the whites of his eyes. His ashen skin. "My flashlight's a piece of shit. Died as soon as I realized you weren't with me. I've been walking back the way I came for fifteen minutes shouting your names."

"You were shouting?" Brigit's heart was a throbbing wound inside her throat. "I didn't…"

"When did you lose Ian?"

She turned back the way she'd come, searching for the direction in which she'd last heard Ian crashing through the trees. Sam's breathing sounded as harsh as her own.

"Not long ago. Five minutes? Less than ten. My flashlight stopped working too. And I fell." She wiped one hand against her thigh. Something wet and soft slid off her palm. Sam shuddered, teeth clacking teeth. Brigit reached with her unclean hand and gave his shoulder one firm squeeze. "Come on. We have to find him."

She started off in the direction she thought Ian had gone, and Sam matched her pace without a word. Brigit didn't call out this time. She hadn't heard Sam, for one, but also something in her couldn't bear the thought of shouting Ian's name, again, and hearing no response. He might not be in danger, she reminded herself. If Ian had woken with a birch tree creeping up on him, Brigit sure as hell would know about it. Whatever was out here, if anything really was, its worst mind games thus far had been with her. Maybe Ian was already back at the Ruritan.

Every noise she and Sam did make was an assault on the silence that now hung against the ground like fog. Nothing else moved in any direction. No squirrels above, no deer racing past. No Ian fumbling in the dark. Despite the path cut by her flashlight, Brigit had the wild thought that she was floating, suspended in the air or deep underwater. Her churning legs, the crunching of her footsteps, all that could be in her head. She could still be in the Super 8. She could still be in the Dell sixteen years ago, holding Emma's icy hand, her face smeared with mud and sticks jutting out of her hair after their very last game.

I won, Emma whispered, or didn't, or once had. *Now you have to come with me.*

It was impossibly fast, this suffocating, dreamlike walk out of the trees. Like only moments separated Sam finding Brigit and the two of them breaking into the moonlit parking lot of the Ruritan. There was the building with its great dark windows, and there to the right was Ian's car standing solitary guard. At the sight of the car, something snapped.

"Ian!" Brigit ran a few steps toward the Ruritan, whirling to survey the low bulk of the building, the rest of the deserted lot. Nothing. Nothing and no one. "Ian!"

"Hey," Sam said, coming up beside her. "Hey, stop."

Brigit ignored him. She ran to the Ruritan and pressed her face against one darkened window, but inside there were only a few stacks of chairs. The night hung still and heavy atop the Ruritan and the trees at its back, empty, all of it empty. She sprinted back to the edge of the woods and cupped her hands around her mouth, shouted so hard her lungs became paper torn again and again until nothing else would come out.

Then Brigit let her flashlight fall against her thigh and stared at the black expanse of forest into which she had led them.

"Brigit." It was Sam, Sam behind her, Sam reaching out and taking her shoulders in his hands to pull her around. She wrenched away as he continued. "We need to get help."

"We need to go back. We need to find him. I can fix your flashlight; we have more batteries in the—" She stopped, horrified by the sudden realization that Ian had the car keys.

"We'll go back in," Sam said after a moment. "We'll find him. We just need more people and more lights."

"I can't leave him out there."

"I know. It's fucking scary, but we can't—"

"No," she cut him off. "There's something in the woods. Do you hear what I'm saying? Do you understand me, Sam? There is something in that forest and if I leave Ian in there with it, if I…"

"He couldn't hear us," Sam said when Brigit couldn't finish. "You couldn't hear me. What do you think we can do?"

Her jaw clenched, muscles working. Sam stared at her for a moment, then took one quick step away, leaned his head back to the moon, and made a noise that sounded like it had been dragged from deep inside his chest.

"I don't *want* to leave him. I'm not—I *came* here to—but if we go back now…like this…" Sam didn't finish. He didn't have to. Brigit heard the fear in his voice. Saw it in the tight line of his shoulders. He thought if they went back into the woods, they'd get separated again and this time they would never find their way out.

She turned back to the forest. Deeper pockets of shadow shifted the longer she stared, a subtle writhing of dark on dark like oil moving over water. Brigit pulled out her phone and called Ian, jaw tight. Voice mail. Then she dialed Alicia Nguyen.

Alicia answered on the third ring, her voice as unreadable as ever. "Brigit. You've found something?"

"Ian's missing. He's somewhere in the Dell behind the Ruritan, and it's not safe to wait until tomorrow to get him out. Can you help?"

To her credit, Alicia didn't hesitate. "Are you out of the Dell?"

"Yes."

"I'll be there in twenty." They hung up.

Brigit tried Ian again, just in case, and hung up midway through his pre-recorded greeting. She hunkered down on the grass, running her hands over her head and tugging at her hair. The short, sharp pain was good. It grounded her in this moment, this space.

"Who'd you call?"

"Alicia Nguyen." Brigit didn't rise, didn't look at Sam. "She's the one who called me here. She thinks the same thing you do. About Gabrielle and James and my sister."

"Ah." Sam came over and sat down beside her. He grimaced. "She's a cop now."

"I'm aware."

From there, they waited in silence for Alicia to arrive. The woods stayed silent too. But not still. Brigit watched those shadows slide against one another, dark on dark on dark, and behind all that, so slim and distant it had to be a trick of her mind, a narrow shard of white.

INTERLUDE: 2003

Livejournal.com
Post from user WhenItsLicia
November 23, 2003

(no subject)

I wish I could close my eyes and wake up last summer. I want it so badly I could throw up. I would call every night. I would read every note she gave me. It's like I've been asleep since it happened. I keep forgetting and remembering and forgetting again.

    I went to the Dell for the first time since the night she got arrested. I thought my head would be full of horrible things but instead I couldn't stop thinking about the 4th of July, when we brought a picnic blanket and saw that doe. People say you shouldn't go in at night and I get that, but it's so different in the sun. Also kids kill themselves everywhere. If more do it here than other places, I don't think we should blame the fucking woods.

    This weekend I saw her family at Food Lion. Her sister had eyes like a dead person. She almost walked right into some woman. Creeptastic. That's what Emma would say. I left without buying anything. Mom was pissed.

11: BRIGIT

When headlights turned off the country highway and into the Ruritan parking lot, Sam and Brigit sprang to their feet. The Ford Focus had lost some of its sheen above the spattered dirt, bright crimson by day closer to purple in the moonlight.

Alicia climbed out of the car and jogged over to them, her hands busy with something blocky and awkward, and slowed when she hit the end of the gravel. "Sam," she said as a beam of strong light cut the dark. "What are you doing here?"

Brigit shielded her eyes against the glare, and Alicia lowered her oversized flashlight.

"I came to help look for James." Sam's tone was a blend of defensiveness and strain. Alicia's dark eyes narrowed but she turned her full attention on Brigit.

"Ian?"

"In there." Brigit pointed at the woods with her flashlight. Its glow carved out a soft bowl of bark and undergrowth beyond which lay darkness thick as tar. "He asked us to meet him here," she continued, nodding to Sam. He opened his mouth, but Brigit didn't let him protest. Speaking was good. As long as she spoke words someone else expected to hear, Brigit could avoid herself. "I could feel the connection as well, between Gabrielle and James and other kids from town who've gone missing from this place. The three of us went into the trees together but got separated. Sam and I found each other but Ian…" Her throat cinched into a knot. "He's not picking up his phone. I don't know if he has service."

"How long since you lost track of him?"

Sam checked his wristwatch, breathed a soft curse. "Two hours."

"What?" Brigit whipped her cell phone back out. She hadn't even registered the time when she'd made those calls, and now stared in disbelief at the numbers on her screen: 11:53 p.m. They'd gone into the woods at fifteen past eight. Brigit shook her head, lifting her eyes to meet Sam's. He looked as sallow and shocked as she felt.

"Did you see anything?" Alicia asked, and Brigit couldn't tell if she sounded more urgent or if everything just seemed heightened now. "Did you find anything that might suggest James is out there too?"

Sam shook his head. Brigit thought of the thing creeping toward her one stealthy step at a time. She pulled her elbows tight with the opposite hands and grasped for the role Alicia needed to see. "I sensed another presence in the Dell. I don't know what it was, but it wasn't friendly."

"You sensed?" Sam asked. Brigit dug her nails into her arms.

"Yes."

"It's a forest. I didn't see anything in there but trees."

"You also shouted and nobody heard. We just lost an hour. What exactly did you think those kids found?"

"I don't know, a bunker or a cult or—"

"People," Detective Nguyen cut in. Brigit clamped her teeth on the tip of her tongue as she and Sam both turned to Alicia. "Brigit, I asked you to come here because of your sis-

ter's connection to Gabi Markham's disappearance. Your…
gifts, whatever they may be, were a bonus at the time, at best.
I won't say they're anything else now. Without hard evidence
I can share with my team—evidence that goes beyond a gut
feeling—I can't call in a search party in the middle of the
night."

"You're the one who put us here," Brigit said. "You're the
lead detective."

Alicia rounded on her, and for the first time something
other than professional tension split her tone. "Yes. I am. And
people who look like you tend not to appreciate off-book
moves from lead detectives who look like me. Such as bringing in a psychic behind their backs and requisitioning emergency resources when she gets in trouble." Brigit opened her
mouth but nothing came out. "We will go after your partner," Alicia continued, her composure regained. "I promise
you. But if you want real help, you'll wait until tomorrow."

"What happens tomorrow?"

"I know you told James's mother why you're here. The
Mulroys are coming in to check on the investigation at nine."
Alicia grimaced, clearly unhappy with what she was about to
say. "So that's when you come to the station and tell me, in
public, how you followed a hunch about the Ruritan and Ian
disappeared in the Dell. That'll give me a reason and community support to comb these particular woods, instead of
closer to where Gabrielle was found."

"You want us to manipulate James's parents?" Sam took a
step away from Alicia and Brigit that threw his whole face
into shadow.

"We'll have a better chance of finding Ian if more people
are willing to look."

"I'll do it," Brigit said. She lifted her chin, daring Sam to
speak again. He shook his head but kept his mouth shut.

The idea of leaving Ian in the trees until the next day made her want to carve herself up, but Sam and Alicia were right. Whatever moved inside that forest was stronger than her, at least in the dark, and Brigit couldn't lie to herself: she was petrified of going back into the woods, of giving whatever had hunted her the chance to tire of its game.

Gabrielle was alive, though. Unconscious, but alive. Brigit had to believe that James was too, wherever he was, and that Ian would also be left unharmed. At least for now.

"I'll be there at nine a.m. sharp. I just need a ride back to—" A thought struck her. Brigit glanced at Ian's car and blew out a breath. "My room key is locked in there."

For a moment, all three were quiet. Then Sam stepped back into the light.

"Crash with me tonight," he said. "I'll take you to the station in the morning." He gestured toward the gravel that extended past the Ruritan. "I'm parked over there. Your car will be fine overnight."

Alicia looked to Brigit. She eyed the woods again. She could stay here instead. Sleep on the dewy grass, let frost creep over her face.

"Yeah," Brigit said. "Thanks."

They split off at Alicia's car. The detective paused with one hand on the door, jaw working in the moonlight. Brigit hesitated too, expecting another promise or an offer of sympathy. Instead, Alicia ducked into the Focus and backed out of the lot without another word.

Brigit and Sam climbed into his hatchback, joining a dismembered bicycle that filled the car with the smell of grease. She tensed and relaxed each muscle in her face as they rolled past Ian's car. Then they were on the empty dark road, leaving him and the Dell behind.

★ ★ ★

"I'm sorry."

It was the first thing Sam had said since they'd left the Ruritan. The faint glow of his dashboard lights turned his expression sepulchral.

"It's not your fault," Brigit said. To her surprise, she meant it. "We were always going to end up in the Dell."

"Not for that. I mean, that too, but I'm sorry for—questioning you. It wasn't cool. Not after what happened. With your friend still in there."

Your friend too. The words hung between them, unspoken but palpable. Sam worked his fingers on the steering wheel.

"You must be wondering," he said as they turned onto a gravel road flanked by squat pines. "Why some random guy would go into the Dell in the middle of the night. What's the deal with me and that teenager?"

Brigit glanced at Sam. A knot of anger lingered in her chest, but inside it was fear, and something in the tightness of his voice caught that knot and tugged: Sam felt the same way.

"And what is the deal?"

"James is a golden boy. Track star. Roots in town for generations, and you can bet that family tree has a history of cutting away any branch that might *run off to San Francisco*, as his mom has literally put it. His parents love him, but he's terrified if they find out he's not their perfect straight senator-to-be, they'll disown him. Gabi means well, but James needed a friend who knows how that feels." They made another turn, and the headlights illuminated a small house with a sagging porch. "This place. It pushes down and down until you can't even twitch. People help it along, of course. Out of fear, sometimes, or that's what we're supposed to tell ourselves so we don't blame them when they fuck with us. Doesn't mean they wouldn't do it again, given the chance. Anyway, it's easy to feel alone in that. I won't let James be alone in this." Sam stopped the car, pushed out a breath. He turned to Brigit, and his dark eyes burned. "Ian either. We're going to find them, okay?"

Brigit couldn't speak as she climbed out of Sam's car. Her throat was suddenly swollen, thick with acid. Those lonely years of high school she'd held at bay outside the bathroom at Tim's Tavern flooded her now with all their gutting, joyful misery, lungs burning, stuck fast in the injustice of finally meeting parts of herself that—at best—no one wanted to see. At least her parents had never wanted her to be anyone she wasn't. They just didn't have it in them to care who she was.

Sam led the way down a paving stone path to a front porch decorated with bird feeders. "Home sweet home," he said, testing the bottom step with one foot before putting his full weight on the wood. "Sorry. Bit of a wreck."

Brigit cleared her throat as Sam unlocked the door. "It's nice."

"I bought it off my parents when they moved, but I overestimated how much time I'd actually have to work on it. So everything is a little broken. Watch your step," he warned as Brigit passed him into a darkened room. "Cat."

She stopped in the middle of the room, eyes adjusting to shadowy shapes: couch, woodstove, armchairs. The cat made an appearance just before Sam turned on the lights, winding between her legs with a soft noise of either welcome or annoyance. Brigit had never been good at interpreting animal sounds. Emma had been allergic, and after she died, the family's preferred pet was grief.

In the warm glow of a ceiling light, Sam's cat turned out to be black with yellowish eyes. He hunkered down and it went to him, butted its forehead against his knee. "This is Gabe,"

Sam said. He scooped up the cat with one arm and carried him past Brigit. "Guest room's this way."

The guest room turned out to be more of a storage closet for Sam's collection of cardboard boxes. But there was a bed, with sheets that smelled faintly stale but not actively unclean.

"Sorry about the junk. This is what happens when you store all the shit you don't want to remember. I think I still have my papers for Mrs. Dudley. That group project approach to close reading? Fucked up."

"Oh, god, I know." Brigit smiled a little. "That was the only English class I ever got a B in." The first thing he'd said to her floated back up: *You never struck me as a team player in school.* "She only taught seniors, though. Were we in the same class?"

Sam wore an odd expression: rueful and nervous at the same time. "Yeah," he said. "We, uh, we were. I sat behind you, actually."

"Oh. Shit. I'm sorry."

"No, it's okay." Sam looked outright pained now. "I look different now than I did when we were in school."

Brigit studied him, the dark hair, the slender build. Tried to cast her mind back to high school and the agony of senior year, when she'd been so close to escaping Ellis Creek. She remembered…a skinny kid in baggy jeans, forever swamped by a too-big sweatshirt or flannel. Always first in, first out of the locker room after gym.

The girls' locker room.

Ah.

Brigit had maybe clocked something back then, but she wouldn't have known what she was clocking. This quiet, watchful kid who almost never spoke but once appeared in the local paper for solving some kind of—

"You won that programming thing the math department put on in senior year."

Sam blinked at her, obviously startled. "Yeah. The Euler Project. I went through a computer science phase. Right after the ornithology phase. Turns out I just like learning things."

"Sure." She shoved her hands into her pockets as warmth bloomed in her chest. Being neighbors on a spectrum of identities shouldn't make her feel closer to him, but Brigit didn't fight the automatic sense of kinship, or the pang of regret: Could she have had this back then after all? But just like coming out to Emma, that was pointless to imagine. "Sorry I forgot who you were. And for the record, I'm non-binary. I've tried a bunch of gender-neutral pronouns and none have felt better than no pronouns at all, which is hard to explain in a social media profile, let alone every time I have a conversation, but yeah. You're right. High school in Ellis Creek was not the best."

Sam smiled, his whole body easing. "No joke. And listen, I get it. Maybe after all this we can talk. You know, about this other hugely complicated thing?" They shared a weak laugh. "Okay, well. Get some sleep if you can." For a moment the relief slipped from his face, leaving something older and graver in its place. "I'm right down the hall if you need anything."

"I'll be all right." Brigit waved him toward the door. "Thanks again. I'll see you tomorrow."

Sleep came slowly but with force. She dreamed of the Dell. Oak leaves drifting. A smell like peat and brackish water. And a noise that shouldn't be out there at all, the sudden bright *SNICK* of—

Brigit woke with one knee jutting off the mattress, angled like a plant toward the morning sun. For one beat all she felt was quiet pleasure. The bed was perfectly warm, and the light on her face was soft as dough. Then the truth of what this morning meant—that Ian had been lost in the woods for a whole night—sent her spilling out of bed. She checked her phone, hopping into her jeans. Not quite 7:45. Plenty of time to reach the police station by nine.

There was no sign of Sam in the kitchen, but Brigit found a jar of coffee grounds beside the stove and a drip pot by the sink. While coffee burbled into the carafe, she finally gave the neck stretches a try. Ian would need them too, if he was awake.

A soft mew alerted Brigit to Sam's cat's presence before he landed on the counter by her elbow. "You're a good boy, aren't you?" Brigit asked, stroking the sleek head. "Is it true what they say about black cats, or are you guys fakes too?"

The strong smell of coffee drew Brigit back to the drip pot. Gabe didn't approve of her shifting loyalties and followed Brigit to the couch once she'd filled a foraged mug. She patted the seat beside her, wanting the comfort of a small, friendly creature who didn't give a damn what she'd done.

Sam padded into the living room when Brigit was halfway through her cup. She toasted with her mug. "There's coffee in the kitchen."

He grunted and vanished, reappearing several long minutes later with a mug of his own as well as a plate of some kind of dark, nutty-looking bread. "Stollen."

"What?"

Sam set the plate down on the low wooden coffee table between the couch and the armchair, taking the chair and nodding at the bread. It smelled faintly sugary, and below that something Brigit liked less—an almost muddy scent, like compost. "Fruitcake, only not gross. You're supposed to toast it but…" He leaned back in the armchair and closed his eyes. "God, my back. I run a marathon yesterday?"

Brigit hummed in agreement. Her whole body was sore, though the stretches had helped. She sipped her coffee, glanced over at Sam to ask when they should leave, and nearly spilled scalding liquid all over her lap. Curled around the right rear leg of his chair, so low to the ground they would have been level with Gabe's yellow eyes, were four red-gloved fingertips.

She couldn't breathe. Couldn't move beyond that first startled jolt. The fingers gripped the dark wooden leg from behind as though something crouched there, crammed into the impossible space between the armchair and the wall, like a child too delighted with its hiding spot to realize it had given itself away. Or like something equally delighted to let her know it was there.

"Sam," Brigit managed. He didn't answer. The room dropped a few degrees, cool morning air invading through the walls. "Sam."

"Probably not as bad as Ian feels," Sam said. Brigit's palms hurt. The mug had gotten hotter, or her fingers had gone clammy and bloodless. "He's been running through those woods for hours now. Or is it weeks?"

His eyes slid open. From that lazy, bent-necked position, he looked like a mannequin draped over a chair for storage.

"I think it's actually years." Sam's lips carved up into his cheeks. "Maybe he'll be older when you find him. If you find him. An old, old man with white hair and weak bones who could still hurt us if we let him." A heavy thud marked Gabe's leap onto the top of the couch by Brigit's head. Cat musk filled her nostrils. "Everything can hurt you if you let it. Do you think your sister felt that way before she died?"

Gabe descended onto the cushion beside her and paused alongside her thigh, eyes fixed on the armchair. As fur tickled her forearm, Brigit listened to the shaky ins and outs of her own breathing, felt the trembling of her joints. With that awareness came the ability to move. She stood too fast. Coffee spilled onto her hand, burning the skin as Brigit pulled back her arm to throw the mug at Sam, at the thing that crouched behind him, moving his mouth and tongue—

"Hey," Sam said. "Morning. That coffee?"

Brigit blinked, her mug arm tensed in the air. The armchair sat empty above the black cat now twining around its legs, his tail stiff and twitching. Sam stood in the open doorway that led to the kitchen, scratching his head and looking significantly more alert than he had the first time he'd walked in.

"Yeah." Her voice sounded shockingly calm. "In the pot."

Sam turned and walked into the kitchen, then reappeared in the cutout window at the bar counter as he poured himself a mug. "You hungry? I've got eggs, yogurt, some kind of fancy bread from my aunt…"

A chill tightened Brigit's nape. "I'm good. Thanks."

She kept her eyes on that window to the kitchen, watching Sam grab something from the fridge and return with his mug in one hand and a cup of yogurt in the other. He set his coffee on the table and perched on the armchair, downing half the yogurt before speaking again. "Get any sleep?" A brief pause. "Any—premonitions?"

Brigit didn't answer, too busy scanning the low, secret parts of the room. Then his words registered like cool hands on her shoulders, pressing her down into the couch. She took a sip of coffee to wet her throat. "It doesn't really work like that. I'm not clairvoyant."

"Then how do you do what you do?" Sam refocused on his yogurt. "I did some googling last night. Couldn't sleep. Found you guys in a couple spots."

She wanted to ask which spots, which stories exactly he'd read. There were the episodes posted on YouTube, personal blogs, a few small-town news reports—but it didn't really matter, not now. Sam already knew the worst thing that had ever happened to her, and he'd lived through the most unnatural events she'd ever faced.

"I have help," Brigit said, and stood. "Is there time to shower before we go?"

Sam found her a towel, apologizing for the low water pressure. Brigit locked the bathroom door and turned the tap as hot as it would go. Steam began to creep across the mirror above the sink, eating through her reflection like mold.

Sam had come out of the woods thinking bunker. Maybe a cult. He had probably rationalized the missing time by now too; either way, he definitely hadn't seen anything in there. Hadn't been *visited*. Neither had Ian, or there was no way in hell he would have set foot in those trees. So whatever had come to Brigit twice now, crowding around Emma's impossible phone call...that was just for her. Taunting her. Goading her onward, into the Dell.

Or maybe not. Maybe nothing wanted her at all. Maybe instead, Brigit had unlocked a door inside herself by coming back here. Maybe she had been living behind a thinner wall than she'd imagined for all these years, the same kind Emma might have lived behind, and that boy in Connecticut with his Sharpie-stained shoes, and maybe now that wall was coming down.

12: BRIGIT

The drive into town was quick for country roads. They didn't speak much, although Sam inhaled audibly once or twice, and tapped his fingers on the wheel. Every time they slowed for a turn or a light she felt his gaze on her profile, but Brigit kept her eyes on the windshield.

There was only one way forward here. One way to find Ian and get him out of the Dell. The lost time was real. So Brigit had to tell herself that what she'd seen and heard and fucking smelled was real too. There was something in those woods. It had killed her sister. Taken Ian. Brigit could not afford to paralyze herself with doubt. At least, not until she got him back.

"Hey." Sam's voice held an edge that told Brigit this wasn't the first word he'd spoken. She blinked. The car was parked outside a brick police station lined with dogwoods, and Sam was looking at her with his arms stacked on top of the steering wheel, knuckles tight on his forearm. "You okay?"

"I'm fine."

"Good. I need you to be fine. I don't want to go in there. Even if cops didn't freak me out, I'm not a fan of James's parents. They're definitely not a fan of me."

Brigit's heart rate eased at his bluntness, her own nerves calmed by the discomfort lining his body.

"Don't worry," she said. "You can wait in the car." In her voice, she heard a person who hadn't left her best friend alone in the dark. A person Sam could trust. "I'll be all right. You don't need to be there for this."

"I want to help."

"You have. You are." She unbuckled her seat belt and managed a smile, one hand on the door. "Don't go anywhere. I shouldn't be long."

Brigit dragged his impression of her across the asphalt parking lot, up to the double wooden doors, and into the small but noisy entrance of the station. By the time the doors swung shut behind her, she'd wrapped it so tightly around herself it was like the rest of her—the real self—had gone to sleep.

At least she'd been right. It didn't take long.

Once the tears and accusations subsided, Mr. and Mrs. Mulroy turned to Alicia and demanded a second search party be mustered for the quadrant of woods surrounding the Ruritan. They'd already done a walk-through after Gabrielle had been found, and now they would sweep the Dell south to the downtown border.

"All right," Detective Nguyen said, after a quick conference with two uniformed officers who'd risen from their desks when Brigit began to speak. "We'll organize a line. Thomas, go ahead and put out the call for volunteers. I'm sure we can get a few pensioners to take a walk in the woods. Brigit, a word."

Alicia's summons interrupted Mr. Mulroy halfway to Brigit. He wore a look she'd seen before, usually on the relatives of clients who suspected she and Ian were using sad people for money (which they only sometimes were). Or, worse, the ones who did believe her and had opinions about what that meant for her immortal soul. Brigit dug her thumbnail into her index finger. "Excuse me," she said to James's father, and sidestepped him to approach the older woman.

"Ride with me," Alicia said. "I have some questions I'd like you to answer."

"Sam is waiting for me."

"He knows the way."

Mr. Mulroy stood beside his wife. She had one hand around his elbow, tugging him toward the door, but he resisted her attempts to pull him away.

"Unless you'd rather wait here," Alicia said, and although she didn't so much as glance at James's parents, Brigit knew a threat when she heard one. Jaw clenched, she allowed herself to be led past the Mulroys and into the sun.

"Now that you've had a chance to sleep on it," Alicia said as soon as they pulled onto the road, "I'd like to know what you saw in the Dell."

"I never said I saw anything."

Four red fingers slipping quickly out of sight. Her sister's voice on the phone, distant and accusatory: *You have to come back.*

So, leaning into the theory that did not involve Brigit losing her mind: if the presence from the Dell could wear the shapes of other people, putting on voices would be no problem. Which was better, her dead sister begging for help sixteen years too late, or a monster aping Emma just for fun?

"Fine." Alicia changed lanes, neatly cutting in front of a large black truck whose driver laid on the horn, and turned onto the road that would take them past the Dollhouses. "Then what did you feel?"

Her voice remained calm, but Alicia's knuckles were yellow and bloodless on the wheel. The sun broke through a skin of clouds and shone against the older woman's throat above her white blouse, and in that stark light the shadow of her jugular thudded visibly. Anger twisted up from somewhere deep, a steady ember Brigit caught and held inside her chest. Alicia wanted something from her. Not help finding James. Something else. Something she refused to voice.

Alicia who had loved her sister. Who had stayed in Ellis Creek all these years after Emma's death.

Who also thought there was something in the woods.

Because it was odd, on second thought, wasn't it? That Alicia would call Emma's sibling instead of their parents. That she would offer Brigit and Ian thousands of dollars to solve a case when she didn't even believe Brigit was a medium.

Ian had known that. So had Brigit, on some level. But she hadn't pushed for real answers because it was easier not to ask, easier to focus on the surface of this mystery than cut into the taped-over wound that was Emma and that final night in the Dell. Even after the call, the dreams, the goddamn ash that coated her tongue whenever she thought too long about her sister, Brigit had circled the edges of this question without daring to look inside.

What was Alicia using her *for*?

Ian had tried to talk about it, before they'd gone into the Dell. She hadn't let him finish.

"I felt something old," Brigit said. "I think it likes playing games. I think it's been there for a long time. I think it knows who I am." They passed the café, and the squad car ahead of them turned left. "But you already know that, don't you?"

"How would I? I'm not psychic."

They followed the squad car. The Ruritan came into view like a shipwreck. Behind it and on every side, the Dell spread out in undulating waves of green and brown.

"She called," Brigit said. "Emma called me on the phone."

"About the forest? About what she was planning?"

"Two days ago." The car went very quiet. Alicia's cheeks were pale and precisely carved as a wax figure, and vindictive pleasure sliced through Brigit's heart. "I don't suppose she's ever called you," she continued, pulse so loud it seemed impossible that Alicia couldn't hear it. She should stop, she knew she should stop, but Brigit's intuition flowed too quickly for her to control. "I don't suppose she called and asked you to bring me here?"

Alicia pulled into the parking lot and stopped the car. Her left hand stayed on the wheel while her right hand went to her forearm and squeezed tight, as if she needed to remind herself of her own solidity. "I haven't spoken to your sister since the day before she died."

For once that smoky voice sounded thin. Brigit opened her mouth, blood pounding in her temples, but a sharp knock on the driver's side window cut her off. Mrs. Mulroy bent to peer inside the car. One fist hovered by the glass while the other clutched her necklace near her throat. Alicia unbuckled her seat belt and shot Brigit one quick glance.

"After," she said, and climbed smoothly from the car.

13: BRIGIT

The Dell by daylight was beautiful. Had always been beautiful. Brigit hovered at the edge of the forest and tried not to let her heart fall out. The last time she'd seen it with sunshine fracturing across the canopy, she'd been eighteen and freshly graduated. That day, all expectations of her—survive high school, survive the wreckage of her family, survive—peeled off like a rind, leaving something raw and tender underneath: the knowledge that she'd done what Emma would never do.

"I have some questions about your consulting approach." Max stepped into the space between Brigit and Ian's car, her tone cautiously wry. Her hair was up in a high ponytail that showed off the vines inked up the back of her neck. "I thought you were here to find missing people, not lose more of them?"

"Call it method investigation."

This won a faint laugh that eased Brigit. After Sam's nervous energy and whatever the fuck Alicia was throwing her way, it was a relief to hide in banter.

Max glanced around. "Lacey here yet?"

And there went the ease.

"Should she be?"

Max made a noise in the back of her throat and stretched both arms behind her, fingers locked. Something cracked. "Well, what are we waiting for? Let's go find your friend."

As soon as she said it, Brigit realized that she *had* been waiting. The Mulroys and Alicia had already formed a line, stretching out with a foot or so between each person, and the cops to her left were doing the same. They were chatting quietly. Someone laughed. Apprehension ran cool fingernails down Brigit's spine.

You promised, Wild Child.

Another memory: Ian's eyes on her in the Whole Foods, and the pang of heartsickness when she'd realized he could see her weakness like a stain.

Max lifted a hand as though to touch Brigit's shoulder, then seemed to reconsider. Instead, she quirked her mouth and tilted her head toward the trees. Brigit unclenched her fists. Together they joined the line.

Even after they crossed the ten or so feet of tree line that blurred between forest and field, the Dell remained less dense than it had seemed the night before. Chilly sunlight filtered through the leaves and turned the tops of maples into a riot of orange and red. Where birches pierced the canopy, their leaves glowed like liquid gold. Still, Brigit tensed at every cracking branch. Twelve hours. That was how long Ian had been on his own out here. Six of them in pitch darkness if his camera light had gone out.

The line of people moved slowly, conversation dying down as they searched for signs of lost boys in the woods. Looking for a body. She didn't want to think like that but it was impossible not to, the silence fog-heavy, weighing them down. Brigit nearly tripped when Max broke it.

"So how many monsters have you found?"

"What?"

"I asked around," Max said, pausing to lift a log with the toe of her boot before letting it drop with a crumbling thud. "Most people we went to school with don't remember you, but the ones who do told me you went to film school and then started hunting Bigfoot."

Brigit laughed. The startled sound felt good at first, then terrible. "No Bigfoot," she said through a new lump. "Spirits, mainly. Although one time we did investigate a lake monster in Tennessee."

"Was it real?"

"Depends on who you ask."

They'd slowed a pace or so from the rest of the line. Brigit kept Max in her periphery as she scanned the browns and reds of fallen leaves for anything metal, anything fabric.

"Weird line of work," Max said. Faint tension in her tone. Because of the topic or the setting?

"I would say I'm not cut out for normal jobs," Brigit said, keeping her own voice light, which was kind of an out-of-body experience given the weight of fear on her chest. "But that's probably obvious. So, I guess I'll just say it was Ian's idea, and there's not as much paying work for mediums as television made us think."

"Right," Max said. "Ghosts and all. Guess I can understand why you kept that quiet. Wish you would've told me in high school, though. I could have helped you market your real talents instead of buying you that tarot deck."

Brigit didn't falter in her steps, but she felt like she'd missed one. Tarot deck? There was plenty of detritus she'd left behind when she moved out, which her mom had wasted no time selling; maybe there had been a deck, now that Max mentioned it, but Brigit certainly hadn't remembered it was a gift… She waited too long to respond, and Max huffed in amusement.

"Yeah," she said. "Checks out. Don't worry. When you dropped off the face of the earth after graduation, I figured my idea of our friendship and yours weren't the same. Any doubts cleared right up when you said hi at the bar like we just sat together in homeroom or something."

Any other day, that probably wouldn't have hit her. Today, the fact that Brigit didn't think it would have bothered her only made the impact worse. Because the truth was, she *didn't* remember being real friends with Max. It must have served her until it didn't, and then she'd moved on, flaying off everything from Ellis Creek that might have tried to keep her.

"Sorry," she said as they continued their slow march, concentrating on naming the different shades of leaves, the way Ian would. His steady gaze flashed through her mind. "I'm not proud of that."

"Hey," Max said. They stopped together. Brigit met Max's eyes, held them. Max cleared her throat. "It's fine. Kid stuff. So anyway, the Dell. Fun fact, my great-aunt Eleanor actually got kidnapped from somewhere out here back in the '40s. Or that was always the story. Speaking as an expert, what do you think is the deal with these woods?"

"Well," Brigit said. Her heart beat stronger through the ache. "I have some thoughts. But now that we're being blunt, you asked about Lacey before, and I know Ian ran into you two talking the other day. Is there anything I should know about her and Gabi?"

It was a gamble. Max held her silence for a beat. The line moved on without them. Then Max smoothed a strand of hair off her forehead, her bright red lipstick carving out a grimace.

"In the name of being blunt… I'm not sure what I should tell you. Not because I know something fucking horrific and I'm scared to say, just—you've been gone a long time. When this is over, you'll leave again. I won't."

A spark lit Brigit's synapses, burning one bright tunnel through the fear. She could see the edge Max teetered on. Brigit opened her mouth to ask the one right thing, the perfect question that would convince Max to share what she knew—

"Hey! Over here!"

The question evaporated. Brigit took off running.

The shout had come from about fifty paces down the line. By the time she reached its origin, enough searchers had congregated that she had to shoulder her way through the crowd, stumbling over feet and undergrowth until a hand caught her upper arm before she fell. Alicia's voice sounded very near her ear. "Brigit. It's okay. He just dropped it. There's no blood."

Yanking her arm out of Detective Nguyen's grip, Brigit dropped to the ground and reached for the camera half buried in leaves, stopping herself just in time. There might be fingerprints aside from hers and Ian's. Evidence they needed to preserve. As soon as the idea entered her mind, she had to swallow a laugh. It came out anyway. People murmured around her, watching. She felt their eyes, little pinpricks, little crow beaks pecking at her back. They'd heard her laugh. Who among them knew who she was, why they'd come? Pressure on her shoulders. Light and gentle and familiar, not the weight but the scent—bike grease and strong coffee. Sam.

"Let's get some room," he said quietly, standing with Brigit. She turned from the circle and took a few steps out of the mosh. Alicia tracked them with her eyes but didn't follow, and as soon as Brigit and Sam exited the circle surrounding Ian's fallen camera, it closed around the gap they'd made like water.

At first Brigit thought Sam only wanted her to breathe freely, outside the claustrophobic press of faces. Then he squeezed her arm. Brigit glanced up, but Sam's attention was focused straight ahead, beyond the backs of the Mulroys, and when he felt her shift he ducked his chin in a small nod. She followed his gaze.

One of the branches on the pine tree nearest the circle had been partially snapped, baring yellow wood like fat showing through a wound. Past that, a spine of white caught the sun. A single birch tree topped in gold.

Brigit glanced back at Alicia and Max. The detective was crouching now, talking quietly to one of the uniformed officers while Mrs. Mulroy clutched her husband's hand and peered over Alicia's shoulders. Max stood a few feet apart. Unlike the others, she was watching Brigit, her pale eyes sharp with concern as they flicked from Brigit to Sam and back. *It's fine*, Brigit heard again, that gruff release of tension. *Kid stuff.* Her chest felt tight. She didn't fight the animal instinct toward safety in numbers. Brigit tilted her head slightly to the left, indicating the broken branch. Max tracked the movement, then stepped out of the ring of onlookers. When she joined Brigit and Sam, Sam shifted on his feet, jaw tight. Max's gaze slid over him and away, deliberately avoiding eye contact; Brigit put a pin in that tension for later. She led their trio toward the injured pine.

Another broken branch stood out several paces up a hillock. This one had almost fully snapped, dangling by the scantest thread of bark. The skin tingled around Brigit's nostrils, the soft hollows of her elbows. She was a bloodhound now. Even as her conscious mind tumbled forward in uncontrollable hope, some part of Brigit fell back through the years to the times she'd felt this before: racing through these woods with a hunter's focus. Had Gabrielle dreamed of that too, or only of the last game—only Emma and her sharp white teeth?

At the top of the short hill, Brigit stopped to catch her breath. The air smelled ancient, like water and smoke. Trees swayed in a gentle breeze, leaves fluttering. "Oh," she said, looking down the hill. Then she was gone, half falling, half sprinting down the slope.

He didn't look up when Brigit skidded to a halt near his feet. His chin rested near his sternum, hair falling into his face; the tree he sat against had dribbled pine needles into his curls. There was mud on his kicked-out legs. Brigit crawled up beside him and, before she could lose her nerve, touched his shin.

Ian burst into movement like a startled quail. Both arms flew up, knocking Brigit's hand away, and he flung himself in the opposite direction with enough force to crash shoulder-first into the ground.

"Hey! Hey, hey, it's me, you're okay, it's just me." She balanced on her knees, hands in the air between them. Ian sat up on his elbows, panting. There was no blood left in his face. Only shades of brown and gray and, beneath his eyes, a sickly greenish tint. It took him a moment to focus on her face, and another for recognition to replace the panic. Brigit knew that look, the awful uncertainty between reality and fiction. While she waited for him to come back to himself, Sam and Max made it down the hill.

"Ian," Sam said, the way you'd talk to an injured dog. Ian said nothing. Only stared at Brigit, lips parted, his breath coming in shallow pants. "Did you find James?"

"Hey," Max said, "chill for a second. Give them some space."

Brigit turned her back on them both and, making sure Ian could see each movement, shuffled closer on her knees. Faint threads of sweat and cheap motel shampoo fought through the forest musk. His scent was here more than he was. She needed to throw him a lifeline.

"Can you give me your hand?" Brigit asked quietly.

The other volunteers were now shuffling leaves and crunching sticks as they followed from where the camera had fallen. Soon they'd come over the rise. Ian's wide eyes flicked toward the incline, back to Brigit. Slowly he shifted forward on his haunches. Reached for her outstretched hand. His palm was clammy as a basement wall but she wrapped her fingers around his and did her very best not to burst into tears.

"You're okay?" she whispered.

He didn't answer. Each movement of his chest was faint and quick. Up the hill someone shouted, was answered. Rushing noises blended together, papery and wet all at once, many feet slipping and running down the slope, but Brigit didn't open her eyes to see them come. All she could do was hold on to Ian's hand.

His fingers, at least, were strong. Cool but sturdy in hers. Her pulse pounded so quickly Ian must have been able to feel it in his palms, and some distant part of Brigit recoiled at that tangible evidence of weakness.

"Ian," she said as the rest of the searchers converged. Sam placed himself in the way with one thin arm out as if he could form an energy wall while Max spoke quietly but forcefully to Alicia. Nobody got too close. "Please say something. I need you to answer me." She tried and failed to smile. "We found your camera, if that's what you're worried about. Not a crack on it."

Nothing. Only a bird kicking off from high above them, and someone asking if this was the missing kid, and Alicia's low voice murmuring something Brigit couldn't make out. Then Ian lifted his other hand and raked it through his hair in a fidgety gesture so familiar it pierced her like a fishhook.

"Thank god," he said faintly, and they both sagged several inches lower into the undergrowth. "I can't expense that. You know?"

"Ian. Are you all right?" Brigit turned to see Alicia stand-ing a shoulder's distance away, her dark eyebrows soft with something that could, conceivably, have been relief.

"He's okay," she said when Ian didn't answer. "We need to get him out of here."

"Did you find my boy? Is he out there?" Mrs. Mulroy shouldered around Sam, followed closely by her husband. The forest held its breath. Ian released Brigit's hand. She looked back to him, fingers unexpectedly strange with the sudden absence, but his gaze had slipped from her face.

"No," he said, and now his voice was sharp as broken slate. "Your son is somewhere else."

INTERLUDE: 1992

Ellis Creek Tribune
February 19, 1992

DEATH IN JUVENILE CORRECTIONS FACILITY:

THE VERDICT, SUICIDE. THE QUESTION, WHOSE FAULT?

Sixteen-year-old Anthony Miuduski was found hanging from a shower bar in the South Roanoke Juvenile Center this Tuesday. The young man was serving a two-year sentence after setting a series of forest fires, one of which succeeded in causing minor property damage to a coffee shop on Route 20.

The case garnered media attention last fall due to Miuduski's age (fifteen at the time of the crimes) as well as the fact that his lawyer called for a period of mandated psychiatric care in lieu of correctional incarceration, which was denied by Judge Helen Samford. "I don't care where he set the fires," Samford said. "Arson is a gateway crime regardless of intent to injure. If we coddle these young men now, we're teaching them they don't need real accountability—they only need to fake it until they come of age."

Now Miuduski's parents are calling for an investigation into the governance of the South Roanoke Juvenile Center as well as a posthumous resentencing of their son. "Anthony was sick," Beth-Anne Miuduski told the *Ellis Creek Tribune* this week. "You see a kid sleepwalking into the woods, you get him medication. You see that same kid try to jump off the roof or light a fire, you get him a doctor. You try to help. You don't lock him up."

Judge Samford has a history of hard-line sentencing in cases involving minors, one which has come under criticism before but never with such severity. Continued on pg. 12.

14: IAN

Narrow fingers gripped his upper arm. Mrs. Mulroy's blue eyes were wide and fierce in the harsh midday light, and although she released Ian's arm immediately, her grip lingered through the knit of his shirt. A man Ian didn't recognize hurried up behind her, his face waxy above a neatly wrapped plaid scarf.

"Sophia," he said, eyes on Ian even as he wrapped an arm around Mrs. Mulroy's shoulders. "Not here."

"Then where?" she asked, rounding on him. "In church? Has God told you where our boy is?" She spun back to Ian, grabbing his hand in both of hers. He froze. Blood pulsed in his temples. He could feel her cold sweat on his palm. *God doesn't live here*, Ian might have told her. *He won't know anything you don't already.*

"Please," Mrs. Mulroy—Sophia—said. "Please tell me."

He shook his head. Her words shifted and danced inside his head. On one level Ian understood what she was asking, but at the same time he was somewhere else, so distant he couldn't make himself care about her fear. Minutes ago, Brigit had gripped his hand like this. When was the last time she'd done anything like that?

She lied. The words reverberated underneath Mrs. Mulroy's plea, thrumming along with his heartbeat. *She lied. She lied.*

"He doesn't know anything," Brigit said, and a harsh sound burst from Ian's chest that startled him as much as anyone. She stepped in close, one arm cutting down between him and the Mulroys like a parking lot gate, and James's mother released Ian's hand. "Please," Brigit went on. "Let us take care of Ian, and then I swear to you, I'll share anything and everything I can about your son."

Mrs. Mulroy rounded on Brigit with bared teeth. "Why should I believe you? I knew your sister. I held my tongue out of respect for the dead, but she wasn't like my boy, she was no kind of innocent—just like Gabrielle—and you! Whatever you have, it's—" Abruptly her face crumpled, her fear and grief as ugly as the rage. "You said you came here to help us, so help us. Help me. I don't care who gave you that power, I don't care if it damns me to ask you, just use it, please, there must be more you can do—"

"Sophia. Andrew." Alicia materialized from the crowd as Brigit stood beside Ian, so still she might not have been breathing. "If you'll follow me back to the station, we can talk about next steps."

She sounded in control, calmly ushering the Mulroys away from Ian and Brigit. As they shuffled past, Alicia caught Ian's eyes for one bright moment that sent a frisson down his spine. There was a warning in that look, one Ian lacked the energy to parse. "Keep your heads down," she said to him and Brigit. "I'll call you soon."

As Alicia and the Mulroys strode away, other people drifted toward them across the gravel parking lot in a hush of murmurs and staring eyes. Max was among them, although she kept her distance, hovering where gravel met grass with her arms folded loosely across her chest. Sam, too, stood a few paces out from the rest of the volunteers. He watched Ian and Brigit with a strained expression, bouncing faintly on the balls of his feet.

"Come on," Brigit said, something deadened in her tone. Ian turned back. She had one hand out, palm up. "I'll drive." He wanted to argue but couldn't find the words, or any words. Goose bumps rippled down his arms beneath the fabric of his shirt, except in the divots where Mrs. Mulroy had grabbed him. "Ian." There were veins in Brigit's eyes, the whites shot red. "We should go."

She was right. He didn't want the onlookers to close the remaining feet between them, and he didn't want the smell of the forest thumping against his senses like a drunken parent trying to get back inside. Ian felt around his jeans pocket, half expecting the car keys to have vanished into the Dell, relieved when his fingers met cool metal and sharp teeth.

They were quiet as Brigit pulled out of the Ruritan parking lot and onto the country highway leading back to downtown Ellis Creek. The silence pooled around his ankles, black water in the car, sloshing here and there with every turn. He knew she felt it too. It was obvious in the catch of air with every aborted word, the cautious glances from the driver's seat—the same breathing quiet they'd shared in the motel room, right before he asked her to stay. And with a cold, lonely spike of intuition, he knew what Brigit wanted to ask now.

"I didn't see her," Ian said.

"See who?" Brigit's voice was hoarser than it had been in the parking lot.

"I didn't see your sister."

She rolled them to a halt at the first red light before town. The sky had turned from pale gray-blue to crystalline, sheer as silk.

"Ian…" Brigit stopped. The light stayed red.

"Listen," Ian said, because if he didn't say something, she might find a way to continue and suddenly he didn't want her to go on, and if that made him a hypocrite, he'd live with it. Besides, it wasn't like Brigit went out of her way to tell him everything she thought. "Can we just get back to the motel? Let me take a shower and have some coffee. Then we can talk."

The light turned green. Brigit nodded, accelerating through the intersection, and didn't speak again. Ian cracked his window and tilted his head toward the rush of cool air, breathing deep. Petrol from the corner gas station. Trash from a garbage truck idling in a right turn lane. The rumble of that massive engine rolled over him in fits and starts, and with it other cars, a horn somewhere, the pumping bass of nearby hip-hop.

He didn't fit inside the car. Couldn't find a way to sit. Couldn't focus either. The world skipped and darted past while Ian stumbled after.

Her hair smelled different. She'd used another shampoo. Not something Ian would usually notice, but his senses were all over the place—starved, perhaps, for anything but the woods.

Time scooped itself away from him. They were at the edge of town and then the Super 8, Brigit standing out of the car, the heavy glass doors, the stairway and its ratty carpet, all of it moving too quickly. His knees cracked as he walked, not the joints but the mud crusting his jeans.

Brigit unlocked her room before Ian could find his door key, and stood there in the door frame with her lower lip caught between her teeth. It was that, more than logic, that helped him into her room—her uncertainty on display. "There's all the towels," she said, opening the bathroom door and backing away like she'd spotted something awful. "They're clean."

She waited between the double beds until Ian entered the bathroom and closed the door behind him. He didn't allow himself to pause once the latch clicked, going straight to the shower and turning on the full spray.

Peeling off his clothes was an insectoid act. He stepped out of his jeans and for the barest sliver of a second, they stood on their own from the knees down. Ian thought of the cicada carcasses he used to find in the summers, translucent pinkish aliens stuck to tree bark and car tires and crunching underfoot. What had come out of those shells? He'd never actually seen the transformation happen. Anything could have emerged.

Cicadas led to summer led to cool nights in long grass. The itch of blades against his calves. And later, the regulation check for ticks, a full-body brush of the hands. He'd done it so many times growing up, at home or in locker rooms while white boys pretended their ticks came from him. He was doing it now.

Hot water sluiced along his back, tracing chaotic lines down his legs. Ian rubbed the dirt off his ankles and calves, up above his kneecaps. Dragged his palms higher, over the sharp, familiar arches of his hip bones and up toward his ribs—

A bump. Just below his lowest rib on the right side of his abdomen.

Ian craned to inspect his flank. The lump wasn't visible at first but he could feel it, a narrow ridge that caught at his fingertips when he brushed them back and forth. He pressed down on the skin below his ribs and pulled it taut, wiping water from his eyes, and there it was: a shadow, a subtle line of raised flesh.

There was something in there.

Ian rubbed a thumb over the ridge. It didn't hurt. It didn't feel like anything. Only about an inch from end to end, it could have been a scar or a particularly gnarly reaction to a mosquito bite.

Yes.

The woods.

He'd been out there all night, warm-bodied and vulnerable, attracting every stubborn bug that hadn't realized it was officially fall, time to die off.

Ian redirected his attention from the welt to the tiny bar of soap on a shelf below the faucet. Water had spackled its cardboard packaging and one corner dissolved in his fingers when he picked up the box; it hadn't occurred to him to open it before turning on the shower. Although of course Brigit hadn't unboxed her soap. The towels were all fresh. So whose shampoo had she used between last night and now?

It didn't matter. She'd needed his car keys; maybe her other things had been locked in the back seat and she'd spent the night—anywhere. A place with a shower. Better than down in the leaves and mud. But that wasn't her fault. She'd asked him not to lose her; no one said anything about not losing Ian.

He rubbed a hand over his face. Exhaustion throbbed around his skull like a loose bowling ball. He needed to get out of the shower and talk to Brigit. Only he couldn't decide what he wanted to say, or how, or what he wanted her to say back. The last twelve hours were blurring in the spray, watercolors running into one another. Had he slept in the Dell? When had he found that last tree, the one he'd slumped against until Brigit had stumbled into his field of vision?

Ian turned off the water and pulled one of the thin terry cloth towels off the back of the bathroom door. It was only after drying his hair and hanging up the towel that he remembered that Brigit's shower and Brigit's towels were, in fact, in Brigit's room. His clothes lay in a stiffly crumpled heap, perfuming the steam with earth and dead leaves and something sour, dank, a basement smell. Ian cracked the door and peered out to find Brigit on her bed, sitting back against the headboard with her knees drawn up to her chest.

"If I toss you my key, can you get my backpack?"

"Oh," Brigit said, sliding off the bed. "Yeah." A fleeting smile. "Or you can come out here, you know. I'll manage the shock."

She busied herself with her phone. Suddenly the odor of the clothes and the welt on his abdomen seemed small, unimportant. Ian wrapped the towel around his waist, scooped up his muddy clothes, and opened the door.

Brigit had reclaimed her spot on the bed, forearms braced on top of her knees with her phone in hand. "Oh, my god." She slapped the phone onto the mattress, staring at him, and fluttered her free hand above her chest. "My virtues."

"Shut up." Ian knew what she was doing, but the smile tugging at his lips felt too good to fight. "You think I'll get in trouble if I burn these clothes in the sink?"

"Only one way to find out." Brigit smiled back, and that warm feeling closed in on itself. Her quick, secretive smiles were rough stones he collected and stored away. This was the other kind: wide and open and entirely fake. Wherever she was right now, it wasn't here with him.

Thankfully no one was in the hallway to watch him fumble in the pockets of his jeans, trying every single possibility before finally locating his room key. Ian didn't burn the clothes (he didn't have a lighter), but he did shove them into the tiny wastebasket by the desk, piling his empty chip bags and candy wrappers on top. His towel from yesterday hung over the bathroom door; he slung Brigit's over it, and a buzz stung his fingers as they brushed the dry terry cloth—not static but sharper, more painful. He'd hung that towel before going into the Dell. Ian wasn't sure which was worse: the knife twist that came with imagining his past self, or the fact that he had no idea why he felt this way. The overwhelming sense was one of disconnection, islands of memory in a flat black sea.

Jeans. Gray T-shirt. Flannel on top, red and orange, the colors of fire. The overshirt was brighter than his usual, but Ian wanted loud right now. A statement.

He ran his hands through his hair, dark brown gone black with water. His face was no longer waxy and pale beneath his overtones, so that was something, and this outfit smelled like his deodorant and nothing else. Most of the fog that had enveloped him since Brigit found him had lifted during the shower, and the rest of it sloughed away now as Ian straightened his flannel and dried his palms. He was here. He did exist. And whatever had happened to him out there, whatever bits and pieces had already dissolved beyond recovery, Ian was certain of one thing: Brigit had been lying to him since the minute they'd arrived. She had reasons to stay in Ellis Creek that had nothing to do with Gabrielle, James, or psychological closure. Worse, he had either been oblivious to those reasons, or he'd willfully ignored the signs. And she had let him.

Ian padded across the hall and knocked on Brigit's door, two firm raps. When the door opened, she had her phone pressed to one ear, and she let the door swing back into Ian's hastily outstretched foot so she could gesture at him to stay quiet.

"Okay," she was saying, "I hear you. Does this have to happen now?"

He slipped into the room and closed the door behind him. She didn't back toward the beds, and Ian's determination faltered. He'd have to duck around her to get by, so instead he just stood there, Brigit close enough to hear the faint rasp of her breath. The voice on the other end of the line was too soft to make out clearly, but it sounded masculine. Her lips tightened, then relaxed.

"All right. I'll be there soon." She ended the call and dropped the phone, already moving to grab her jacket from the foot of one duvet. "That was Sam. I have to go."

"I?" Ian repeated, still blocking the door. Brigit stepped left; he mirrored her.

"Come on," Brigit said. "You should get some real sleep." Her gaze drifted somewhere over his right shoulder, her mouth tilting down at the corners, and when she moved to pass him again, Ian didn't think. He reached out and caught her shoulder.

Brigit jolted to a halt. Her hazel eyes flickered to his, too wide to hide her shock. For two beats of his heart, there was only the warm ridge of her clavicle. The hollow just beneath. Impossible that she could be so fragile, her bones this close to the surface; for a moment Ian couldn't breathe. For a moment it was her who'd gone into the woods and had not, would not, come out. Then Brigit firmed her mouth and lifted her chin, only a fraction but that was enough. Ian dropped his hand and stepped away, bumping into the door. Reached back and twisted the knob as if he'd meant to do that all along.

"I'm coming with you," he said, half-strangled, and pulled the door open behind him with an uncomfortable bend of his elbow.

Brigit didn't move. What was her expression—disgust? Anger? His own mind raced in horrified circles from the warmth of her shoulder to the incomprehension in her eyes to the fact that he'd stopped her by force. He'd put out his arm and invaded her space like it was nothing. A metal base-ball trophy slammed into the wall inches from Ian's ear, and he flinched—except there was no trophy. Just a car door closing outside, because they were here, today, in this motel. His back ached. There was an itch below his ribs.

"Fine," Brigit said, and stepped past him into the hall. "We'll need the camera."

He followed her out, barely listening to his own words as they came. "Do we have a new location?"

"Better." Brigit was already at the stairs. "We have a confession."

15: BRIGIT

She almost went to the passenger side of Ian's car, redirecting herself at the last possible step. He hadn't reclaimed his keys as they left the motel, and Brigit hadn't acknowledged that she would drive; in fact, neither of them had spoken since hitting the stairs.

Brigit needed a beat to reacquaint herself with the distance of the pedals, the jimmy it took to shift out of Neutral. None of this was difficult an hour ago. Her shoulder thrummed. Not with pain, exactly, or soreness, or even an itch. What lingered there was deeper, like someone hovering a finger so close to your skin you swear you can feel it. She fought the urge to rub the spot, to knead her knuckles into the flesh as if the ghost of Ian's hand were a stitch from lifting too much weight.

He'd never touched her like that. Even in the earliest days of their friendship, when they were young and dumb and getting drunk in their sophomore year off peach vodka and whatever other bullshit the upperclassmen deigned to buy them, Ian had always been so careful about physical contact. Brigit was used to navigating those particular waters, steeped in the irony of the fact that she was great at casual hugs and reassuring touches when it came to people she didn't give a damn about, but as soon as there was some kind of connection, the idea of bringing their bodies close to hers triggered a bone-deep unease. But with Ian, it was a conversation they'd never needed to have. He'd gotten it from the start, had never made her feel ashamed or lacking by forcing the topic. It had taken Brigit longer than she cared to admit to understand that Ian's respect for her boundaries didn't stem just from his good nature, but also from something private, a scar that hurt him as much as it helped her.

And that, too, was a conversation they hadn't had. Not really. Not more than the broad strokes, although they were damning enough. She'd always thought that was her way of showing respect as well. But now, with Ian's handprint burning on her shoulder, those aborted conversations rose up in Brigit like bile.

It felt so wrong that contact, even tense contact, should be this sharp-edged between them, his shock at the touch as visible as hers. Max's little scoff rose up without warning: *My idea of our friendship and yours weren't the same.* Because Brigit was the one who'd set the rules, well before Ian ever heard the name Ellis Creek. She was the one who'd left him in the Dell for twelve hours too. Who'd led him in there in the first place after lying about why. Brigit didn't know what Ian suspected about the woods, or Emma, or her own muddy brain. She didn't know what flavor of fear he felt right now. Had been afraid to ask. That felt wrong too—but now, set against the guilt and confusion over other ways Brigit had fucked up over the years, at least it felt possible to address. Here in the car where they'd spent so many hours together, Brigit forced herself to speak.

"If not Emma, what did you see? Out there?" Ian didn't reply. She glanced sideways. He was looking down at his abdomen, fingertips pressing gently against his side, like a doctor examining a patient. "Ian?"

"Oh," he said, and sat back against his seat. "I didn't... I don't think I saw anything." They stopped at a light.

"Do you remember hearing us? Sam and me, shouting for you?"

"I shouted too." Ian rubbed at his eyes. "No. I didn't hear you."

The light turned green. Brigit accelerated carefully, paying attention to the way her pulse had begun to speed as well. The splinters in her brain were turning viral. Sam hadn't heard either. They'd both lost hours. Maybe, please, god, maybe Brigit really and truly wasn't imagining any of this. Like Gabrielle hadn't imagined any of it. Suddenly there was Mrs. Mulroy's anguished voice: *Just like Gabrielle—you said you came here to help us, so—*

"Did you find any birch trees?" Brigit asked, cutting off the memory but not the ravenous pressure that made it hard to breathe. She wanted very badly to trust her eyes and ears. But if she could...

"I was in the woods."

"It would have been a ring of them. Like James described."

"No. Are you asking because you did?"

Tell him. Tell him. Tell him tell him tell him tell—

"I'm thinking maybe after this you should head up to Maine," Brigit said. "If we're going to do that inn, we'll need some good footage of the grounds. I can finish up here, collect our check, and follow in a couple days."

"Stop," Ian said sharply, scratching over his shirt. "Don't do that."

Brigit pulled into the parking lot of Tim's Tavern. Her whole body felt lighter now that she'd chosen to lie, which itself had been easy as breathing. Because if she could trust what her brain told her, there was no choice at all. She'd already failed Ian once. Now she needed to get him out of Ellis Creek. Whatever else was going to happen here—*You have to come back*—he would be safe in his ignorance of it. Brigit would make sure of that.

"Look," Brigit said, pointing with her chin. "Lacey's already here. We'll wrap this up, she'll tell us whatever she needs to tell us, and we'll pass it on to Alicia. Then we can get the fuck out of here. You did say Maine, right?"

Brigit heard the calmness in her own voice, the confidence, and her heartbeat slowed to match it. Ian was scratching at his side again, high up near the ribs, shaking his head.

"No," he said. "I mean, yes, I did, but I don't understand what you're saying right now. Look, I'm sorry I—"

"Come on," Brigit interrupted, climbing out of the car and lifting a hand toward where Sam stood a few awkward feet from Lacey. Behind them both waited Max. "Get the camera. She's ready to talk."

"Thanks again," Lacey said to Max as the blond ushered Lacey, Brigit, and Ian into her office. "I didn't—I couldn't think of another place."

"It's fine," Max said, resting her hip against the side of her desk. She caught Brigit's eye as Lacey stared at the galactic print on the back of the door, and shrugged. Whatever this was, Max wasn't sure either. She had a good enough idea to let it happen here, amid her books and art and the much tidier shelf of records in one corner, but there was something off about her stance. A discomfort Brigit couldn't place. As if sensing the scrutiny, Max cleared her throat.

"You want me to stick around?" she asked Lacey.

Lacey bit her lower lip. A large bag was slung over her shoulder, and she clutched the strap where it crossed between her breasts. She'd drawn her hair back in a severe ponytail that exposed the dark shadows beneath her eyes.

"No. If that's okay." She stepped back against the wall beside the record shelf.

While Lacey's attention was on the placement of her feet, Max looked back to Brigit, who nodded. She had a feeling that whatever drove this unease—the big secret Max hadn't told her in the woods—was about to come out.

"Sure," Max said. "I'll just…spot Sam a round." Her red lips twisted then, as if she'd made a joke, but she wasn't laughing. "If you change your mind, I'm right out there."

When the door closed again, Ian backed into it and checked his camera. Lacey threw up one thin hand. "No cameras."

"Right," Ian said, and Brigit remembered that, of course, Lacey had refused to be filmed during their first interview. "Sorry. You still good if I just record audio?"

He sounded almost normal aside from a scratchy pattern on his voice. Lacey grimaced but nodded. "I don't want to get you in trouble."

Ian fiddled with the camera, then gave them a thumbs-up.

No one spoke for a long, uneven moment. The clinks and rumble of the lunch rush filtered in from the bar. Grease and whiskey fought with the warmer, lived-in scents of worn carpet and decaying cardboard. The smell reminded Brigit of a motel after too many days with the "do not disturb" sign on the door. That brought her back to the Super 8, what felt like months ago. Her and Ian on the bed as he insisted they could do something good here, something real. *People* want *to tell you stuff, Bridge.*

Looking at Lacey now, her obvious need to speak, Brigit's chest eased. Ian was right. Lacey had sought her out for a reason beyond the lies that Brigit had told, or maybe not beyond them but within them, and this was one promise on which

WHAT GROWS IN THE DARK   159

Brigit could deliver: Lacey would tell her things she wouldn't tell others. And even if those things wouldn't help Brigit find James Mulroy, they might make Ian leave Ellis Creek before she got him killed.

"No rush," Brigit said. "Do you want to sit?"

"I'm all right." But Lacey didn't continue, instead licking her lips with a quick dart of tongue that reminded Brigit of something cold-blooded. She considered touching her, a light hand on the arm, but discarded the idea immediately. Lacey was too tense, too fidgety, a fellow wild creature on high alert. Instead, Brigit pushed Max's desk chair out of the way and lowered herself to the floor.

"Do you mind? I've had a long week."

Slowly, Lacey joined her on the carpet, pulling her bag into her lap like a child. A rustling of clothes told Brigit that Ian was doing the same behind her. "Take your time," she said when Lacey had settled into position. "Wherever you want to start is okay."

"I wanted to talk to you." Lacey pulled her lower lip into her mouth and chewed it again, released. Her lips were chapped to the point of bleeding in one spot at the corner. "I've been thinking a lot. Some things are clear to me now, that weren't so much before. I couldn't see them. Or I wouldn't let myself. But I didn't— Your number, I lost it. I'm sorry. Sam was all I could think of."

Brigit recalled the way Lacey had looked away when she'd first mentioned Sam. Lacey said his name differently now— less harsh, but still disquieting.

"That's all right." Brigit smiled faintly, nothing extreme that might spook her. "Lots going on. I'm glad you got back in touch."

Lacey nodded and took a breath. Her fingers worked at the seams of her bag, picking, smoothing. "I wanted to tell

you… Shit. Shit, shit, shit." She stood in one abrupt movement, swinging her bag back onto her shoulder. "I'm sorry,
I don't know what I was thinking. I can't do this in here." A
brittle laugh erupted from her throat. "Jesus. Yeah, I'm sorry.
I need some air. A cigarette. Can we go outside?"

"Hey," Brigit said, getting to her feet, "it's okay. We can
talk in the parking lot. Or if you want to smoke first, that's
cool too."

"No, I—I'm ready. I'm sorry, this is just, it's hard, you
know? Owning up to things." Lacey ducked around Ian to
open the door, slipping into the hall before Brigit could answer.

"Come on," she muttered to Ian, annoyed with herself for
miscalculating.

Lacey was waiting past the bathroom door. She led them
through another metal door that opened onto the rear parking lot. Sam was there too, leaning against his car with head-
phones in. He pulled the earbuds out but didn't approach, and
Lacey ignored him completely.

She strode a few paces away from the tavern, pulled a pack
and a lighter from her bag, and knocked a cigarette loose
against her palm. First, she flipped it between her fingers,
rapid-fire, then clamped it between her teeth and lit it. Took
a deep drag. The nicotine seemed to straighten her shoulders.

"First I wanted to tell you she was sorry." Lacey inhaled
again, blowing smoke through the corner of her mouth so it
wouldn't hit Brigit.

"What?"

"Maybe that's just what I would say if I were her."

A cold stone turned in Brigit's belly. "What do you mean?
I'm not sure who you're talking about."

"Your sister," Lacey said, eyes flicking behind Brigit and
back in a flash. "Emma."

Nothing moved except the cars driving past, a bird swooping toward a pizza crust. Brigit had no way to respond.

"I'm certain she was sorry for what she did to you. I wanted to say that in case it makes a difference." Lacey's eyes glistened, unshed tears bringing out the emerald. "Tell Max I'm sorry too. Oh, god, I really am. She doesn't know what I did. I didn't even know what I did at first. I was high, okay? I was fucking high when I found it, so I just went with what it showed me, and that's no excuse, but someone should know." She raised her voice, glancing back at Sam. "And I had no idea James would go with Gabi. I didn't mean for that to happen. I didn't believe any of it would until they were gone. I thought I dreamed the whole thing, or Gabi was making up *her* dreams, except of course that didn't make sense either, because how could she have known?" Lacey laughed, eyes wide and frantic. "But I didn't want to admit that. Even if I had, it wasn't like I could tell anyone the truth. So I told myself we were just kind of bleeding into each other. You know when you spend too much time with another person and it goes weird, and eventually what they think turns into what you think or the other way around, and you can't tell what's real anymore? Max yells at me for that. It was so easy to pretend it's what happened to Gabi, at least for a little while."

Lacey's mouth jerked into a dreadful, humorless smile. "Then you got here. And things kept getting worse, and honestly… Honestly, I'm just really, really tired of lying. So here's the truth: Gabi's not like me. She's sure of herself. If she decides something, as far as she's concerned, that's it, because Gabi Markham says so. Lucky for her, she's pretty much always right in the end. But she does it with things that don't concern her. She can't help getting involved—she can't just stay out of it. And I wanted her to stay out. I wanted her to stop talking about my business, stop pushing, just *stop*, be-

fore she made real trouble. That's all I asked for! It seemed—
god, it doesn't matter how it seemed. I don't expect you to
forgive me. I wouldn't forgive me. But I'm going to make it
up to her. To all of you." Lacey took another pull from the
cigarette and dropped it to the pavement. "I hope this will
count. I can't remember exactly what I said but I'm pretty
sure this will count."

One second both of Lacey's hands were busy with her bag.
The next, she'd reached inside and pulled out something metallic. Sunlight flared, impossibly white—were those trees
behind Lacey? Thin branches sprouting from her nape?—
and as Brigit blinked it away, Lacey put the gun to her temple and fired.

16: IAN

Someone was screaming. Not Brigit, nor Sam. A woman on her way to the parking lot. Lacey lay on the ground. Her bag gaped, a cell phone partly visible. Tampons rolled onto the pavement. Her head was no longer a head. Blood mixed with other things spread out around her shoulders, soaking her hair.

Ian reached for Brigit, pulling her backward and up. "Don't look," he said. Sam had dropped into a crouch and was now vomiting onto the asphalt. Running feet. People. A siren wailing, not nearly close enough.

"What the fuck?" Max sprinting from the tavern's rear entrance, a stained towel flung over one shoulder, face white as milk. "What happened?"

"I don't know," Brigit said. Her voice was very soft. Max took the towel and draped it above Lacey's neck.

"Don't look," Ian said again, and it tasted like a prayer. "Don't look, come here, come with me."

They turned together. The skin of his face felt hot and damp. Brigit's collarbones were flecked with matter. Sam stood and spat and staggered to join Ian and Brigit as they approached the tavern wall. They waited with their backs against the bricks while Max paced in front of the entrance, wheeling toward Lacey and sharply away as if on a track, her fingers fisted in her hair. The sun shone high and magnificent above, turning the body into a matte lump in a shining red sea.

It was strange. The moment before the gunshot had broken everything apart, Ian had been sitting near Brigit, focused on the tarmac because there was no need for him to frame a scene. He hadn't seen Lacey pull the gun from her bag. But he'd felt something. A pang in his side, a pinch of muscle below his ribs. Ian's stomach had already dropped by the time the weapon fired.

Tires squealed, exhaust belching into the air as an ambulance followed by a cop car spun into the parking lot. The siren wailed over them all, its high note slapping Ian again and again until he couldn't hear his own thoughts and thank god for that. Before the officials jumped out, Pete burst around the corner of the tavern. He wore the same baseball cap he'd worn the morning before, when Lacey had perched on his knee in the back of the bar.

"No," Sam said roughly, the first word he'd spoken since Lacey pulled the trigger. His shoulder jutted into Ian's as he pressed back against the wall. Max crossed the parking lot in three long strides and placed herself between Lacey and Pete, arms out.

"Don't come any closer," she said, voice shaking but loud enough that every word carried. "You leave her alone now."

The small crowd of people who'd poured from the tavern stilled. Max's words seemed to have broken something so fundamental the air itself responded, congealing around Ian like blood. Pete stepped forward, and at least four onlookers flinched. Ian did too. The movement felt somehow obscene, the whole parking lot poised on the edge of something irreversible.

And then two EMTs leaped from the back of the ambulance, rushing around Pete and Max, and the blistering tension broke. As one of the EMTs lifted the towel from Lacey's face and quickly let it drop, Pete's arms milled through the air as if he thought he could catch himself on something, or catch Lacey maybe, grab her on her way into nothing. Max held her ground. The rest of the people in the parking lot began a slow, listless retreat, as though someone had wound them up and pressed them gently back toward their places.

"We need to go," Brigit said. She was very pale, but her jaw was set. Ian followed her gaze. Alicia wasn't among the uniformed police now clustered around Lacey's body, but one of the officers had raised his head and was looking over at where the three of them sat.

"They might have questions," Sam said, but the upward tilt at the end made him sound like a child asking for permission.

"There are plenty of people to ask." Brigit nodded toward the woman who'd screamed and was now drifting back to the tavern entrance. "Ian and I are already way too visible here. We need to delete that interview before the police decide we had something to do with Lacey's death."

"Ah," Ian said. He rubbed a hand across his mouth, staring toward Max and Pete. There was something in Max's stance that seized him like iron. "You're right. We should lower our profile."

Sam barked a laugh, high-pitched and humorless. "Lower it? You have blood on your face." He pointed to the woman Brigit had indicated. "And they *know* you, Brigit. Maybe you don't remember, but that's Evelyn Shepherd. She's been the chief librarian since we were kids. Her son is the cop on the left, and half these people either go to church with the Mulroys or work for Pete's dad."

Officer Shepherd placed a hand on his partner's shoulder, spoke briefly and quietly into his ear. Gestured toward the tavern, toward them.

"They know you," Sam was saying, "and they sure as shit know me and Lace—"

"Sam. Please." Brigit's voice didn't break, but it could have.

Ian felt that somewhere deep. He focused on breathing in and out, letting Brigit lead him and Sam toward the sidewalk—but it wasn't Lacey's blood or Lacey's brains that Ian saw as he followed Brigit like a duckling. In the black space behind his lids he watched, over and over, the way Lacey had flipped that cigarette.

Nobody shouted for them to stop or get back there and explain. Ahead, Brigit glanced to her right and back, scanning the cops and the EMTs who were now lifting Lacey onto a stretcher, one holding the blood-soaked towel in place with a gloved hand. Ian barely registered this tiny horror.

Every time he'd encountered Lacey, Ian had looked but not looked. He'd seen but not seen her fingers flicking, the nervous, wary set of her shoulders and the way she watched for Pete in the tavern. All the signs his body recognized while his brain pretended otherwise, though for him it had been pens, not cigarettes, that absorbed the energy of not screaming every time his father walked into a room. He'd carried that habit for years after the last—and worst—punch.

"He hurt her," Ian said. The itch on his side was back. He scratched it. His throat felt hot and full, and the words surprised him too. "Pete. He hurt Lacey."

Sam flinched beside him, a full-body contraction, but said nothing. They kept moving. The sun laid cool hands against Ian's cheeks. It was around one, the sky spotty with clouds, no traffic whatsoever on the road they paralleled. Something was making noise that wasn't footsteps on cement. A muffled buzz. Brigit pulled her phone from her jacket pocket. She held the phone face down for two more rings, breathing deeply. Then checked the screen. After confirming the caller, Brigit answered quickly.

"You heard?"

Silence as Brigit waited for a response. Her short hair curled gently at the nape of her neck, which bent in a graceful, attentive curve. She slowed, then halted. Sam caught Ian's eye, but Ian shook his head. They would all need to wait. He scratched absently at his ribs over his shirt, not digging too deep, afraid of splitting skin and causing an infection.

"And still nothing?" Brigit asked. "Where—" She stopped and listened, nodding, mouth thin. "All right." She hung up and faced them with a bracing breath. "Gabrielle's awake. Sam, thank you for everything. Ian, now that Gabi might be able to tell someone where James is, I think we've done all we can here." Brigit's expression twisted. A spot of blood moved with her cheek. "Maybe too much. We should let people grieve in peace."

"You want to leave?" Sam asked, a little shaky.

"I think it's time," Brigit said, and Ian heard it in her voice—the serrated edge that betrayed her gentle tone. She was angry. More than angry. She was *scared*.

He opened his mouth, and the itch turned into agony so sudden and complete he couldn't scream. Ian didn't feel his legs crumple, but his field of vision shifted, tilting wildly as he collapsed onto the sidewalk.

He tried to breathe, lungs like needles pressed beneath the iron weight of his ribs, but only managed painful slivers of air that tasted like mud. He wanted to cry out. He wanted his mother. There were no mothers. Brigit's face swam into view, her features blurring, snapping back into focus.

Wide eyes, open mouth saying words that weren't important, and then they weren't words but branches breaking. Dead leaves underfoot. He'd been stabbed, ripped in half; he was salt in a wound, and then Ian was nothing at all.

17: BRIGIT

There was a second—just one—where all Brigit felt was exhaustion to her marrow. Then Ian slumped from his knees to his side before tipping onto his back, and she dropped to the ground beside him. "Get the car," she snapped at Sam.

"Whose?"

Brigit rummaged for Ian's keys and held them up. "Blue Subaru."

As Sam's footsteps pounded away, Brigit hovered over Ian, unsure of what to do or where to touch him. She knew to roll people over if it looked as though they might vomit, and to put a wallet between his teeth if he'd been seizing, but Ian lay still and silent. He was breathing, at least, shallow but steady.

Brigit dashed the back of her hand across her face, but her cheeks were damp with more than tears. Suddenly frantic, she used her sleeve to scrub away blood and thicker flecks. Things were clearer with it gone. Ian's skull had hit the ground when he fell. Not hard, from the sound, but this fear was specific and actionable. Brigit slid a palm beneath his head, checking for wetness. Nothing. Only it felt wrong to lay him back down on the concrete sidewalk, so she lowered herself to sit cross-legged, awkwardly maneuvering Ian's head into her lap. It was heavy, an inhuman weight. Brigit craned her neck to watch the sky, where dark birds wheeled across the gray.

Forever passed, or thirty seconds, before Ian's car pulled up to the curb. Sam hopped out and opened the back door.

"Okay," Brigit said, repositioning to loop her arms beneath Ian's shoulders so his head lolled back against her chest. "Help me get him up."

Sam bent and took Ian's legs. Together, with difficulty, they hoisted him upright and into the car. His left arm flopped out, and Brigit caught it by the wrist and laid it gently across his stomach before setting his camera in the footwell.

"Can you navigate for me?" she asked Sam, too drained to second-guess it. He nodded and passed her Ian's keys.

"Where to?" Sam asked once they'd joined Ian in the car. To his credit, his voice didn't shake now. She relayed the address Alicia had given her over the phone, resentment burning in her chest. Brigit hadn't intended to take Alicia up on her offer of a safe spot to wait out the aftermath of Lacey's death, somewhere no police or reporters would follow. She'd intended to grab Ian and drag him out of Ellis Creek, bodily if necessary.

"So, not the hospital," Sam said. It wasn't quite a question.

"Not the hospital." She stopped for a light, glanced in the rearview. Ian was still unconscious, his lashes dark and thick against his cheeks. "I can drop you off wherever once you point me the right way, or loop back around and take you back to Tim's if you want. I guess your car is there."

"No," Sam said, and his voice was thready but clear. "Lacey, she—she said something about James. About how he went with Gabi. Whatever this is, I'm in it until we find my friend."

Brigit had no response to offer. But her grip on the wheel did ease.

★ ★ ★

Sam's phone directed them to a cozy cul-de-sac not far from their old high school. Brigit recognized a few of the street names they passed—Elm Hollow, Maple Court Ridge—from hours spent walking around these neighborhoods instead of sitting in class.

"It's this one," Sam said, pointing at a tidy one-story house with a bright yellow door. St. John's wort and meadowsweet lined the yard, while the inner lawn was matted with the same creeping thyme and mint Brigit's mother had cultivated once. An unexpected pain pressed into her at the memory.

She parked on one side of the double driveway and opened the back door of the car. Ian made a low noise when sunlight slanted over his face. "Hey," Brigit murmured, crouching so their faces were level. "I need you to work with me here, okay?"

Sam came around the car. "Should we pick him up?"

Brigit studied Ian's closed lids, the rapid movement beneath. Part of her wanted to recoil, she realized—an atavistic instinct. The urge to avoid disease. "Ian," she said, too low for Sam to hear. "Come on. Help me out."

He didn't.

Brigit and Sam got him out of the car with effort. Ian felt heavier now—less like a sleeper, more like a corpse. They each looped one of his arms around their shoulders and half carried, half dragged him up the short sidewalk.

"Can you hold him?" Brigit asked at the steps. "Just for a second."

Sam grunted, adjusting his stance, and she gave him Ian's full weight long enough to feel around the toe of one of the work boots by the door. A key was slotted into the lining. Brigit straightened and steadied Sam, who'd begun to lean precariously to the right, then took Ian's left arm again. They hefted him up the stairs so Brigit could unlock the door.

Inside was a stubby foyer, complete with coatrack and what looked to be a handmade shelf for shoes. Brigit and Sam forged ahead to a compact living room. They shuffled Ian to the sofa and tipped him down, Sam catching his legs just before their weight dragged Ian onto the floor. Finally, panting, they stood back and looked around.

Alicia's house was as deliberate and confident as the woman herself. None of the furniture was part of a set, but all the colors worked together—pale blues with deep burgundy accents, walls the color of a tea egg. The room held the pleasant ghost of burning wood. Nights were only just beginning to grow cold enough for a fire. Someone who lived here enjoyed them for the ambience more than the heat. Brigit approached the fireplace mantel, a handsome stack of slate topped with photographs.

Alicia standing in a line of white men, all smiling, all uniformed.

An elderly couple who must have been her parents, grayhaired and smooth-skinned until you reached the nests of wrinkles around their eyes.

Alicia and a woman with close-cropped black hair and high, round cheekbones, the detective standing against a low stone wall while the other woman sat behind her with her arms draped around Alicia's neck.

And finally, the same woman in a stunning red jacket over tailored black slacks, beaming at an Alicia Brigit hardly recognized: one smiling widely, dressed in a floor-length blue gown with a high lace collar.

Brigit's heart. There was something in it, or around it, a tightness that drew her hand up to press against her ribs. She'd thought of Alicia as a static artifact. Another piece of Ellis

Creek that had survived Emma. But that, of course, was the point. Alicia had survived. She'd grown up, had other girlfriends, fallen in love. Gotten married. She'd built a life here, one that was healthy and happy and distinct from Brigit's sister, and now Brigit wanted to set this cozy house ablaze.

"The Dell did this to him." At Sam's voice, Brigit turned away from the mantel. Sam stood a few feet from the couch, arms wrapped around his chest, looking down at Ian's silent form. "Right?"

She ought to lie. She'd already gotten one person hurt in that forest, and whatever chance there might have been to stop Lacey, Brigit had been too preoccupied to see it. Really she should have taken Sam back to the tavern no matter what he said. The more people knew how deep this rot ran, the more opportunities Brigit would have to fuck their lives up too. Except… *Stop*, Ian had told her in the car, just like he'd told her in the Dell. *Don't do that.*

"Yeah," she said to Sam. It felt like an offering. Brigit went to the couch. She pushed through that low revulsion that told her, *Stay back, stay safe*, and laid the back of her hand against Ian's forehead. It was cool and gave the impression of dampness, like a mushroom.

Sam sank onto an armchair opposite the wooden coffee table. He rubbed both hands over his wan face, bringing faint color into his cheeks. "He spent one night in there. Doesn't look good for James."

"Gabi's awake," Brigit reminded him. "Alicia said she'll come here after talking with her. She would have called me if something was wrong."

Sam nodded rapidly. "Okay. Good. That's good. So it goes away. Like…an allergic reaction, maybe?"

A soft, fretful noise cut off Brigit's reply. She hunkered down, surveying Ian. His eyes remained closed, the orbs mov-

ing in darting patterns. His skin had gone the waxy brownish gray of raw pecan shells. And there was a smell, now that
she was closer and adrenaline had stopped numbing out un-
necessary details about the world around her. A faint, peaty
sweetness. Her heart jumped like his wandering eyes.

"Is he awake?"

"I don't think so." Brigit leaned closer. Ian's inhalations
barely moved his T-shirt. She thought of Gabrielle, bathed in
that same scent. According to Alicia, she'd woken from her
coma less than twenty minutes after Lacey died. No immune
systems had arranged that coincidence. And she thought of
the scratching too. Ian's fingers working at his ribs.

Dizziness spotted her vision. Brigit realized she'd practically
stopped breathing, sipping air through her mouth to minimize
how much of that scent got inside her; the blare of her phone
nearly knocked her off balance. A local number, unfamiliar.

"Hello?"

"It's Max. Can I meet you somewhere?"

"Now isn't a good time. Ian's having some trouble."

"Lacey had trouble," Max said. "Lacey had trouble and you
were going to help her, and now she's dead." Brigit took a
beat to absorb the impact. Max broke it. "I know it isn't your
fault. It's *his*. And mine. I didn't say anything before because
I didn't know if I could trust you, but also I didn't—I didn't
want to *deal* with it," she finished, voice raw. "I wanted those
kids to be in some shitty motel on the beach. I wanted Lacey
to lose a friend because she wouldn't stop lashing out when
Gabi tried to talk to her about Pete, because I figured that
would get through to her without me having to do anything,
and wow, when I say it like that, it makes me sound like a
real fucking coward. Or lazy. Or both, whatever, it doesn't
matter, I screwed up and let a goddamn teenager do what I
should have done. I told myself if I didn't see it happen, and

Lacey kept refusing to say it happened, it was better if I didn't get involved."

Max paused, swallowed audibly. When she spoke again, her voice was rocky. "But listen. Lacey was scared of Pete at the end. Like, finally legitimately scared. She told me, *What if Gabi did something stupid?* I bet she found out Gabi confronted him, and he hurt her, and maybe James got in the way and Pete hurt him too, I don't know, and Lacey couldn't take the guilt. It's his fault she's dead. He probably knows where James is too. I just need you to prove it."

"What do you mean?" Brigit asked carefully. She wasn't dizzy anymore, but her thighs burned from holding the crouch.

"You can—see things, sense them, whatever. I don't care how it works or what you call it."

"Max," Brigit said, standing, "I can't read minds. If you think Pete did something—"

"Ask her."

"What?"

"Ask Lacey. That's what I'm saying, okay? I want you to do a séance and ask Lacey the truth." Cold sweat beaded underneath Brigit's arms despite the warmth of the room. She glanced at Sam, found him watching her with new intensity. "Isn't that why you're here?" Max asked, each word a slash across the phone line. "Aren't you getting paid for this?"

Brigit wanted to swallow but couldn't. Saliva pooled at the back of her throat. Her brain felt as heavy as Ian's skull, and she couldn't think of a single lie.

"Just tell me where you are," Max continued, thickly. "I'll come to you. I closed the bar. Brigit, please. If you can speak for her now, please do it. Don't let him get away with this."

Except Pete hadn't come up once in Lacey's final moments. Brigit would put good money on him knowing nothing at

WHAT GROWS IN THE DARK 175

all about Gabrielle, James, and the Dell, and even if not, she sure as shit couldn't make certain.

"Fuck you, then," Max said into her silence. "Wait! I'm sorry. I didn't mean that. I know we're all, you know, traumatized right now, but there's no one else I can call. I was literally going to drive around looking for you if you'd changed your number. I don't know what else to do, and Alicia played all her cards already—"

She continued, but Brigit stopped listening. All at once, her mind careened past the fear and shame in pursuit of an idea, and this idea bloomed larger than everything else. Alicia and her cards. They were certainly not played out.

"All right," Brigit said, and Max caught her breath. "I'll do it. We're at Alicia's house. Let me give you the address."

"What's going on?" Sam asked as soon as Brigit hung up, that nervy energy back in his shoulders. "What about Pete?"

"Max blames him for Lacey. Maybe for the kids too." Brigit turned back to Ian, checking the rise and fall of his chest. The funny smell was fainter now, or at least less oppressive. Assured that he wasn't going to stop breathing the second she left the room, she started toward the open door frame leading to a kitchen. "Help me look for candles."

"But—what's going on?"

We're going to make Alicia talk, Brigit didn't say. *And what the hell, why stop there?* Lacey hadn't mentioned Pete before she died. But she'd mentioned Max, and she'd connected Brigit to Sam more than once—who, Brigit now recalled, had been uncomfortable around Max during the search for Ian. Her gut would have lost those details if they weren't important, and what Max had just shared over the phone felt like some, but not all, of why. This séance could be her path to answers.

"You told me you're in this," Brigit said. "Did you mean it?"

"I'm still here." Sam sounded one shade of defensive and several more of scared, but he wasn't wrong. Brigit nodded.

"All right. Max is coming here, and so is Alicia. When they do, we're going to do something a little fucked up."

"Which is?"

"We're going to ask Lacey why she killed herself."

She left Sam standing with his mouth still open, trying not to feel too satisfied on top of the self-loathing, but as she crossed onto the tiles of a small, neat kitchen, a raspy voice said, "Bridge?"

18: IAN

He was lying on something soft. Noises whispered in his ears, rhythmic and strange until slowly they settled into shapes he could identify: footsteps on wood, cloth rustling. "Bridge?" Ian asked as he opened his eyes. The world was too bright for a minute. Colors shifted like constellations in a backward sky.

"Hey," said someone who wasn't Brigit. "Holy shit. That timing. How do you feel?"

Ian blinked until his vision pieced itself back together. He was in a living room, sprawled on his back on a long sofa, and crouching near him was Sam Levy. The other man's narrow face was drawn with concern but also excitement, or maybe severe relief.

Brigit appeared over Sam's shoulders. "Move," she said, and Sam rose and stepped aside. She took his place on the floor, her slender forearms resting on the tops of her knees.

"Hi," Ian said. Brigit searched his face, her eyes moving from the cut above his brow to the pulse point at his throat before finally meeting his gaze.

"What's the last thing you remember?" Her voice was soft, but there was a flicker behind that carefully blank expression. An urgency that didn't look right on her.

"I remember Lacey," he said, sifting through images that struggled in his grip. "All of us walking. And…" Ian frowned as he tried to remember. There was Brigit standing near him, expression closed, her phone pressed hard against her ear. "You got a phone call."

"Then what?"

Pain. Pain and absence.

Ian shook his head and started to sit up. Dizziness spun him, but Brigit moved before he could slump, one arm catching him by the shoulders and the other hand hovering as if she thought he might roll off the couch. The only people she touched so readily were clients. People she thought she could use. Ian sank his teeth into the tip of his tongue and sat up fully this time, moving away from her arm. Something shifted in Brigit's eyes, a flash of hurt buried so quickly Ian might have wished it into being, and she got to her feet.

"Whatever happened," she said, pushing past Sam, "we'll deal with it. Max and Alicia are on their way here now. Are you feeling well enough for that? If not, Sam can drive you to the motel so you can get some real rest. Or the hospital. If you want that."

"Well enough for what?" Ian asked, noting how Sam did not object to being volunteered as one of Brigit's troops. Funny how quickly that happened.

"I'll take that as a yes," Brigit said. She exhaled. "Good. We're going to try and talk to Lacey."

With that, Brigit strode through the open door frame into a quaint tiled kitchen. Ian recognized the energy falling off her now, a snowstorm of self-assured intent, and suddenly he needed a door he could close.

"Is there a bathroom?" he asked Sam, who hovered between the living room and kitchen, clearly torn.

"Uh." Sam looked around the room. Pointed left, down a short hall past the couch. "Maybe there?"

"This isn't your house?" Ian stood gingerly, wary of a head rush, but all seemed well enough now. "Where are we?"

"Alicia's. Brigit brought us here after you—yeah." Sam wavered, then appeared to change his mind about speaking further. "Do what you gotta do. Shout if you need help." He joined Brigit in the kitchen, where judging by the sounds, she was rifling through cabinets and moving dishware. Preparing to set up the scene.

Ian went down the hallway Sam had indicated, and sure enough, the first door on the right stood open to reveal a sunny bathroom. The walls were the color of daffodils above pale floor tiles. Closing himself inside the room felt like stepping into an egg. He locked the door and went to the sink, splashing his cheeks with warm water and scraping tiny flecks of dried blood free with his nails. He used the hem of his T-shirt to dry his face, pressing soft cotton into the hollows of his eyes. As he brought his hands down, Ian's breath caught in his throat and he froze with his shirt half-raised. On his side, creeping down from the fabric toward the arch of his hip, was a lacy network of white lines.

Ian shrugged out of his button-up and tugged the T-shirt over his head, letting both fall in a heap. He stared at his reflection for one long beat. His breath came too loudly, an embarrassing rasp at odds with the room, and Ian lunged for the toilet just in time.

Despite a round of heaving, all that came up was colorless bile. When he was sure his stomach would hold, Ian cleaned himself off with toilet paper and flushed it all away. Then he put both shirts back on before returning to the mirror. He found mouthwash in the cabinet. Rinsed his mouth and spat. His heart ticked along at uncontrollable speeds, carrying his blood through the intricacies of veins and muscle and trembling hands. As Ian steadied his palms on the porcelain sink basin, he thought he could see it beating in his sclera.

"This is not happening," he said to that heartbeat, that fluttering panicked animal. Water dripped down his chin. "This cannot be happening."

But he could feel it in him now. He saw it when he closed his eyes. The welt below his ribs, which had opened, just a little, barely the size of a fingernail. Just enough to let the nub of white wood breathe.

When Ian returned to the living room, Brigit was setting unlit tea candles at the corners of the coffee table while Sam did the same to the fireplace mantel. She looked up as he entered, and for a moment, as their eyes met, Brigit's seemed to shimmer. Then she bent to place the last candle. "All good?" she asked him, and her voice betrayed nothing.

Sweat tickled his forehead. The air was close, about to get closer once they lit all those candles. Once he noticed, the compulsion to get them both into open space was overwhelming.

"Can we talk for a second? Outside?"·

"I can leave if you want," Sam said.

"Oh," Ian said, afraid he wore his terror like a neon sign, but Brigit had already straightened and was shaking her head.

"That's all right. I could use the air. We'll be right back."

Ian let her take the lead, unsure of which direction to go, and they walked in tense silence through Alicia's house. That it was the detective's home didn't really sink in until Ian passed the photographs in the hallway leading out: Alicia swimming somewhere tropical, two mud-spattered women screaming at the edge of a cliff. Discomfort of a much more mundane variety crawled along his skin.

Once Brigit closed the front door behind them, she set her back against it and folded her arms. It would have looked casual, maybe even nonchalant, if not for the tightness of her jaw.

"Are you okay?"

Out here, without Sam to perform for, the question hit the air between them like birds into glass. Ian was used to feeling that way with Brigit, but this was the first time he'd been on this side of the window. The feeling wasn't all bad. There was a power in it. He could see how a person might build up these glass panels and live behind them for years, just watching other people try to batter their way inside.

But he wasn't Brigit. He wouldn't allow himself to be.

"No," Ian said. Anxiety welled faster than blood from a wound, saliva choking him before he could go for his shirt hem. He coughed, chest convulsing, just as the rumble of a car engine drew Brigit's eyes past him.

"Shit," she breathed. Ian turned, cough subsiding though his eyes still watered. Alicia had pulled into the driveway. "Hey," Brigit said loudly as the older woman climbed out. "Sam's inside and Max is on her way."

Alicia flipped her keys around one finger, snapping them against her palm on her way up the steps. "Max?"

"Sam will tell you," Brigit said. "We'll be right in."

Ian's head swam. He nodded, and Alicia went inside.

"Okay," Brigit said. She looked up at him, eyes bright with at least half the old anticipation. She wanted to step back into the role Sam and Alicia saw, go in there and pretend at them until they revealed themselves to her. It was a smart move too. Alicia was holding something back, Ian had sensed that from the start, and yes—the séances he and Brigit conducted could be shockingly intimate. People said things Ian was pretty sure they'd regret if they thought about it too hard later. It was one reason he'd thought Brigit would like this work to begin with: window dressing for the act of unveiling and inspecting vulnerability. Not that Ian had explicitly called it that, or ever would, or thought it was a bad thing, even, something she misused, really. This séance was one way to compel Alicia to reveal things she might not otherwise, and it would bring the others closer too, bind them tighter to Brigit's orbit. If there were important threads left unspoken, now might be an unraveling. He wanted that as well. Wait. Did he? Yes. He'd gone into the woods because of these people and their secrets, and come out with—with—

Right, he'd gone in, he'd come out, and he'd brought with him—

It stopped there, the cycle, his brain stuttering like scratched film. He was supposed to be telling Brigit something important. She was about to go inside and be Brigit at the rest of the group, and he was the only one who knew that she wasn't just Brigit, or Brigit wasn't just that, so if anyone could interrupt her now, it was him, and he was going to, he was, only his brain was foggy and his chest hurt from coughing and he felt extremely, distractingly, warm.

"Look," Brigit said before Ian mustered his voice. "I'm sorry. I should have waited for you to wake up. I know this is so far from all right. You don't have to be involved if you don't want—you can rest. You should rest."

"No, it's—I get it," he said, and his heart pounded. "I'm not mad." His side throbbed to the beat of his pulse, not quite pain, more like an insect bite after you scratch too hard. He shook his head, trying to clear it. His side. The thing in it. *Yes.* He had to show her, except his arms felt numb. Brain too. Brigit's face clouded, watching him.

"Okay. Well, let me... I just..."

She stopped, frustration passing over her face; he almost

smiled despite himself. Brigit hated not knowing the right thing to say. She stood there glaring at him, and Ian stared back at her, and then her expression softened and it all— quieted. Slowed. The long dark hours, Lacey's blood on the ground, the piece of his body that already felt alien, and this smothering, dreamlike haze, it all pressed in from every angle, but they'd entered a small and fragile space where nothing else could reach. Where it became possible for Brigit to shock him completely: she put her hands on his shoulders, carefully, and pulled him into a hug.

There was sweetness. The warmth of her arms. Her cheek soft against his, for just that moment, and the way she had to stand on tiptoe to reach.

There was pain, an old, cruel voice in his head that hissed, *Enjoy this while it lasts.*

But stronger than both was the terror that Brigit would feel something shifting under his shirt, or worse, that it would feel her. Ian slid his hands from her back to her waist, and moved her gently away.

The moment didn't break immediately. Like all mistakes, Ian lived inside it for a good long while. What had been subtle inside, when he'd sat away from Brigit's arm, was now a raw and bleeding slice across her face. In the hazy afternoon light, Ian thought he might see bone. It only took her a breath to stitch the wound. Shoulders that had been stiff with shock loosened into confident lines, wide eyes shuttering in that way that so few people understood. Anyone else could look at her now and see a person who knew them, someone who could make them feel like a shipwreck survivor sighting land. Ian saw the glass slide back into place. It was a bread knife to him, sawing through the fog.

"Bridge," he said, abruptly lucid and shivering. "We need to get out of here. Please."

"I told you." She was already reaching behind her for the doorknob. "Sam will take you wherever you want to go. You should let him. I want you to be safe."

"I'm not leaving you."

"Then stay," she said, pulling open the door, hesitating with her face half-turned away. "I'm doing this for you too. I'm going to find the truth."

The fog closed back in. He let her go. The séance would happen. After, Ian would get Brigit alone again, back out here or even farther, somewhere he could breathe. Together, they'd figure out what to do.

Sam and Brigit had chosen seats by the time Ian walked in. Alicia remained standing. All three looked his way as Ian crossed into the living room, though only Sam met his eyes with anything like welcome—but that had nothing to do with Ian. Sam would be thinking of James now. Hoping that if Ian could make it out and start walking around with only minor setbacks, just a small collapse or two, so would his friend.

"How're you feeling?" Sam asked. Ian felt his hand drifting toward his ribs and masked the movement by rolling one sleeve to the elbow.

"Fine," he said, joining Sam on the couch as he rolled up the other sleeve. "What did I miss?"

"Gabrielle's awake and talking." Alicia didn't move away from the mantel. "She doesn't remember anything."

A sharp pang tightened his lungs, something he wanted to call disappointment, but it was fiercer than that, and less fair. "At all?" he managed when no one else spoke.

"Not quite," Brigit said, and their eyes met before she busied herself crossing one ankle over the opposite knee. "She remembers you."

"She remembers the car," Alicia corrected. "Being in the

road, hitting the ground, a man's voice. No specifics. Nothing about the three days before that, or about where James is now."

Ian nodded, dropping his gaze to the coffee table and Brigit's knees so he wouldn't have to craft a facial expression that made sense. He hadn't thought about it directly until now, but Gabrielle had been a given. She would wake up eventually, and when she did, she would help him understand what the fuck was happening to him. Now that assurance was gone.

"That's not uncommon," Alicia continued, "with trauma. Memories shift around. The brain tries to protect itself."

"If nobody else will do it…" Sam made a noise that could have been a laugh, and his tone sounded light enough, but Alicia's face smoothed into a total blank that could have rivaled Brigit's best.

"Are you sure this is where you want to put your time?" she asked Brigit.

"Doing my job, you mean?"

"Is your job playing with Ouija boards in my house?"

"I don't know, boss." Brigit sat back in her armchair. "You tell me."

Ian narrowed his eyes. Nausea crept around his belly, and his head felt moldy, and those things plus the horror in his side turned his voice sharp.

"We need to find James," he said. The tension in the room didn't break, but it did redirect as he spoke. Beads of sweat tickled Ian's forehead, his arms beneath the loose fabric of his overshirt. He clenched his toes hard, focusing on the tiny musculature at work in his feet, and fought to speak without trembling. "That's what matters right now. You brought us here to help, so let us help."

"Yes." Alicia straightened away from the mantel. "I brought you here to help. Now a woman is—"

"Oh, no," Sam said, and Ian had been wrong; his voice

wasn't light, it was *brittle*. "Not a chance. You don't get to blame them for Lacey."

The air had thickened, growing even warmer. Ian wished he could take the plaid overshirt off without risking movement showing through his T-shirt. He couldn't let them see. Not Sam, who would panic. Not Alicia, who would hurt him. (Where did that thought come from? She wouldn't. Would she?) His hips ached near the base of his spine. Every vertebra made itself known.

"Nobody's blaming anyone," Ian said. He was speaking too loudly, or maybe not. But everyone was looking at him. Ian blinked hard, fighting a wave of brightly colored dots amid black static. He felt like he was floating, like he'd slipped out of something vital. Another sentence found its way out. "We're all trying to do the same thing."

"And that is?" Alicia asked.

Brigit uncrossed her leg, black-and-white Chuck thudding onto the floor, and a deep bell tolled through the house. Ian heard it too many times, the sound coming faster and faster, knocking around his skull like the recording he and Brigit occasionally used. Someone laughed but nobody was smiling.

"Hello?" a muffled voice called from outside the front door. "Let me in, you creepy motherfuckers."

19: BRIGIT

Brigit leaned back in the armchair as Alicia went to the door, her spine protesting at the angle. Sam unfolded his legs, planting both feet on the ground so he took up more space. Brigit filed this away for further examination, as her attention kept straying to the one place it really needed to avoid. Ian sat in the corner of the sofa, elbow resting loosely on the arm of the couch. A comfortable pose, if you didn't look closely. If you did, you'd see the sweat beading beneath his dark sweep of bangs, and how he wouldn't hold her gaze.

It was fine. It made sense. He'd figured out at last he shouldn't get too close. That she was someone for whom true closeness was disease no matter how hard she tried, and lord knew she was unpracticed at trying. Ian was right not to trust her. That didn't matter at the moment, though, because she still didn't know what the fuck had happened to him in the Dell, and after Max's phone call, Brigit only had one more real lead. She had to break Alicia.

Except they just kept slicing through her *head*—shards of memory so whisper thin she barely felt each cut. His arms around her, his height for once painfully apparent. The smell of hotel shampoo and lingering peat. Her pulse jagging from anxious, to relieved, to gutted as he moved her away.

She couldn't think about it. She could not.

"Jesus," Sam said in a low voice as Alicia opened the door. Brigit leaned closer to hear, and he rubbed at his face with both hands before giving her a quick, helpless smile. "I don't know what I'm doing here."

That checked out. Brigit didn't know what he was doing there either. No, that wasn't true. Sam was trying to do a good thing for a person he cared about. "You're helping," she said as though her heart weren't a sick and burning coal. "You're helping James."

"Am I? Are we?"

Max strode into the room. She'd redone her makeup and looked ready for battle. "Hey," she said to Ian. "You look alive—that's good." Max waved her hand at the candles Brigit and Sam had appropriated from Alicia's kitchen pantry. "This is…something."

"You ask," Brigit said, "I deliver." She stood and held a hand toward the wide expanse of couch that stretched between Sam and Ian like a highway barrier. "Sit?"

Max glanced at Alicia, who strolled over to sit at the far end of the couch, her coat shifting over her gun. This seemed good enough for Max, although Sam stiffened as she lowered herself down between him and Ian. Nobody spoke.

Brigit pulled a book of matches from her pocket, also pilfered from Alicia's kitchen cabinets, and lit a match. She held the tiny flame to the nearest tea light, and when it caught, tossed the matchbook across the table to Ian. Pretended she didn't breathe easier when he snatched it from the air with startling quickness.

"If we're going to do this," Brigit said, lighting a second candle, "we all need to be on the same page about what exactly it is that we're doing." Heat licked her fingertips. Brigit let it for just one instant before shaking out the fire. "What happened today was—" She had to stop and swallow a sudden bulb of air that rose up her throat out of nowhere. "Trying to contact Lacey won't change anything. It won't make any of us feel better. If we do manage to reach her, and she is able to tell us something about Pete, it obviously won't be admissible in court. At best, this will confirm that you should go after him through legal means."

Max's expression tightened, the red lipstick cracking faintly, bleeding away from the upper edge of her mouth. Ian leaned past her to light the candles at the far end of the coffee table while Brigit took the mantel using a lit wick.

"If we can't reach Lacey, because this is not an exact science and trauma is impossible to predict, even more so when you're talking about spiritual trauma…" Final candle lit, Brigit turned back to the others. "Then we move on to something more concrete."

"The fuck does that mean?" Max asked as Brigit retook her chair.

"The Dell," Alicia said for her.

"The woods aren't going to help Lacey."

"No one's going to help Lacey," Sam said quietly. "We should focus on the one who's still alive."

"Hey." Alicia's voice cut the room in half. Her on one side, everyone else on the other. "James has been gone five days. If this is going to happen, it needs to happen now." She rounded on Brigit again. "Do you believe holding this séance will help us find him?"

"Yes," Brigit said without hesitation. Alicia's secrets were crucial; Brigit was sure of that. She would winnow them out. Ian sat in her peripheral vision, matchbox in his hands, but he didn't back her up. His eyes remained on the flames.

Max sat forward. "So how does it work?"

Brigit measured her inhales and exhales. Otherwise her heart would beat too quickly and it would show in her voice. "Tell me about Lacey. The first things you think of. Max, you start, but I'd like everyone to say at least one thing. This connection won't want to build. It'll need all of us to keep it strong."

Max nodded and kept nodding. Traced one finger along the black lines of ink scrawled across her left wrist and up toward her elbow.

"Yeah. Okay." She blew out a breath. "Ah, shit. All right. Lacey was…a real twenty-four-year-old twenty-four. She had this aggressive optimism that drove me up the wall. But it made her kind, most of the time. She saw the best in people, even when they didn't deserve it, and if she decided she was on your side, nothing would change her mind. I just assumed she'd get taken advantage of a couple times and learn to protect herself a little better, you know? By the time I started realizing how bad it really was with Pete, he had her absolutely wrapped around his finger. She knew he was playing her on some level, based on how defensive she got about it, and when Gabi started noticing the abuse, I guess Lacey just doubled down because that was easier than facing the truth. She definitely didn't want to talk to me about it. But she started working late when she didn't have to. Closed up with me when it wasn't her shift, that kind of thing. Maybe she did want help but didn't know how to ask. Not that I knew how to give it."

A cold thrill of recognition shivered in Brigit's abdomen. How many times had she lain awake and wondered the same thing about Emma? *You were eleven,* she reminded herself. *Max is an adult.* As if that mattered. As if Emma would have confided her secrets at any age.

"This last week," Max went on, "she was clearly fucked up about Gabrielle. They'd been fighting about Pete again, but Lacey seemed different. I didn't put together why. God." She ran a hand over her hair, yanking strands back into the ponytail. "I think she wanted me to say something this time. If I had, maybe she would have—whatever. I don't know. Is that enough?"

Max thumped back against the couch. The candle flames guttered. On that gentle gust of air, Brigit smelled smoke and something else, that twisted sweetness again, like rotting wood.

"Definitely. Thank you," she said, voice calm even as her heart rate picked up. "I know that wasn't easy. Sam. Would you mind?"

"Ah…sure. I didn't know Lacey well." Sam glanced back at Max, who met him with a hard stare. "I knew Pete, though. He and his dad, they have that construction business that built half the county. His dad would ask for help sometimes, historical records. Deeds and stuff."

"She said about Lacey," Max muttered.

"Oh, now you want to speak for me? For either of us? Right, I forgot. You want information so you can go after Pete through *legal means*. Fun about-face."

Max shut her mouth. Brigit studied the currents between them. Sam and Max. Alicia and Max. The three of them and Lacey. She glanced at Ian, looking instinctively for his quirked brow, but his eyes were closed.

"If I had to pick some words," Sam went on a little louder, looking back to Brigit, "I'd say Lacey was stubborn. Protective. Not of the right people, but it's true she had that going for her. I don't think I have much else. Not about Lacey directly. I don't, uh, feel like I have the right."

"What makes you say that?"

"I…" Sam waved his hands in the air in front of him. "Sorry. I'm not good at this."

"That's okay. There's nothing to be good at." That peaty smell was in Brigit's mouth now, tacky on her tongue. She swallowed. It didn't help. "If there's anything you feel strongly that connects to her, it could help me forge a bond. We're all here for a reason." Brigit looked around the room, allowing a quick pass across Ian's face. His eyes were still closed. "We all have the right to speak. I hope you will."

Sam nodded. Heaved a sigh. "Okay. I don't love talking about this. But here you go. Like I was saying, Pete knew me from work. We never really met as kids. Two years ago, he walked in on the wrong conversation between me and a girl I was dating. Things got bad. Then they got worse. Last summer, he got drunk enough to follow me out of Tim's Tavern, and there was…an altercation. I tried to press charges. Lacey covered for him. She didn't know what really happened, only whatever he told her. People already think I don't fit in here. Easy to believe I provoked him. And look, I know you didn't know the full story either," Sam said to Max, whose face had gone a little gray. "But when we couldn't get your testimony, Alicia thought the only way to move the case forward was if I told everyone about the harassment after he found out I'm trans. Made it clear this wasn't just a one-time act of violence everyone could write off as a drunken mistake. I said no. It wasn't me hiding who I am, I just—I do live here, you know? I didn't want to be a martyr. I thought we could still get it heard, at least, except Lacey blamed me for everything. I got angry. I said some stuff. It damaged my own case more than anything, but I don't think she saw it that way." Sam grimaced. "I didn't know he was hurting her too. It's so obvious now, but back then, all I could see was myself. So… I feel like if she's here, or could be, I might not be someone she wants to help."

"She called you, though. When she wanted to speak to me, and she didn't have my number, you were the person she asked."

"That makes sense to me," Alicia said quietly. "Lacey loved Gabi. She knew Gabi loved James, and that James trusted Sam." She tilted her head toward Sam, black hair sliding over her cheek. "And I imagine she also hoped that if there was anyone in town who would understand why she pushed Gabi away so hard—who would see it, eventually, for what it was—it might be you."

This seemed to strike Sam deep in his chest. Beside him, Max inhaled a ragged breath.

"Yes," Brigit said, her own heart twisting, spots burning on her cheeks where Lacey's blood had spattered. But she'd started. She had to continue. "Hold that here." To Alicia: "I take it your impressions of Lacey were nuanced as well."

"I think she was confused and trying her best."

"Can you give us a little more than that?"

Max crossed her legs at the knee. Meanwhile Ian hadn't moved since lighting the candles. Brigit dragged her attention back to Alicia, but it niggled at the edge of her senses, like a heat source just out of reach: Ian's silence, but more than that, his stillness. It made her think of the way his head had felt in her lap, heavy and inanimate.

"She seemed like a good friend to Gabrielle," Alicia said at last, "based on what her parents told me. Picked her up when she needed a ride home from clubs in Richmond. Made sure she didn't drop out of school."

The first candle Brigit lit had burned hot, a deep well melting away from the wick. Clear wax pooled against the tin.

"Pete used Lacey's good heart against her. I think he got

into her head to a degree that would have been difficult for anyone to claw free of. It would have been easy for Lacey to see Sam as a threat, at least consciously, and Max as a potential ally."

Ian watched that candle too. Its miniature flame danced in the dark of his irises. Damp warmth seeped onto her pointer finger. Brigit realized she'd been picking at her scabbed thumb, down where nobody could see.

"What about Gabrielle?" she asked, recalling Lacey's words: *I just wanted her to stop.* "Not an ally in the end?"

Alicia's lips twisted. "I thought that's what we're here to find out."

Brigit placed her palms flat on her thighs. Cool sweat pressed into her jeans. "Ian. Your turn, if you would?"

Hatefully, an upward lilt curved that final word. As if she weren't sure he would at all. There was a pause. Brigit's heart stuttered in her chest, and Ian raised his eyes to hers.

20: IAN

They were looking at him, all four of them, their attention brighter than the candles. Heat against his skin. Brigit, though, watched him with ice behind her eyes. "Whatever you can offer, please."

His side ached from ribs to hip. It was kinetic, this pain, rippling out from the hole in his side like worms forcing passage between his muscles and dermis. Ian tried to blink. Perhaps he should step outside. Cold air might numb the nausea, slow whatever infection was clearly and rapidly getting worse. Then he could find the right words to make Brigit leave this house. It should have been easy. One little sentence.

"I think Lacey was brave," Ian heard himself say. "It took courage to do what she did today." His voice sounded smooth, quiet, a little sad.

"Kill herself?" Max asked sharply.

"Try to make amends." It was his tongue moving. He could feel the vibrations in his chest. "She felt responsible, so she took action. Not all of us can say we've done the same." Blood pounded in his ears, violent and shockingly loud. The pain had vanished. Now warm air filled his lungs and left them in a steady rhythm. Couch fabric brushed against his forearm as Ian's body repositioned itself, leaning into the corner of the sofa without any conscious interplay between his spine and his mind. "I didn't know her, obviously, but that's my strongest impression."

How was this happening? How the fuck was his voice coming out in calm, thoughtful tones, sympathetic to the stricken expression on Max's face? Panic filled his vision with screaming dark colors and he couldn't see, couldn't breathe—but he *was* breathing. Ian felt his mouth curve on one side, a rueful half smile. "I think that's all I've got."

Brigit, he tried to say. He pushed the word against his lips but they lay slug-like on his teeth.

"That's fine," she said, and looked away. "Thank you all for your honesty, and for being open to the process. Now I need quiet, please. I'm going to try and reach her."

She closed her eyes, settling deeper into the armchair, her muscles loosening at the shoulders. A long, slow exhale. The candles flickered all around, tiny hisses below the surface of the air, but Ian couldn't pull his gaze left or right. He sat frozen, white noise blaring in his head. His bones tightened around him. He could feel his heartbeat pulsing in the plates of his skull, his brain inflamed, threatening to ooze through the seams like gum.

"Lacey Rollins," Brigit said. "You're falling, far away. We've built a net here for you, a place for you to rest and catch your breath. All you need to do is let us help you find it." She spoke with a rhythm that eased the others into a regular pattern of inhalations and exhalations. Yoga breathing. It was a trick Ian had come to recognize and resist without really meaning to, but his unfamiliar lungs slipped into the flow. The heat of the room. The smell of wax and smoke. "I'm sending someone to find you, Lacey. You know her already. You spoke for her, to me. Let Emma help you now. Let her bring you somewhere safe."

"Oh," Ian heard himself say, "I don't think anyone would argue this is safe." A moment of silence. Brigit's face flickered with doubt. "I was wrong," his voice continued. "I do have something to add on the subject."

"You have more to say to Lacey?"

"No. Lacey's dead. I have more to say to you." Something tweaked beneath his meniscus as one of Ian's ankles crossed over the opposite knee. An elbow found the couch arm, his jaw dropping onto the propped fist. "I think we should talk about responsibility. I think it's interesting, how people deal with feeling responsible. Don't you?"

Her face recomposed itself into a blank canvas. *It's not me*, Ian shouted inside his head. *You know me. You know me!*

"For instance," his voice went on, "it's your fault I got stuck in the woods for twelve hours. And yours," to Sam, who sat frozen at the other end of the couch. "But neither of you have done a single thing to make amends for that. Or, no, I guess that's not right. Brigit did offer me her shower."

"Ian," Brigit said calmly, and if he could have punched holes in his chest he would have. "You're angry. You're right to be. But you said it yourself, we're here to find James. We need to focus on that."

"We need to focus on the fact that you don't have a clue what happened to your sister, which is genuinely fucking funny, and the fact that Alicia over here has wasted her life trying to stop it from happening again, except nothing she's done has made a difference. If anything," he continued, facing Alicia, "no matter what grand story of change from within you tell yourself, your endorsement of the thin blue line enables the conditions that led a twenty-four-year-old to shoot herself in the head. No way around that one, am I right?

"But back on topic, the reason we're all here—the only one further from the truth about *that* is Max, with this ridiculous theory about a man who's going to die of liver disease before he reaches fifty. Although I guess in a roundabout way, she's got a point that Pete did push Lacey to it, which, Sam, I'm sure you've thought about, given what might have happened if you'd only had the spine to admit how small and scared he made you feel before he ever broke your handsome nose."

His voice remained pleasant and relaxed, so much so that Ian didn't absorb his own words for a beat. Then several small things happened at once. Alicia stood, coat flapping, the gust of air blowing out two of the tea lights on the coffee table. Max said, "Okay," and bristled from top to bottom beside Sam, who clenched his fists, ashen-faced. Brigit's eyes flashed as she sat forward in her chair, and her lips curved in a cold and vicious smile.

"Ian," Alicia said, "what the hell was that?"

The thing controlling him did not look away from Brigit. She didn't look away from it either. Only shook her head, very slowly, just once. "He's not here," she said. "Is he?"

"Yes," Ian's voice corrected her gently. "He is."

"Hey," Max said. "Is this some kind of psychological thing? Because it's not fucking cool."

Ian's heart drummed faster even as his mouth twisted up, slowly, the infestation inside him discovering each muscle in turn. Brigit's smile had faded with his reply, all emotions retreating behind the mask. When she spoke again, her words were simple.

"Why are you here?"

"Because you were going to leave."

Something flitted across her face, gone so fast he couldn't pin it down. "What do you want?"

Ian felt himself lean forward. He took up an insouciant

pose, hands dangling between his knees, forearms resting casually on his thighs. Whatever expression had carved itself onto his face made Brigit's nostrils flare.

"You know what I want," the thing inside him said. "You've always known."

"Excuse me," interrupted Alicia, and movement registered in his periphery. Ian's eyeballs swiveled right. The detective's hand was now on the butt of her gun. "One of you needs to explain what's going on. Right now, please."

Ian's body sat back, hands lifting, palms up. Brigit didn't so much as flinch as she said, without looking away, "Can we have the room for a minute?" Alicia scoffed, and Max's lip curled up. "I need to talk to my partner," Brigit added. "Please."

And there was something in her voice despite that *please*, a cool note of command that set the hairs on Ian's forearms trembling. The room bristled.

"Five minutes," Alicia said. The other two followed her out of the living room and down the hall, Sam still visibly shaken, Max white with anger.

"All right," Brigit said. She placed her palms on her thighs. "No more bullshit."

"Are you sure?" Ian heard himself ask, coyly, as though his nape weren't tight as drying leather. "Are you *ever* sure? How much bullshit can you spin before you forget how to do anything else? Maybe that's the wrong question. Maybe the real question is something like…oh, what *is* the difference, for liars, between 'monster' and 'not'? Is it empathy? Do you think you have that?"

Her knuckles curved and whitened but her words remained even. "Why did you take Ian?"

Brigit didn't falter on his name. That stung him somewhere deep.

"I haven't taken Ian anywhere. I haven't hurt him either. Not really. If anything," his mouth continued with a silken tone Ian had never even attempted, "I've helped him."

"Oh?" The sneer on her face. He'd never seen that either. At least, not aimed at him. "Do tell."

She was goading it. Instead of forcing the answers or trying to sweet-talk them out, instead of begging this thing to let him go, she was *goading* it. Ian's father had favored this tactic, and eventually Ian figured out why: if you push someone into throwing the first punch, it's not your fault when you retaliate. His brain throbbed, anger slapping thick and bloody against his skull with every beat, and suddenly he was standing. For one fraction of a second, Ian thought he was back in control. Then his feet slammed gracelessly across Alicia's hardwood floors. The swift movement must have startled Brigit too, because she froze head to toe as Ian's body lunged around the coffee table, slammed its palms down on the arms of her chair, and caged her like an animal.

"I've helped him see you," Ian said. Brigit stared at him, wide-eyed, so close her breath puffed light and rapid against his jaw, and god, what a violation to have this intimacy now while his skin felt like rubber, owned by someone else, like he could peel gobs from his cheeks with a putty knife and feel nothing. "I've helped him understand what you really are."

She swallowed. Afraid. They were too close. It wasn't him, it wasn't him, but he was scaring her, his legs bracketing hers, claiming her space. When she spoke, though, her voice was a soft but steady slice across his throat.

"And what is that?"

His body leaned in. His exhale ghosted across Brigit's neck, and she shivered. She didn't move as Ian's lips brushed against her ear.

"Why, a Wild Child, of course."

Locked inside his head, Ian couldn't catch hold. Everything whirled, points and edges scraping at his swollen mind. That shiver had been subtle but impossible to miss. Did she like this, on some level? Did he? Was he even the one wondering, or was it the thing controlling his body and voice?

Stop it, he thought, or *Stop me*, or nothing, nothing, just the gleam of her eyes, the impossible hammering of his heart. His mouth curved against the shell of her ear. His right hand slid from the chair to her shoulder, the side of her throat, drawn to the rapid-fire flutter of her carotid. There was his thumb, rough, not him, not him, at least not only him, tracing the line of her pulse, and her hand drifting up to rest at his hip, trembling and warm… And then, so suddenly he could do nothing but gasp in stunned agony, sharp nails dug into the vulnerable place below his ribs. She'd slipped her hand beneath his shirt in an instant, clawing at his abdomen with vicious precision, and Ian toppled sideways to the ground.

"Get in here!" Brigit shouted, loudly enough to bring the others crashing back into the living room. Ian's head pulsed, tremors racing up and down his spine, his vision bleeding white and then reverting in a sickly wheel of colors. Without thinking, he raised a hand to his forehead.

He raised a hand.

As soon as he realized what he'd done, the world blanked out in another burst of black and red and his limb jerked back down, shoving his body upright but not before he found his tongue. "Cut it out," Ian gasped, even as his gaze tore itself away from Brigit and circled toward the others, furious, a wolf in a trap. His jaw snapped shut so hard that had his tongue been between his teeth, he might have bitten it off.

Brigit didn't hesitate. She grabbed his arm and yanked, off-balancing him enough to keep him from fighting as she snapped, "Help me!"

Alicia moved first. In a blur of coat and dark hair she grabbed Ian's other arm, and together they dragged Ian to the floor.

"What the fuck?" Max said from the doorway as Ian thrashed like an overturned beetle, one knee slamming into the coffee table. Sam lunged to stop a tea light from skidding onto the rug.

"Knife," Brigit gritted out. Ian's forehead snapped up for her jaw; she dodged just in time. "Knife!"

"How deep?" Ian heard himself ask, jeering and frantic. "How deep will you cut?"

"What the *fuck*," Max said again, and over her Alicia barked, "Sam! Hold him!"

Sam dropped like he'd been hit. All his slim weight came down on Ian's thigh where Alicia had pinned him while Brigit wrenched at his arms. Ian stared straight into Sam's terrified eyes, his cheek skin stretching with a painful grin, as in his periphery, Alicia worked something out of her pocket and passed it to Brigit. Whatever it was jolted Max into motion.

"Stop!" she shouted as Alicia found a new grip around Ian's shoulders, and then Brigit yanked Ian's shirt up as his torso writhed and struggled. Max staggered to a halt so abrupt she nearly crashed into the couch.

"Help us keep him still," Brigit said, and if she'd trembled in that chair, she did not tremble now. Ian's eyes homed to her, the pocketknife she now held, its blade flipping out with a bright *snap*. There was a low moaning noise from somewhere, maybe Sam, a drone that Ian felt in his teeth, both real and fake. His lips drew back. If anyone came closer he would bite them, bite down and tear, not because this thing wanted so badly to stay in his body, but because it was a feral creature, or not a creature at all. It was something living underneath his skin, threading out along his veins and sprouting weblike across the soft jelly of his brain. Anything close to human had

fallen away the instant it came under real attack, leaving only
a lattice of mucilaginous will to survive.

"Max!" Brigit snapped. It broke something, that word—
pure distilled noise. Everyone moved. Alicia pulled Ian's wrist
and he grunted with pain, breath coming harder as she twisted
his right arm up behind his back, his spine curving to leave
his right side bare and vulnerable. Sam redoubled the pressure on one leg and Max collapsed onto the other, strands of
platinum hair sticking to her bared teeth.

Please, Ian thought as Brigit bent over his ribs, her mouth
thinning into a determined line, but god, if those weren't
tears at the corners of her eyes... *Please. Please.*

The digging of the blade. A sick, searching motion underneath his skin. The wet sound of ripping flesh. That peaty,
inhuman stench of the deep wood, the mud, a plume of
it, like he'd carried a scent gland around inside him which
she had just stabbed clean through. Brigit dropped the knife
with a clatter, still working, his blood instead of Lacey's on
her cheeks. She put her hand inside his abdomen and pulled.
And pulled.

Ian didn't scream. He couldn't even breathe. Or maybe
he'd been screaming the whole time. There was a wrench-
ing, threads being torn from the soupy fragile core of him, the
edges of his flesh peeling up in protest—and then it was over.

Brigit sat, or fell, backward. She was panting. Sweat mixed
with the blood on her face. In her hand, not moving, was
a red-spattered something. Ian tried to face it, but his mind
didn't want to let him; it wanted him to turn away and curl
up and never open his eyes again. But it was his mind, and
he controlled it, and he forced himself to look.

A sapling. Or something close. White trunklet, thin as a
No. 2 pencil and about as long, with a mess of roots at the
bottom. Dozens of them. Some like carrot tips, some as fine

as spider silk. Gluey resin clung between the strands, blood sliding off a darker slick. The five of them sat in complete stillness, silent save for heavy breaths, staring at what Brigit had yanked out of Ian's side.

"Jesus fuck," Max said, and the spell broke.

Brigit hurled the sapling into Alicia's fireplace. Alicia released Ian's arm and crossed to the mantel, grabbed a starter brick and handful of newspaper from the kindling bucket beside the hearth, and threw them both onto the stone. She held up her hand. Brigit snatched the matchbook that had fallen near the couch and threw it neatly across the room. In seconds, the papers and the sapling were engulfed in flames.

21: BRIGIT

"Stay here," Alicia said, and her voice was raw but steady. "I'll get the first aid kit." She stepped away from the burning hearth, then paused. "Is he…"

Sam and Max still pinned Ian's legs. He lay flopped on the glossy wood floor, breathing hard, blood slowly soaking through his shirt where it had fallen back down over the wound. "It's me," he said. None of that strange, mocking silk to the words. "If anyone doubts it, I don't care—I'm not moving."

Brigit looked up at Alicia and nodded. Alicia strode from the room. Brigit's gaze fell back to Sam and Max. "Get off him."

When they didn't move immediately, Brigit flipped onto her knees. She found the pocketknife beneath her palm, hilt slippery. Max and Sam released Ian, scooting backward. Brigit slid the knife toward the center of the room. Her body continued without her brain, that same hand rising, reaching for Ian's cheek. She caught herself, leaned forward, and pressed both hands to his wound instead. Ian hissed through his teeth, trembling under her palms as she held the cut closed, her pulse still screaming with panicked adrenaline. Brigit kept her eyes on her hands, the dark blood welling up between her fingers, running down toward the floor—and then she felt other fingers on her forearm, very light. As if Ian was afraid he'd hurt her if he gripped too hard.

"You knew," he said, too quietly for anyone else to hear.

Brigit's chest squeezed, a violent cramp from heart to belly. She had known. But not for the right reasons. Not because she could look at him and distinguish whatever defined Ian from something else stealing his body, at least not right away. She'd known because the thing in the woods was fucking with her. Because it was taking her perceptions and the things she cared about and warping them, whether in Sam's house or in her own motel room. This wasn't that, but it had used Sam's likeness to taunt her with exactly the same sly, mocking tone—and Ian *had* spent all that time in the Dell…so it came with a flash of brutal clarity, the idea that whatever lived out there might have escalated to a physical intrusion on her life by way of her best friend. Horribly, Lacey's voice played through her head—not Lacey with the gun, but days earlier, still in that parking lot with her fragile, drowning smile as she explained about Gabi: *She likes to be the main character.*

So did Brigit. And she was suddenly quite certain that whatever had used Ian like a puppet knew that too.

Ian's warm, dry fingers were no longer on her arm. Her vision had blurred so badly she couldn't watch him lift his hand to her face. She could only feel a knuckle brush the tears from her cheek. It split something in her, that touch. Cracked it like a geode. Inside, as with all geodes, was sharp stone. She sat back on her heels, forearms straining to keep the pressure steady, as Alicia returned with a red zippered duffel in her arms and a spool of black thread balanced on top.

"Luckily for us," Alicia said, kneeling beside them and

neatly unzipping the bag, "I just recertified. This should be fast."

Brigit waited until Alicia threaded a needle, then eased the pressure off Ian's side and stood. "I'm going to go clean up," she said. "Can you help him without calling this in?"

"You can't possibly imagine I'm calling this in," Alicia replied, dabbing blood from the cut. "I'll explain that stain to my wife, and no one else."

"Where is she?" Ian asked, grimacing as the first stitch went in. "Hopefully not home soon."

"Philly for the week. Developer conference." Alicia's voice dimmed as Brigit left the room. "In case you needed more proof that Hannah's the smart one."

Brigit found a bathroom by sheer luck, walking in the one direction that led neither to the front steps nor the kitchen. She fumbled the door closed, catching the knob and turning it so the latch wouldn't slam and betray her. Bad enough they'd all seen her crying, reaching for Ian like a goddamn Renaissance painting. "Fuck," she bit out, and then she said it a few more times because it was only herself in here, and herself was the worst company of all.

Her cheeks were bloody again. Her hands were worse. Tiny clots of skin clung beneath her fingernails. Brigit went for the neat square of hand soap first, then stopped herself just before she ruined the bar and elbowed on the tap for a rinse. She wasn't sure what pressed her into this pointless, forgettable nicety, especially considering she'd just spilled blood all over Alicia's wooden floor. Maybe it was her quickness to act when Brigit had shouted for help. The tense jolt of understanding they'd shared before Alicia left to retrieve her first aid kit. Or maybe it was the far cleaner evisceration Ian (not Ian) had managed with nothing but a few words: *Alicia over here has wasted her life.*

The blood washed off easily enough. Brigit dug her nails clean and rinsed all traces of red from the sink. Judging by this house and its cute porcelain soap tray, the adventurous photographs…well, Alicia's life didn't seem all that wasted. But she was still in Ellis Creek. And right now she was out there in her living room, stitching up the person Brigit most wanted to remain whole.

In the mirror cabinet, Brigit found a bottle of heavy-strength migraine medication, and took one with a scoop of water. She could still feel the roots against her palm. Thin, spidery tendrils fighting her fingers, slippery and hard to pinch. A whole cancerous network of them. That thing had been inside Ian, webbing out along the filaments of muscle in his abdomen and higher, all the way to his tongue. Brigit leaned her forehead briefly against the door.

Back in the living room, Ian was grimacing as Alicia finished tying off a neat black stitch. Sam and Max stood as far from the fireplace as they could get while remaining in the room, wearing expressions so similar it would have been comical had they not also been so pallid.

"There," Alicia said, her voice the barest ghost of satisfied. "I'm no doctor, so I'd advise you take that to a hospital for a second look when you can."

Ian sat up with a grunt, peering down at his side. Four stitches closed the uneven gash Brigit had sliced below his ribs. The flesh around them was clean but blotchy, red with offense. Fresh blood welled slowly from between each dark thread. Alicia pressed a gauze pad to Ian's side; he held the pad in place while she secured it with surgical tape. Brigit watched from the doorway, some unwelcome emotion closing off her voice.

"You okay?" Sam's voice was too loud, startling over the crackle and hiss of the fire. Someone had added more kindling to keep the blaze going. It took Brigit a moment to realize the question was directed at her.

"Oh," she said, stepping into the room but keeping her distance from the scene on the floor. Her voice didn't shake. If her hands did, no one could see. "Yeah. All good here?"

"I'll live," Ian said, and allowed Alicia to help him to his feet. He swayed and she steadied him, not taking her hand from Ian's elbow as she pinned her gaze on Brigit.

"So."

"Kitchen?" Brigit nodded at the bloodstained floor as if it didn't make her stomach churn. "We'll help you clean that up, but I don't think any of us wants to be in here for this."

"Oh, what *now*?" Max asked, and again, the annoyance in her tone would have made Brigit laugh if she hadn't also sounded like she'd gone four days without sleep.

"I had some thoughts about how all this would go." Brigit ran her fingers through her sweaty hair, which stuck where she raked it. "But after what we just saw..." She shook her head. "We all know bits and pieces of what's going on here. Time to share."

In that sense, this had actually gone rather well. People in shock were more likely to blurt out truths they might otherwise try to hide, and now Brigit didn't have to sell an actual conversation with poor, dead Lacey in order to convince everyone that Ellis Creek was fucked. It didn't hurt that whatever Alicia was hiding, the horror on her face when Brigit had called her back into the room had been real. Same with the tight fury and guilt that gripped her when Ian called her out. She knew something, yes, but it wasn't parasitic trees, and that made Alicia more trustworthy than Brigit had found her since their very first call.

While Brigit and Sam sat at Alicia's kitchen table, Max went to the stove, lifted the kettle, and shoved it into the sink.

"What are you doing?" Sam asked. Ian took the chair to his right, one hand at his ribs as he eased himself down.

"I don't know about you, but I could use some tea." There was a warning in Max's voice, in the rigid line of her shoulders as she filled the kettle. Alicia opened a cabinet beside the fridge and pulled out a glass jar stuffed with tea bags. She set it on the countertop at Max's elbow, then padded out of the room.

Brigit worked to keep the irritation off her face. She couldn't force them to hurry up and tell her what she wanted to know. What she *could* do was create a different kind of trust than the one she'd spun in the living room, a kind where Brigit didn't hold all the power and therefore could be spoken to with greater candor. That required patience.

Wheels on wood announced Alicia's return moments before she pushed a tatty swivel chair into the room and sat across from Brigit. Max fumbled with the burner dials until one produced a whoosh of blue flame. Metal clanked as she placed the kettle on the stovetop and leaned beside it, folding her arms.

Brigit surveyed the table. Everyone met her eyes as they passed. No one spoke, not even Alicia. The satisfaction of that warred with Brigit's visceral discomfort with what she was about to do. She'd just pulled a living thing out of her best friend's torso. How was it that the idea of sharing what had happened to her since landing back in Ellis Creek felt almost as invasive?

"All right," Brigit said, to herself as much as anyone. "Diving in. I've been seeing things since I came back. So far I've had three...encounters, aside from this and what happened in the Dell." Ian sucked in a breath. She didn't let herself linger on him, instead moving her gaze from person to person as she spoke. "One almost could have been a dream. A birch tree in my room, and—" Red fingers. Choked laughter. "—something hiding behind it. I only figured it was real because before that, I got a phone call from my sister." That sound on the line, phone receiver dragging over packed earth. Brigit could hear it now, mingling with the kettle's low static. "But I don't think it was her. I think it was that thing."

A sharp twist of grief cut into her chest. *You have to come back.* She'd needed to believe that voice was really Emma's. That Emma thought Brigit could help save Gabrielle and James.

"What about the last one?" Ian prompted when Brigit didn't speak again. He sounded more worried than betrayed, but she couldn't look at him. Granted, he'd lied too; he could have told her what was underneath his shirt anytime after his shower. Except reaching for anger only made her tired. Ian had lied to protect himself. Brigit made him want protection.

"The morning we found you," she started, and the teakettle shrieked. Max yanked it off the heat, then cut the flame and glanced at Alicia as the whistle died.

"Mugs?"

"Above the sink." Alicia seemed to understand that it would be kinder to leave Max this task than to get up and help. Brigit leaned her head to the left until the pull seared through her muscles. Held for a beat. Switched directions.

"Who wants what?" Max asked.

"Herbal," Sam said. He hadn't regained much color, but he managed a tight smile. "Something soothing. I need some fucking chamomile."

"Cosigned." Ian's voice held a note of humor that Brigit couldn't resist. She snuck a peek in the guise of another rolling stretch. He was smiling too, not enough to crease the circles underneath his eyes, but enough to send a spike through her heart.

"Caffeine for me." Brigit sat back in her chair and willed her shoulders to relax. "Thanks."

"So," Ian said. "You were saying?"

"It made itself look like someone else to mock me. About you."

Brigit couldn't help the way her voice broke that sentence in two, and she accepted her tea from Max with more relief than she cared to show. Ian's smile just now—was it real? Did it carry from his mouth to his eyes, and deeper? For the first time since she'd known him, Brigit wasn't sure. She sat frozen in her skin, the dissonance crushing. Cold rills tightened her nape.

"The point," Brigit went on, forcibly even, "is that my family appears to be the linchpin for a lot of what's happening. Detective, can you shed any light on why?"

Max retook her spot by the stove. "And what any of this has to do with Lacey. What even was that, back there? Before the tree monster? I want to know what the fuck is going on, and not just with that—that *thing*."

"I think it told the truth," Sam said, drawing everyone's attention and evidently regretting it as soon as he had. He focused intently on his mug, but forged ahead. "Pete drove Lacey to kill herself, but only in the abstract. The real shit is in the woods. Something out there."

Brigit nodded. "I don't think Pete knows anything about this. Lacey told me she was sorry for what she'd done to Gabrielle. She was just trying to keep her out of her business."

She paused, filtering her mind. At the time she'd been so stunned to hear Emma's name come out of Lacey's mouth that the rest of what the girl said had gone hazy, quick to dissolve, and then the gun…

Ian cleared his throat. "She said she didn't know James would follow Gabrielle. Into the Dell?"

"To the spinney," Brigit corrected without thinking. In her head, Emma bared her teeth. *I won. Now you have to come with me.*

"The what?" Alicia asked. Instinct told Brigit to rein the words back in, cover them up somehow, but that was the weak, defensive self talking. Not the self who could make up for everything she'd done wrong since setting foot back in this town. Not the self who could finally learn the truth about what killed her sister.

"Spinney," Brigit repeated, tasting each syllable. "It's just a fancy word for a grove of trees. We have one in the Dell."

Cold ground beneath her knees, jeans already muddy from the chase and the capture, the journey through the woods. Emma's fingers are tight around hers, and tight around them both are seven white trees with trunks like bones and roots like—

Veins.

Her heart sped up. She could feel it fluttering, a small thing enclosed within the white curving birches in her chest. Sweet, painful warmth spread through her with every beat because as she spoke, Brigit finally understood, and understanding felt so goddamn good it almost made up for how long it had taken her to put this together.

"What we just pulled out of Ian is part of something else. It's lived out there a long time. My sister found it. I bet your great-aunt did too," she said to Max, recalling the oldest missing person notice she and Ian had found at the library—little Eleanor Temple, vanished from a picnic in 1941. Max stiffened away from the stove. "And so did Lacey."

"That's what happened to Gabrielle," Ian said, the same knowledge dawning in his voice, and this time when their eyes met, neither of them looked away. "Lacey wanted to keep her from reporting Pete for abuse. With her testimony on top of Sam's, something might have stuck. Lacey said she wanted

Gabi to stop. That was all she 'asked for.' What if Lacey asked whatever's in the spinney to *make* Gabi stop? What if she made some kind of bargain, and ending her own life broke it? So then… Gabrielle's dreams about Emma and the woods could have been bait, to get her to the spinney. But also bait for you," he said to Brigit, horror slowing his words. "Like I was. When it was—in me, even before it took over completely, all I could think about was getting you outside. The next step was probably the Dell."

"Bait," Sam echoed, nodding. "That tracks. The nightmares made Gabi crazy, James too. It was the first time *he* was the one keeping *her* secrets. Of course he jumped at the chance to help her find the source."

A beat of quiet, pulsing but strangely companionable. Then Brigit set down her mug. "We can't prove any of this. But I'm sold."

"Gabrielle did wake up after—after what Lacey did," Sam said. "So why is James still out there?"

Brigit didn't let the silence hang between them now. "That's my fault."

"No," Alicia said. "It's mine."

INTERLUDE: 2003

Psychiatric Admissions Note

Date: 10/23/2003

N/S/A: Emma Weylan, female, 18

Chief complaint: court ordered evaluation following attempted violent action

History of present illness:
   -Suicidal ideation: no
   -Harm to others: no
   -Paranoia: not persistent
   -Hallucinations: patient told witness there was a monster at location of arson attempt; has not made similar claims to police
   -Focused ROS: patient sleep deprived, appetite seems regular, mood stable on admission

Past psychiatric history:
   -Diagnoses: cyclothymic disorder
   -Treatments: therapy (weekly, one year), parental mandate
   -Hospitalizations: none
   -Medications: lithium, extended release, 600 mg 2 times daily

Current medications: patient has not been taking recommended dosage, claims medication makes it hard to think

Substance use/abuse notes: no reported drug or alcohol use, no signs of either

Mental status exam: patient clean and showered. Cooperative but distracted, no repetitive actions, no lasting paranoia. Language clear, no slurring, no memory loss. Affect depressed, mood impatient, anxious. Wants to see her sister.

Incident details: patient used gasoline to set fire to area of woods outside the Ellis Creek Ruritan. Witnesses describe manic behavior. Patient was covered in dirt and sticks, claimed to be doing "what had to be done." No injuries on scene save minor scratches on patient's friend (female, age 17, name withheld). No damage to property. Charges pending psych eval.

22: IAN

"Or our fault," Alicia amended. She hid her expression well, but Ian detected a faint wrinkle on her brow. "So you had no idea about any of this before you got back?"

Brigit shook her head. On anyone else, her watchful, deliberate silence could have been a way to process shock and alarm. On Brigit, Ian knew it for recalculation. He could practically see the gears spinning in her head as she slotted new information into her knowledge base. To think he'd accused her of trusting Alicia too readily before they first entered the Dell. He'd been thoughtless. So distracted by concern for her, he'd forgotten who she was.

Alicia had begun to speak. Ian refocused on her voice, low and smooth, heartening in a way he didn't trust because he knew, even as it affected him, he was experiencing a psychological response to her self-assurance. He had the uncomfortable thought that this was one reason he kept doing the exorcisms, the ghost-busting, even after they'd made a few episodes and Ian's rose-colored glasses started to crack. Why he kept setting lies into motion, then watching them unspool from behind the curtain of his camera. It was because Brigit had a similar effect, when she wanted to. And every time it worked, every time Ian saw her manipulate their poor, hopeful clients into believing her bullshit, a cozy, vindictive splinter would whisper, *You're the victim, and I'm not.*

He'd thought what he and Brigit had made him special. Before Ellis Creek, he'd thought they were a team. Although, she went into the Dell for him, didn't she? On the living room floor, she'd reached for him with bloodstained fingers, real tears on her face.

"—how to be supportive," Alicia was saying, an unusually pained note in her voice that drew Ian back to this room, this table. "I wish I could say it wasn't draining, but that would be a lie. I don't know how much you knew about any of that at the time."

"My parents tried to keep me out of anything unpleasant," Brigit said. "Which, I later learned, was pretty much everything."

Alicia nodded, then continued.

"I thought therapy was helping, and so did Emma, usually. Sometimes downswings would coincide with a fight between us or your parents, and she would refuse to go. Or she'd stop taking her medication because it took too long to feel the effects, or she'd feel them and think she was better. So when she told me about the woods, that some kind of monster lived out there feeding on kids…" Alicia pressed her lips together. "I told myself hallucinations were part of her illness. I've carried that mistake for sixteen years."

Sam sat back. "So you knew what took James. You knew this whole time."

The bright kitchen lights betrayed Alicia's throat as she swallowed. "Not immediately. And not entirely." She glanced at Ian. "What happened to you was unexpected."

"'Not entirely,'" Sam said, "still means you lied. To me. To his parents."

"Why didn't you tell me any of this when I first got here?" Brigit asked. Before Alicia could respond, she rested her elbows on the table, mug between her palms, and leaned in. "Wait. Let me guess. You wanted to see how much I already knew."

Alicia hesitated. Then she closed her eyes. "After Emma died, I…struggled. There was a note. She gave it to me the day before it happened. Things were bad between us. After I stopped her from burning the Dell, they got worse. I was exhausted by it. I thought she was trying to play with my head again, so I didn't read the letter. Then, when they found her body… I couldn't. I threw it away."

"That's why you didn't come around after," Brigit said. "You felt guilty. Is that why we're in this kitchen right now? Are you on a redemption arc?"

"I felt guilty because I thought I was part of why Emma killed herself. I never believed there was really something out there." Alicia looked from Brigit to Max to Ian, and finally to Sam. "Not until Gabrielle and James. I had other reasons to stay and fight my way into this job. I met my wife here. Hannah's family has lived in Ellis Creek for generations. We could have left anytime, but she thinks we can make it better, if we make it *ours*."

She cut herself off there, perhaps remembering the words that thing had said with Ian's tongue. Max opened her mouth, but Brigit held up one hand like a blade. It was a deft move. All attention swung back to Alicia, and now whatever she said next would sound like an admission. The detective's eyes narrowed almost imperceptibly—she recognized the power Brigit had just wielded—but she rallied.

"When James and Gabrielle disappeared, it didn't take long for their friends and family members to mention those dreams. A blond girl covered in mud, chasing Gabrielle. Voices in the

Dell. A ring of white trees. I remembered everything Emma told me about that place. I went looking."

"And found?"

Alicia's full lips parted, but for the first time, it appeared as though her voice had failed her. She blinked once, breaking their gazes. "I don't know."

"Not good enough," Max said. "Lacey is dead. Sounds like she's not the first desperate kid we all gave up on. Whatever you saw out there, fucking say it."

"I don't know what I found," Alicia said again, stressing each word. "I don't even know how I found it. I haven't made it there again. But…in the birches, something spoke to me. It told me it would let them go. I just needed to do one thing."

"You sold Brigit out." Ian hadn't meant to speak, but Max's anger was contagious. "You called her and asked her to come back here, and you told her to look for them. You used Emma to convince her to stay."

Of course, so had he. But that wasn't the same. He hadn't known what was really out there. He never would have pushed for them to stay if he had. Although…if Ian was right, Brigit's presence in Ellis Creek was the only thing that could save James Mulroy. They'd found Gabrielle right after telling Alicia they couldn't help, as if whatever lived in the Dell could sense Brigit trying to leave. So it had returned Gabrielle as an enticement. Then, when Brigit took the carrot, it infected Ian and sent him back out into the world as—not just bait, but an *insurance* policy? A way to guarantee that Brigit wouldn't skip town before she accomplished whatever it was the spinney wanted.

Thinking that, he wanted to rip himself apart. He'd lost control of his body and his voice, handed over something so intimate he hadn't known he could lose it, and it wasn't even about him. Worse, so much worse, was the memory of crowd-

ing Brigit into that chair. Of finally making her dependent
on his choices, his actions—only he didn't know if he was
the one who thought that, or if the infection had put it there.
Did his father feel something akin to that when he remembered hurting Ian, fear and satisfaction in equal measure? Was
it something Ian carried too, embryonic but ready to grow?

"I thought Brigit was involved from the beginning," Alicia
said quietly. "Why else would it want her so badly? And there
was the connection to Emma. I didn't realize Gabrielle and
James were out there because of Lacey instead. That she made
some kind of deal of her own, and the thing in the woods
just—saw an opportunity, I suppose. Then you arrived—" her
eyes finding Brigit "—and…you were Emma's kid sister—
sorry, sibling. Of course I knew that before, but seeing you was
different. You were so young when she died. How could you
have been involved? I couldn't just send you out there to—do
whatever it wanted with you. But I couldn't risk those kids,
either, and I had no idea what you remembered, or what you
were like. I didn't know if you'd disappear if I told you the
truth. And finally… I started to think that maybe you really
could do the job I hired you to do."

Brigit nodded slowly. Her expression was unreadable. Ian
wasn't sure how to take Alicia's confession either. She'd tried
to walk a line between giving Brigit to the Dell, and not
sending her blindly into the arms of whatever was creeping
around out there. She hadn't done a great job, but he understood the trap she was in—not only because of her past with
Emma, but as the lead detective on a highly visible case. The
female, Vietnamese lead detective with a loving wife.

"So it's still valid," Brigit said. "This deal you made."

"Things have changed," said Alicia. "Obviously."

"For you and me, maybe." Brigit's eyes flashed toward Sam.
"For James? Not so much."

"Yes," Sam said, "let's talk about that. My friend is stuck with a monster in the woods. It's been there for decades. Longer. I'll do the rest of the archives later. What do we do *now*?"

"We all go." Max swiped a lock of hair off her temple with one impatient hand and tucked it behind her ear. The youthful gesture made something twinge in Ian's chest. "You said you'd bring it Brigit, so we bring her. And us. And a fuck-ton of gasoline. Then we light it up."

When nobody spoke for a long beat, Max barked a humorless laugh.

"What are we waiting for, evidence? I know I screwed up last time," she said to Sam. "I could have testified when you brought charges and I didn't, because I'm a coward, and I'm sorry. But that's the fucking joke, don't you see?" She set her mug down too hard. Liquid arced onto the floor. "I was sorry when I saw those bruises on Lacey's arms. I was sorry when she called in sick for three days and showed up with a broken rib. I was sorry when you got beat up, too, but I didn't see it happen, and I was scared of getting up on that stand and telling everyone in Ellis Creek I think the guy whose dad signs half the paychecks that fund mine is an abusive piece of shit. So I didn't." Her voice broke. Skin pulled taut over her cheekbones as Max worked her jaw. "And now he wins. That's what you're all saying. The statute of limitations for assault is one year, and Lacey's dead, and he didn't even kill her. So here's where I'm at: either this place will keep closing in on people until all we can do is breathe our air and shut our eyes tight like it's all fine, and whatever's out there in the woods will keep—taking advantage—which, holy shit, you guys, I have not even begun to process that my grandma's sister is probably buried out there too. But either we just let it all keep happening, or we try and fix even one thing. I want to try. For once."

"You couldn't have saved Lacey," Sam said, and Max went perfectly still. His knuckles were white on his mug, but his voice was intent. "You know that, right?"

"We can't burn down the Dell." Alicia's voice was cool and quiet. "Plenty of people have tried."

"Max is right, though," Sam said. "We have to do something." He nodded to Ian. "He was in there for one night. If we don't find James soon…"

His words trailed into uneasy silence. In it, Ian heard the question Sam refused to ask: *Will there be anything left to find?*

"I don't want any more people going into those woods than necessary," Alicia said, moving Ian crisply past the image of a boy, conscious, rooted to the earth while his body decomposed around him. "In fact, I'm going to ask you all to stay put. I brought this down on us. I'm also the only one who carries a weapon, so—"

Max scoffed. "What, you're going to shoot a tree?"

"You can't just put us in time-out," Sam said. "We're not the children here. And we have more information than we've ever had. That has to help, right?"

"I'm not saying a gun is the answer," Alicia said, "but I do have training you don't, and when I took my oath of service, I agreed to do what it takes to protect this town. I let you all down in that. If anyone is risking their life today, it should be me."

"Did you seriously think that was going to work?" Max folded her arms. "You don't get the honor of claiming all responsibility. You were just as much a pawn as Lacey, and I don't think any of us needs a fight about who's the biggest fuckup in the room right now."

Alicia tensed. "I can't have more civilians running off to get themselves possessed."

"Too bad you don't call the shots," Max snapped back. Ian

braced himself to speak, but before he could, Brigit pushed her chair back and stood.

"Hey," Ian said, half rising. Skin tugged at the stitches below his ribs.

"Relax," Brigit said from the threshold of the room. "Bathroom break."

She eyed the others, then quirked her mouth at him and padded off. A door closed quietly down the hall. Tension crackled in the kitchen, visceral enough that Ian wished he'd thought of the bathroom first. But he doubted Brigit had left to take a breather. She was sending a message.

Sure enough, her blatant dismissal of the argument snapped something loose. Alicia sat back first, then Sam, and finally Ian. His side pulsed with steady furious pain, but already the memories were jagged: the knife, Brigit's fingers working underneath his skin. Six years ago, when he changed his last name and took that final punch, Ian lived with the cracked incisor for weeks. When he finally went for the emergency extraction, he'd wondered if the false tooth would ever feel more real than that agony, but he'd grown used to it almost at once. Hadn't thought of the pain at all, really, until walking into the hospital in Ellis Creek.

This felt different. More like reels of his mind had been removed, leaving only negatives he lacked a way to view. The only exception was Brigit, her eyes on his. That fucking shudder.

"Okay," Ian said, because if he stayed silent his brain would protect itself into a hemorrhage. "So, we agree—we're all going." He paused, waiting for Alicia to argue, but she only pressed her lips into a line. "And that fire is out. We shouldn't destroy the whole forest anyway, not if we can help it. That'll put a lot of people at risk, and there are plenty of trees around here that aren't...that are fine. I don't want to kill anything I don't have to." Ian turned to Alicia. "Would you be able to find it again? The spinney?"

Alicia moved her head to the right, not quite a shake. Her lips twisted down at the corners. "I—want to say I could. I should be able to say that."

And even with his conflicted loyalties, Ian's heart ached at the familiar blend of confusion and self-loathing that gnawed through her control. Alicia was right: she *should* be able to remember. Just like he should be able to remember exactly where he'd spent those long hours in the Dell before something propped him up like a doll for Brigit to find. Ian nodded.

"You found it once," he said, "and apparently Lacey managed. Other people over the years. I think it has to want us to find it, and we have to keep looking long enough to get there. If we can manage not to lose Brigit, we should make it. And then maybe we can…"

"Dig up the trees? Salt the earth?"

He cast a narrow glance at Max, anticipating a sneer painted with her half-eaten lipstick, but she stared back with clear eyes. Ian raked a hand through his hair, fingers catching as always in the curls behind his temple.

"Salt," Sam said. "Yeah. Okay. If those trees are where it lives, what *makes* them? I might…" He stopped, tapping a finger at his lower lip. "You don't have to salt the whole ground. Just the roots you want to kill."

"How do we salt roots?" Alicia asked.

"A drill." Sam patted the air in front of him, finger still extended, and flicked his gaze from one of them to another. "We drill the roots and fill them with salt. My parents used to do it to honey locusts, because of the thorns. It kills the trees, all the way down."

"Every root?" Max worried at her lower lip, front teeth

tearing away another stripe of red. "That's going to take a lot of time. I don't like a lot of time."

"Not every root. The bases. Where they connect. If it's distracted with Brigit, away from the spinney..."

"I have a drill," Alicia said.

Max tapped the counter. "I have rock salt. We keep it for the parking lot."

A car engine turned over, loudly enough that Sam and Ian both craned their necks toward the front door. It sounded close. Too close. Ian met Alicia's eyes and saw the comprehension flash. They stood at the same time, chair legs scraping. Ian ignored the pain as he hurried toward the hall down which Brigit had disappeared while Alicia made for the door.

"Bridge?" he asked outside the bathroom, knocking. No answer. "Hey. Brigit. You okay in there?" Nothing. Ian knocked again, then braced himself and tried the knob. It turned easily. The door swung inward. The bathroom's frosted window had been shoved all the way open. Late-afternoon sunlight streamed in along with a crisp breeze. He stared at the window for one painful beat, then turned and jogged after Alicia.

Max and Sam stood on the stoop, Sam shivering without his jacket. Ian's car was gone. Alicia stood over her Ford Focus, the hood of which had been propped up with a metal bar, and when she spun back toward them there was violence in the set of her mouth. "She took the spark plug."

"Not mine," Max said, pointing down the block at a black motorcycle. "She doesn't know what I drive."

"Great." Sam ground the heels of his palms against his eyes. "We have one bike, half a plan, and the most important part of that plan just left."

"What's the rideshare situation in this town?" Ian asked Alicia. His heart thrummed against his ribs, pulsing fire at the edges of his wound, but something hotter and more urgent flared inside his chest.

"Let's see." She pulled out her phone, thumbed it open, and waited. "All right. We could have a car in ten minutes, but that doesn't help us if we don't know where she went. The Dell is huge. She could have gone in anywhere. Unless, the Ruritan again?"

"No," Ian said, shaking his head, the words coming out before he could think them through because if he stopped long enough to think, if he gave this any time at all, the panic would rise up and crush him like an elder god. "I know where to go. Max? Can you take Sam to the bar and get his car and the salt?"

"What about you?"

"We," he said, nodding at Alicia and trying to channel Brigit's unflappable confidence, "are going to call a ride and save my idiot friend, and then we're all going to stop this thing for good."

Ian regretted his words immediately, fear and embarrassment like acid in his mouth. He wasn't her. He'd never be her. He couldn't get these people to follow him. But Max was nodding. Sam was nodding too.

"All right, then," Alicia said. "I'll grab the drill."

23: BRIGIT

She didn't feel bad about the car. It wasn't guilt that stung her lungs. Alicia would find the spark plug soon; Brigit hadn't hidden it particularly well. Just well enough to give herself a solid head start. No permanent damage done.

Although, she had been tempted to take the plug with her. For half a breath she'd considered bringing it to the Dell and hurling it into the trees, one more artifact for curious kids to find in twenty years. Problem was, stealing the plug would have levered Alicia right back onto the high road. Also the plastic would never degrade. Also maybe there was no high road.

Fuck it. Fuck the psychoanalysis.

Ian finally knew everything, or everything important. Sam knew what happened to James. Max knew why Lacey pulled the trigger. Alicia had confirmation of what she'd done wrong with Emma, and what she'd done right today. It was the perfect time, in other words, to be a hero. Because Alicia, of course, was right. Someone *had* brought this down on them, starting sixteen years ago.

The sun hung low as Brigit turned onto the highway leading north out of Ellis Creek. To her left, above the lazy, sinuous mountaintops, the sky bled orange light across the horizon. It was appropriate that she reenter the Dell at sunset, and in fact the day felt shorter than it should. As if each minute she spent driving toward the Dollhouses also took her back in time, to a place where there was only that one night spooling out forever.

"Wow," Brigit said to Ian's familiar mix of spicy deodorant and cheap shampoo. She was spinning out. "Do I need to get my shit together here?"

This was the right thing. Had to be. It was at least *a* right thing, because instead of five people getting hurt tonight, there would only be one, and that was basic math. And Ian would think about her, after. Not as a liar or a traitor, someone he couldn't stand to touch because he'd finally seen what lay beneath the pretty mask. He would think of her as a person who had been brave. For all of them.

Brigit glanced at the rearview mirror as she slowed for a bend and saw that her upper lip had curled away from the teeth. She hadn't meant to sneer. Hadn't even realized she was doing it. Apparently not even the promise of certain death could match her inability to stomach her own bullshit.

The Dollhouses revealed themselves around the final bend. Brigit squeezed in beside the Caterpillar excavator, easing Ian's car onto the overgrown lawn. She took a moment before climbing out, both hands on the wheel, searching for any indentations left by his grip. There were none, but that was all right. It was enough to sit in his seat and breathe his air. Her brain was doing its best to make her change her mind, a last gasp of self-preservation, but Brigit was nothing if not stronger than her brain. Motive mattered, but only in that she needed to believe in herself for long enough to walk into the Dell. Belief mattered, but only because she needed to stay in these woods until she found the spinney.

Brigit reached into the back seat and found the flashlight she'd brought with them before, then got out of the car. The slam of her door sent a flurry of black birds up into the sky. They'd roosted on top of the nearest Dollhouse, nesting in the fragile crook between the chimney and the roof. She watched them wheel, heart hammering in sympathetic panic, and realized she was afraid. She'd been afraid a lot since coming back here. Since long before that. She—

Dirt on her tongue. Thick and sudden and caking the inside of her mouth, filling up her cheeks and pressing back, pressing deeper, tickles of it crumbling down her throat and into her stomach so she'd be buried in it, buried from the inside out, where things might grow—

Brigit spun away from Ian's car and heaved into the grass. The blank Dollhouse windows watched as she bent at the waist, gagging. Black spots danced in the saw grass. The world juddered wildly. The lump in her throat grew, swelling up to meet the impossible earth that choked her tonsils. Her legs buckled. Cold, damp ground seeped through her jeans as Brigit clawed at her neck, her own wet noises smacking at her eardrums, and then, abruptly, she could breathe. On her knees, massaging the tender ache at her larynx that burned with every inhale, Brigit stared up at the Dollhouses. Where someone, something, stared back.

A pale, emaciated figure, obscured by dust and glare, stood behind a second-story window in the farthest house. As four grackles settled back onto the roof in a noisy rustle of wings, it raised one long arm and waved. Brigit blinked. When the house swam back into focus, the figure was gone. Because of course it was. It was playing with her. Not trying to kill her, just…letting her know it was watching. That it could have kept pace with Ian's car on that first day, and now, if it chose, could reach that arm all the way down and twine its spindly fingers around her throat.

Her back no longer hurt as she got to her feet. The crick in her neck had eased. Her throat remained sore, but everything else—the bruised hip from her homecoming night on the floor, the oozing gouge in her thumb—all that faded away in the face of her outrage. If that little trick was meant to knock her off balance and weaken her resolve, the thing behind the birches didn't know her as well as it thought.

Brigit squinted past the empty houses and shook off the last of her nausea. The sky was leaking daylight. Ian and the others would figure out a way to come after her soon, and he would guess where she might go. Heart still drumming but lungs full of brisk clean air, Brigit strode past one Doll-house, then the other, into the welcoming arms of the Dell.

At first the trees were widely spaced, single hickories tower-ing above sporadic clusters of cottonwoods and beech. Lovely golden light filtered through the branches, catching on flashes of color: tiny red berries, the deep green of occasional holly. It smelled like holiday wreaths, the dry, musty scent of dead leaves overpowered by that richer green. Quickly, though, the forest thickened.

Nobody lived on this side of the highway. That was one rea-son her father had been able to purchase the land when they moved to Ellis Creek. It must have been a steal back then, un-tilled, wild, and getting wilder. Too bad he hadn't checked the geophysical situation until after their finances had been rapidly and comprehensively screwed. As Brigit picked her way past bushes now clotting into thickets, she felt a startling ripple of sympathy. Her parents had sunk everything into those houses, and if they'd been a tough sell before Emma, the way her body was found would have been a death knell for sure.

It wasn't something Brigit thought about often, even here, this past week in Ellis Creek, save that first awful moment when they drove past the Dollhouses. Her mind glanced over the knowledge with fierce determination. She hadn't even seen the corpse. Though she hadn't needed to see it to imagine it. Blood on the grass. A girl face down, a body's length away from an empty house, caught between that false semblance of safety and the black, yawning depths of the wood. Now, for the first time in a decade but not since coming home, Brigit wondered why. Not why Emma had done it— or (please, please) why something had done it to her—but why *here*. This spot.

They came to the Dollhouses that night, as she'd told Ian, to play a round of Wild Men. Brigit could see it in her mind's eye, how they'd… How *had* they gotten there? It was a long walk for winter. So Emma drove. Yes. And she must have taken Brigit home afterward, as well, because she remembered waking up the next morning in her own bed. That first hour was so vivid, looking back, marking as it did the line between Emma alive and Emma dead. Brigit could still taste the cereal she'd eaten for breakfast. Reese's Puffs, a rare treat. Emma must have gone back to the Dell alone.

The sun sank lower. Trunks grew tumorous and fat with ivy. The air thickened too, threads of mold creeping into the pine, and Brigit followed that scent more than anything else. This deep in the Dell, a strange lightness chased her heels. As though she were following along in someone else's story, and that person knew where to go.

"I do know this place," Brigit whispered to herself, remembering those countless afternoons she'd played in here without Emma. Walking home from school when her sister forgot to pick her up. Abandoned at the Dollhouses as her father paced and shouted on the phone. It had been easy, then, to morph the Dell into a fairy-tale realm. A world outside human time.

You want to be the wild child, Wild Child?

Laughter broke against her skull, brittle and brief. Except— that memory wasn't right. That wasn't Emma's laugh.

Her body understood first, legs coming to a halt before her brain knew why. Then the giggles came again. They drifted down from the tapering spruce tops, too high for a person to climb; those branches would be thin and pliable as old carrots. Oaks and maples stretched into a sky the color of fresh bruises, but nobody perched in their canopies either.

Red flashed in the corner of her eye. Brigit followed it, neck twinging, and swallowed a yelp. Fifteen feet away, four crimson fingers pressed against a beech tree's pale, flaking trunk. This time they didn't jerk out of sight. Instead the fingers hitched another inch up the trunk to rest at what would be around Brigit's hip height—except the tree wasn't broad enough to conceal a person Brigit's size.

"Hello?" Immediately Brigit wished she could roll the word back. Her voice came out soft, almost breathy. She took a step forward, pulse thumping in her throat. "This is what you wanted, right? I'm alone. I'm ready to play." That sounded better, stronger, but the fingers didn't move. No more laughter either. Nothing but dead leaves on dead leaves. "Hey." Too loud this time. Her body felt off, like the skin didn't fit, her bones pushing out at the seams. She could feel herself vibrate. "Answer me!"

The gloved hand slipped behind the beech. Brigit lunged forward before she lost her nerve, flashlight angled as though it were a hatchet, closing the distance between herself and the tree in three long strides. Her foot caught on an uneven patch of ground and she tripped, fell, caught herself hard against the trunk. She lurched around it, palm stinging, but there was no one. No dropped glove.

Brigit switched on her flashlight and crouched. As best she could tell, the ground above the beech roots hadn't been disturbed. But something else had. She saw it just as she was about to stand, and her stomach flipped. Far lower than the hand had rested, dark and viscous against the gray bark, was a jagged smear of blood roughly in the shape of a palm.

She touched the pad of her right forefinger to the stain. The tacky, half-congealed feel of it remained even after she rubbed her hand clean, but Brigit had needed to know. She'd needed, even now, to be sure it wasn't only in her head. Although, she'd felt the birch branch on her cheek, that morning in the Super 8…and Ian. Ian and the sapling, its wet and veiny roots, the sucking sound they made pulling off his oblique.

Brigit dug her forefinger nail into her thumb, reopening the scrape. Centered by the pain, she swept her flashlight in a low arc. She searched the trunks ahead, scanning bark and knobs of moss, and sure enough: on a young white oak to her right, another splash of red. A path, then. Leading her deeper. Coaxing her into a game.

"Cute," Brigit called to the deepening black. "Very cute." Then she crouched, pinned her flashlight between her teeth, and got to work.

24: IAN

Buildings slid past him on the left, storefronts closing and lights turning out. It wasn't dark yet but it would be soon, maybe before they reached the Dollhouses.

"How long have you known her?" Alicia asked.

It would definitely be dark before they found Brigit.

"We went to college together," Ian said quietly. "But we've only been working together for a year." He waited long enough that if Alicia wanted to say more, she could have. Then he asked, "Is Brigit what you expected?"

Alicia didn't answer right away. She had one hand on her thigh, tapping out a slow rhythm with her index finger.

"Yes and no. I didn't really know her, growing up. Emma told me stories, and of course there were her claims about the Dell. But after she died, I couldn't bring myself to go anywhere near Brigit. I kept tabs, though. Some of our friends overlapped when she was in high school. You know, the scene kids."

They stopped at the last light in downtown Ellis Creek. Ahead, trees blanketed a rolling landscape that seemed to go against gravity, pouring up into the mountains where the sun hovered inches above the Blue Ridge. Something twitched in Ian's mind, a tiny flag springing up at Alicia's words, but it was overpowered by the image of a surly teenage Brigit in black dye and fishnet gloves.

"I hear there was a goth phase."

"Oh, definitely. That's the yes."

"And the no?"

"Emma was an emotional powerhouse," Alicia said slowly. "Volatile, but at least what you saw was what you got. She could also make you feel whatever she felt, though I'm not sure she always knew she was doing it." The rueful note in her voice kept him quiet as she breathed for a moment, thinking. "I suppose I thought Brigit might be exactly the same, or completely the opposite."

Ian huffed a laugh. "Yeah, well. Pretty sure some of that runs in the family."

The image of baby goth Brigit terrorizing high school jocks soured as the light turned green, its nostalgic sweetness twisting out of reach. Now Ian pictured that same teenager alone, layering eyeliner onto her face to black out the features that reminded her of someone else.

They turned onto the northbound highway, and the radio went fuzzy. The driver switched stations.

"You're not angry with her." Alicia pitched her voice low despite the music. Ian did the same, as if it mattered. Their driver hadn't even blinked when Alicia had slid into the back seat with a power drill in her lap.

"I wouldn't say that." His hand, unbidden, rose to his flank. Alicia had given him some painkillers before they left her house, so the fire had banked into an oscillating warmth that sharpened when he moved too quickly. "It's complicated."

"You're willing to go into that—" Alicia indicated the darkening trees outside her window "—for her."

Ian followed her gaze to the forest, the shadows between

each trunk like gashes in a charcoal tapestry. "I lost a night to that," he said, mouth suddenly dry.

Another laugh strangled itself near his lungs. A night. As if that loss was what Ian would take with him when he left this town, if he left it. *Ellis Creek is sticky that way.*

Alicia nodded. They didn't speak again until they rounded a wide serpentine bend in the road and Ian's car came into view.

"There," he said, clenching his teeth around a grunt as the seat belt dug into his hip. The same place he'd bruised himself nearly hitting Gabrielle. "Just let us out at the houses."

"What?" the driver protested. "You sure? Nothing here for you, man."

"Clearly there is." Gone was the softer, contemplative tone Alicia had used when discussing Emma. Back was the woman who'd made Ian consider skipping town before they filmed their first interview. "Pull over."

"All right," said the driver, "no problem. Here you go." He swerved across the opposite lane, coming to a smooth halt in front of Ian's rear bumper, then executed a perfect three-point turn once they'd climbed out into the cold.

"You going to knock stars for that?" Ian asked, watching the car peel off in the direction of Ellis Creek. "Hey, I don't suppose you can do that window jimmy thing…"

Alicia flipped the drill and held it out to him hilt-first. "He did his job, and that depends. Do you care about your windshield wipers?"

Her palm had left the plastic drill handle warm, but as Ian watched her snap off one of his wipers and use it to break into his car, the chill crept back. At least they'd beaten the sunset. Ribbons of orange and purple and crimson unfurled above the dilapidated houses Brigit's father had built. Way off, the mountains loomed black, their ridges crisp and lined with flame.

"I see it, you know," he said. "Why you'd fight it out here."

Alicia glanced at him, one dark brow cocked, and worked the wiper up and down the inside of his driver's side window with quick, efficient motions. Something clicked in the door depths. She smiled almost imperceptibly.

"Don't let a pretty sunset fool you. I never said I was wise to stay."

Ian snorted, stepping forward as Alicia opened the door and backed away. "Oh, trust me. That much I know."

He set the drill on the roof and unbuckled his duffel from the back seat. Vaguely, as if from a movie seen in a childhood fever, he recalled being poured onto this same back seat before waking up on Alicia's couch. Brigit must have moved the camera bag from the footwell when she took the car. She'd even strapped it in for him, taking care not to compress the lens cap pocket with the seat belt.

Ian clenched his jaw against the sudden ache at the back of his throat, and pulled out the camera itself. He felt better with its familiar weight tugging at his forearms. The air itself tasted cleaner, less like woodsmoke and more like the promise of snow.

"Going to film the finale?"

In lieu of an answer, Ian raised the camera toward the first house and flipped on the flashlight attached to the top. Bright white light cut through the dusk.

"Ah." Alicia stepped up beside him, drill back in hand. She cast a pointed look at his feet, and Ian realized he'd been testing his footing on the grass. "If you all insist on doing this," she said, "we're at least going to do it right. You were separated before. We don't have a contingency plan."

"I know."

"Am I going to have to stop you from going in there on your own?"

"I wouldn't be on my own," Ian said. He met her gaze, held it. "But no." Cold licked at his cheeks. With the camera in his hand and the great dark forest looming over them both, he felt the urge to speak plainly. "Listen. What you said in the car, about me and Brigit? You're not all wrong."

Alicia studied him as the sun slipped away. "What are you trying to say?"

"We have an idea I think is worth trying. Salt's a classic monster killer, or at least a protective agent. We've got decades of horror movies and gardening tips to back that up." Ian turned back to the woods. From a broad oak tree, something clattered with frantic violence. "But you should know, if things go sideways, I'll choose Brigit."

Alicia made a small noise, not quite a snort, not quite a hum. "Yeah, well. I wouldn't bet against her. Not in there."

And there was something about the way she said it, an odd, furtive shadow, that sent the little flag from their conversation in the car jutting back into Ian's brain. She'd mentioned something, folded up between other pieces of information, something about Brigit that hadn't quite clicked. He squinted at the trees. "What did you mean about Emma's claims?"

"What?"

"You said you didn't know Brigit as a kid. Just what you got from Emma's stories about the Dell."

"Oh. Don't worry, she's proved herself."

"Proved herself what?"

The older woman sighed. "I know it was bullshit now, all right? There's something real in the woods, but that doesn't mean Emma wasn't...that she didn't have her own problems. I'm aware that by not talking openly to Brigit, I put you both at risk. I'm not proud of that."

"Alicia," Ian said. He'd never called her by her name, not to her face. She seemed to realize that too, because her shoulders went very stiff and very still. "Tell me."

"It's just… Emma said it was Brigit's idea. Back then. This game they'd play."

"Wild Men."

Dark eyes flickered back toward his. "It was some kind of psychological projection, I suppose. That's part of what made the whole thing so easy to discount. Emma said Brigit learned that game from something that lived in the Dell. She was obsessive about it, blaming her, even though Brigit was only a kid. She got trapped between what's really out there and her own paranoia, which definitely came in cycles. That seemed so obvious the night she tried to burn down the woods."

Ian kept his face as neutral as possible. Alicia had touched on this at her house, but maybe now she'd let something else slip. Maybe it would be whatever Brigit had risked that séance to learn.

"She called me, sounding completely out of control, and I drove down to find her. There was mud all over her face. She looked…she looked insane. I don't use that word lightly. And she lashed out when I tried to stop her, so I left. I should have done more. I should have read her letter." Old grief roughened her voice.

Ian frowned, trying to recall what Brigit had said on their first day in Ellis Creek. An older sister, teasing. Late nights and hurt feelings. Very little about the Dell itself. The woods featured incidentally in Brigit's story about that last night. They were a setting, not a character. She and Emma, though…

We had this game.

Worms in his gut. Dark coils, moving. Because she hadn't finished that story. They'd found Gabrielle, sprinting from the trees, and Brigit… Brigit had leaned over the girl in the road, and then she'd gone missing. Stepped right out of her head. Ian could picture her clear as Alicia's silhouette, how she'd crouched there, not breathing, her eyes completely vacant. Before looking straight at the Dell.

A roar broke the quiet, one bright headlight screaming around the bend from Ellis Creek. The figure on the motorcycle was difficult to make out past its glare, but the car following close behind lit Max's blond hair silver as both vehicles pulled onto the flattened patch of grass that marked the Caterpillar's path from the road.

"Hey," she said, killing the engine. The headlight died slower, fading to a sickly yellow before it winked out.

Beside her, Sam pushed open his door and turned to lift something white and blocky from the passenger seat before climbing out of the car. He hefted the bag with both hands. "We bring salt."

"And these." Max swung her leg over the bike and stood, reaching into her coat to pull out a handful of gleaming butter knives. When nobody spoke right away, she flushed, the color visible even at dusk. "They're real silver. I don't know. That was some straight-up fairy-tale monster shit we pulled out of you today."

Sam pinned the salt to his hip like he would an infant and plucked one of the knives from Max's hand. Wordlessly, Ian followed suit. Alicia took hers when offered, pausing for the barest moment as her fingers met Max's palm. She dipped her chin, and Max returned the nod.

"All right," Ian said. He checked his film situation out of habit. If anything happened in the Dell tonight, at least they'd have it on camera. "You guys ready?"

Max held up one finger, spinning back to her pannier. She rummaged for a moment, then turned back with two headlamps, tossed one to Alicia, and snapped the second band around her own forehead. Yellow light caught the shaky curve of her grin. "Yesterday, I was big into camping. Keyword, *yesterday.*"

"So." Sam fell in beside Ian, tossing his butter knife from palm to palm and nearly dropping it. "What's the new plan?"

"We won't just stumble on the spinney," Alicia said. She

and Max turned to face the Dell as well, their flashlights cutting circles from the dark. "It has to want us there."

Ian panned across the two silent houses that watched them
with black and dust-choked eyes, remembering now how
Brigit had twisted in her seat to stare as they drove by. Nothing moved in the trees, or behind those cracked and fading
walls. Whatever she'd seen there was gone. Perhaps it had followed her. *A birch tree in my room*, she'd told them, *and something hiding behind it.*

"Okay," he said, adjusting his grip on the camera, feeling
all the buttons and dials exactly where they should be. His
voice sounded shockingly calm, almost light. "Easy. We just
have to give it a reason to let us in."

"And how do you propose we do that?"

We had this game.

In a surreal disconnect, Ian recalled his own warped voice
speaking to Brigit: *You don't have a clue what happened to your
sister, which is genuinely fucking funny.*

Emma had told Alicia that her sibling was learning from
something in the Dell. She'd been scared of it.

*Kind of like hide-and-seek meets tag. We played that game the
night Emma died.*

Ian rolled his shoulders. It would be fantastic if someone else
would do this for him. Or if Brigit would stroll out of the forest with her small, private smile, the one that said, *Yeah, you got
me, I'm feeling the same things you're feeling and we don't have to talk
about it, but we don't have to pretend either.* The smile that promised she hadn't played house with a monster sixteen years ago
and retconned all her memories when it got her sister killed.

A bat swooped from one roof to the next, flitting through
their flashlight beams like a paper airplane. Ian blew out a
short, hard breath and turned to the group. "Unfortunately,
I have an idea."

25: BRIGIT

The flashlight tucked into her back jeans pocket bit into her flesh as Brigit pressed herself against an oak. The handle would leave an imprint in her skin. Another bruise to join those from the floor and Ian's crash.

Her eyes had adjusted quickly, at least, and Brigit didn't linger long against the tree. This deep in the Dell, the world was a fragmented hash of thin branches and fallen logs, mossy stumps looming out of the black like half-rotted shipwrecks. Autumn had skinned enough trees to let the moonlight in, but even without it, Brigit had run these woods before. Nothing was familiar, and everything was. Her feet knew where to dodge, where to lift an extra inch to clear the granite outcrop camouflaged by fallen leaves. The forest bared itself to her in shades of charcoal and gray and blacker splashes of blood.

Brigit had thought about turning off her light. She'd measured the pros and the cons as she clawed through the topsoil and into the pliable mud beneath. Spiking her hair with leaves and rubbing soft earth across her cheek, she'd weighed the wedge of bright light against how opaque it turned everything else. Now, darting through a copse of small pines that screamed regrowth after a fire, Brigit could hardly remember why she'd brought the flashlight at all.

Last night—Jesus, only last night?—had been different. She'd been different. Ian had been with her, somewhere, the knowledge of him, anyway, and so had Sam, and she'd been scared for them, scared they would be separated, scared she would leave without them or they without her. Emma had been everywhere. The sound of her laughter, its cruelty. How Brigit loved it most when it felt earned and also just a little angry.

Her foot came down on a soft patch, a warren entrance hidden by leaves. Last night she would have fallen. Now Brigit danced away from the pit, whirling forward to maintain momentum. She flung out a hand to brace herself against the nearest trunk, and her palm met something warm and breathing. The noise she made was half scream, half snarl. Brigit jerked her hand back, teeth bared, fingers already a fist, but there was nothing. Only a tall evergreen whose branches began a few feet above her head.

The clouds shifted obligingly as she stood there, panting, so moonlight painted the trunk in stark lines. Brigit touched it again, pressing her fingers to the rough surface to mask any trembling. Cool bark chafed her skin. Behind her, a twig snapped. She whirled, tugging the flashlight from her jeans, and raised it like a club. A small furry creature bustled past her feet and vanished into the murk. "Oh, fuck you," Brigit said, and stalked past the pine.

"Are you out there?" something asked. A girl's voice, light, almost teasing. Brigit froze. "Oh! I can see you, Wild Child."

Her thumb moved without her permission, the urge to turn on the flashlight so strong that Brigit only barely stopped herself before she ruined her night vision. "Emma." It came out a croak, the first vowel catching in her throat.

"Brigit!" her sister hissed, suddenly much closer, cold breath slicing past the shell of her ear. "You have to come back!"

She couldn't move. Her fingers twitched on the flashlight grip, tightening convulsively, and a faint gust of air lifted her bangs. As if someone had swept an arm out in front of Brigit's face. Warm liquid spattered her cheek. The air around her tightened, shock waves of pressure that squeezed and relaxed and squeezed harder. Her face felt numb except where the liquid dripped, slow, thick, trails of heat oozing toward her throat. It smelled of copper.

"I did," she managed. The droplets on her lip itched and burned. The desire to dash the back of her hand across her mouth was so strong that Brigit's whole arm shook. "I'm doing what you want."

Black spots teased the edges of her vision. She couldn't get enough oxygen. If she'd been able to look down and inspect her arms, Brigit knew she'd find her hairs all standing on end, as they had in Sam's living room when this thing had worn his skin instead of her sister's. The pressure worsened as her ears tried and failed to pop. Her flashlight fell, bouncing off her right foot. Brigit sucked in a breath, and the pressure snapped. She wiped her lip and smeared her hand against her jeans.

"This is not what I want," a new voice murmured from somewhere around her ankles. Not an approximation of her sister, nor any other person Brigit knew, and the teasing lilt was gone. This voice was soft, almost confused. She looked down. In the fuzzy dark she could make out the silver rim of her flashlight, her ghostly shoelaces, and past them, a crouching shadow. Or was it a patch of undergrowth? "You're afraid," the voice continued in its odd, sibilant whisper. It was behind her now, still low to the ground. "You don't like it?"

"I don't know." Her own voice keen as broken glass. "You did throw my dead sister in my face."

Something sharp touched the back of her neck, the tender spot just below her short hair. Brigit jumped, spinning again. Her foot came down on her flashlight and she slipped, arms pinwheeling, and landed on her ass with a painful jolt. Movement rushed for her through the dark, black on black and skittering over the ground. Brigit scrambled underneath her, found the flashlight, and turned it on in time to illuminate a pale, fractal *something* with too many limbs and no eyes to speak of. It veered to the left, vanishing the instant before she made sense of it. She squeezed her eyes shut, blinded, the impression of the thing burned white against her lids: arcing lines like a spider's legs, gaping black fissures in what could have been a face.

"If you weren't scared, you would be bored," the creature called from farther away. The mocking note had returned, as if it were quoting someone else, and the taunt did sound familiar...

"You were supposed to be hiding," Brigit said, getting to her feet. Joints popped like firewood. She gestured at her mud-streaked face, the leaves sticking out of her hair. "I'm the Wild Man tonight, not you."

"Yes. Yes, of course," said the rustling of leaves, first slowly, then faster. An eager hiss. "We play this your way."

"My way?" Brigit smudged the wetness on her cheek into war paint, baring her teeth despite her rabbit heart. "If we're playing my way, I have some notes."

A flash of white slipped between two pines ahead. "I will hear them, but we must respect the game. I was found. The spinney is Safe. Catch me if you can."

Some deep emotion pulsed beneath those words, audible even through the creature's multitonal whisper. Brigit had no time to parse it before another sound came, one she hadn't heard in sixteen years but knew as well as her childhood phone number: the high-pitched beeping of a watch timer. She flicked off her light. Faint green shone through the trees to her left, wavering at waist height, no bigger than a firefly.

Her heart dropped. Even as Brigit screamed at herself that it wasn't real, it wasn't Emma, a familiar silhouette took shape out of the dark. The figure wasn't spectral, just blurry because Brigit's eyes were still fucked from the flashlight, and now from tears. It—she—turned and flitted into the trees, disappearing almost at once, and Brigit did the only thing she could. She followed.

26: IAN

"This is gross," Sam muttered as they picked their way past the Dollhouses. "I'm going to shower for years when we get back."

Max grunted, running her hands across her own mud-streaked scalp. "At least your hair's already dark. I might have to shave my head."

Ian ignored them from his place at the head of their phalanx. The Canon was heavy in his hand, a reassuring discomfort settling into the muscles of his arm and shoulder like fingers gripping him, urging him on. The viewfinder pressed against his eye socket revealed an alien landscape of blacks and grays, twisting shadows that mirrored the worry coiling around his gut. Brigit had gotten an alarming head start. She was somewhere deep in these woods, right now, without him.

Or was she? When they'd gone in with Sam, before the separation (before hours in the dark, before the trees, before) there had been some kind of...rift. A slowly growing distance between the three of them, and not just physically. Voices sounding softer than they should, or farther away. Lights bobbing visibly yet, when he'd shouted, nobody hearing at all.

None of his father's scripture could explain that, and if his mother's beliefs might have, Ian would never know.

The saw grass threaded through his hair prickled against his scalp. Grass, dirt, and gravel dust competed with the richer smells of the forest. He and Sam had both stuck fallen branches out of their shirt collars to create a sort of antler protrusion, and Max had camouflaged her hair as best she could. Alicia had torn a web of dead vines off the side of one house and wrapped it around her neck and head, over the bridge of her nose, leaving her looking like a nightmarish pencil sketch from the shoulders up.

"Wait," the sketch said. Alicia's hand swept out and caught Ian in the side, thankfully not the one with stitches in it. He stopped, the others coming to ungraceful halts behind them. "Look."

She ducked her forehead, vines rasping, and aimed her light directly at a pale beech tree a few paces ahead. Ian frowned into the viewfinder. All he saw was a gray trunk streaked with darker striations in the bark. Alicia placed one hand on his forearm, applying firm pressure; he lowered the Canon and squinted. Then sucked in a short, soft inhale. There, a foot or so above the ground, was a smear of blackish red.

"Is that blood?" Sam asked.

"Fuck," said Max. "What the fuck." The butter knife twitched at her hip. Alicia and Ian approached the beech, Max close behind, and crouched to peer at the stain. It had appeared matte through Ian's camera but now, up close and in the eggshell glow of the headlamps, the red glistened here and there. About four inches long, the slash looked as though someone had knelt on the forest floor, cut open a palm, and dragged it across the tree.

His stomach roiled. That peaty smell was back, the one from

Gabrielle's clothing and, this morning, his own. The camera knocked against his calf, and Ian realized he was trembling.

"It's not Brigit's, right?" Max asked, getting to her feet. "Why would she... There would be something else. Other signs."

Alicia released a quiet sigh and stood. Ian hadn't quite joined her when another woman's voice broke the silence at his back.

"Max? Is that you?"

Ian shot upright. Alicia didn't seem to move at all except that suddenly her hand was under her coat, eyes bright and gleaming through the vines. Sam stepped backward, turning, the silver butter knife sweeping the air in front of him. Max alone stood frozen.

"Max," the voice came again, familiar but not. There was something wrong with its enunciation, a mushy hesitance to the *m*. "You found me."

A branch snapped behind Ian. Max stared past him, face white as the beech except for the dirt and her cracked red lipstick. The drill hung useless by her thigh. Ian couldn't turn around. His body had gone cold, veins weighed down with frozen lead. Alicia managed what he hadn't, turning smoothly—but then she took one sharp step backward and thudded into the bloodstained tree.

"Oh," Sam said. "Shit."

"I knew you would find me. I didn't even try to hide." More rustling, followed by a wet noise like papier-mâché sloughing onto the leaves. "I never tried to hide from you." A new scent wafted toward Ian, cold and organic, like raw hamburger. The back of his neck began to itch, his skin humming with awareness of someone standing behind him, almost close enough to touch, as Lacey Rollins asked, "If I had, would you have helped me?" Her lips couldn't quite form all the consonants. "Or would you still have thought I was a silly little girl who needed to learn on her own?"

"I did try to help you," Max said softly. Every ounce of bravado was gone from her voice. Her eyes stood out from her ashen skin like marbles. "I wanted…"

"You didn't help anyone. Not Sam—" Something soft and damp brushed the outside of Ian's arm, but he would not look down. "Not me. You could have stopped me from hurting Gabrielle. You could have helped me send Pete away before he sank his hooks so deep in me I couldn't rip them out." He could hear the tiny clinging smacks of her lips sticking and parting, the wet slap of her tongue against the ruined roof of her mouth. Minuscule drops of liquid flecked the back of Ian's neck with every *p*. "Instead you made me look for my own kind of help. I don't think playing dress-up in the woods makes up for that, Max."

All his fake calm bled into the dirt. Ian felt it go, and in its place was the knowledge that he'd made a mistake coming here. Brigit might be able to walk through these trees without falling through them forever, but he wasn't her, and she wasn't here. She didn't need him, she'd made that clear, and she sure as hell didn't—

It made itself look like someone else to mock me. About you.

Max stared past him at the thing wearing Lacey, her red mouth trembling. Beside her, Sam looked sick. But Ian was on the floor again, wood boards against his back. Brigit's eyes burning into his as she cut him open.

"It's not her," Ian said, or tried to say. The words caught in his throat. He swallowed, tasting blood, and when he spoke again his voice was rough but strong. "It's not Lacey."

The thing behind him leaned closer, undergrowth crackling beneath its shifting weight, and soft flesh tickled the hairs at his nape. "They know that," it whispered, almost a croon. The way it had spoken to Brigit through his mouth. "They don't care."

"Yeah, we fucking do," Sam said, and three things happened very quickly.

Sam stepped in front of Max, his slender frame breaking her line of sight as he held the butter knife out, the bag of salt still pinned beneath his arm. Alicia pulled out her gun, aiming over Ian's shoulder. Ian flipped his own knife in his fist and jammed it straight backward at hip height.

The blade sank into something, but it wasn't skin. Whatever stood behind him let out a rasping cough as he struck a solid internal barrier. Cool, waxy fingers pressed against his hand, sliding over his knuckles toward his wrist. Ian released the metal handle and dove forward, whirling as Alicia fired. He swung his camera up, holding it between himself and the thing he'd stabbed with the same ferocity with which Sam held his knife. The shot rang out across the forest, echoing twice.

One: a woman-shaped figure, lit by all three flashlights and the hazy moon, its head a clot of red and fatty yellow at the cheek.

Two: not a person at all, instead a mass of spindly white wood, brownish rot eating away from the place where a silver knife protruded.

She'd hit it dead in the face, or where the face would have been had it been anything close to human. As the gunshot ricocheted around Ian's skull he got the impression of a spiderweb, intricate lines thick and white as bone, collapsing in on itself like a dying star. An odd noise rustled from its torso, almost rhythmic. Pale branches reknit themselves in a whipping rush as the thing skittered backward, vanishing into the dark and taking Ian's butter knife with it.

"Did you kill her?" Max asked, shouldering around Sam. "It."

"Don't think so," Sam answered for Alicia, who was staring at the place where the thing had been with an expression so blank it could only be disbelief. "No body."

"I don't know if there would be one," Ian said. "I don't know if that was really here."

Max made a noise that approached a laugh and pointed at him. "You have blood on your neck. Is that real enough?"

"I shot it in the head." Alicia stepped away from the beech tree, gun lowered toward the ground. Her voice sounded thin, but she'd regained enough control to look stern instead of slapped. "It rebuilt itself. Why did it leave?"

"Maybe you did hurt it," Max suggested hopefully. She wrapped her arms around herself. "Maybe it ran off to lick its wounds."

Ian shook his head. He replayed the noise it had made, that unnatural rasping, even as its head caved in. The sound was alien but the rhythm, that was familiar. "Or maybe it got what it wanted."

"Which was what?"

"Our measure." He strode in the direction the thing had gone, heart racing with equal parts certainty and dread.

"'Our measure'?" Max repeated, jogging to catch up. Sam and Alicia fell in behind them. "Is this a duel?"

"Not a duel. It's—"

"A game," Alicia finished. "Of course."

"It…wanted to see if we were fun to play with?" Sam tripped and caught himself against Ian's shoulder, nearly dropping the bag of salt. "That's good, right? I mean—it's what we were going for."

"I think it laughed at us," Ian said, steadying Sam and then upping his pace. His palm was slick against the camera grip. "When you shot it."

"We never thought bullets would work. That's why we have the salt."

"No, I know." Ian struggled to find the words and force them out. His mind was already skipping ahead, chasing after a fear whose shape eluded him. "It let us go. It could have hurt us, or split us up like it did the other night. It didn't even have to confront us."

"But we're playing Wild Men," Max said. "Didn't we all agree it's into that?"

"It's into Brigit playing Wild Men," Ian corrected, weaving through closely knitted pines. Twigs snapped against his legs and torso. "I thought it might decide we were part of the game, or that it would ignore us completely and we'd never find the spinney. But it just toyed with us for a minute and let us go."

"Maybe that was only round one," Alicia put in. She sounded out of breath for the first time that night. The dead leaves were growing deeper, rifting around tree stumps like richly scented snow. "Why play with one person when it could have five?"

"Maybe. Just—all this time it's wanted her back." A flash of white caught their lights ahead, and Ian broke into a jog. "Sixteen years," he added between breaths. His right side throbbed with every footstep. "But it let her go last night. The circumstances weren't right. What's different now?"

"I don't know," Sam said, "but if it *is* all about Brigit, there's only one reason I can think of for it to bother with us."

"It has her," Alicia finished for him. "It's already won."

"Hey." Max's pale hand cut through Ian's field of vision. "Is that the fucking thing?"

Ian didn't bother to answer. He just curled the Canon into his stomach for safety and started sprinting toward the birches that had materialized like bone spurs from the dark.

27: BRIGIT

"Brigit!"

Her sister's voice tore through Brigit, gutting her defenses and leaving her gasping. It wasn't Emma she was chasing. Emma hadn't shot herself, and if she had, that gunshot wouldn't have been this gunshot cracking through the trees. But the pain and fear in her sister's voice sounded real, *felt* real, so much so that when the gun fired and not-Emma shrieked, Brigit nearly screamed too. Nearly. Instead, teeth gritted, she ran.

Plenty of people owned guns in Ellis Creek. Deer season wouldn't begin for another few weeks, but that had never stopped half her neighbors growing up. It was the reason their parents had made a point of outfitting Brigit and Emma in bright colors, royal blues and glaring oranges and traffic-light reds—but no hunting rifle had made that shot. It had been too light a crack, reverberations rippling out across the Dell at too high a pitch. A handgun, then. And who did Brigit know with one of those?

The shot had been close, and a one-off. That meant either Detective Nguyen had hit what she'd aimed at, or she'd missed with no time or reason to squeeze off another. Brigit cycled through the possibilities in rapid fire, thin branches whipping at her cheeks and throat, her night vision not yet fully recovered from her brief use of the flashlight.

If Alicia was here, so was Ian. No screaming—no human screaming—had followed the gunshot, so she hadn't hit him or anyone else. It also seemed unlikely the two of them were facing a prolonged assault; the thing behind the birch trees could affect what people heard and saw, but if punishment was its goal, there was no point in letting her hear the shot but not the aftermath.

"Brigit, please," Emma's voice came again, laced with agony. "You have to come back!"

Brigit's foot slammed into a rock and she dropped the flashlight. She left it where it fell. The clouds stirred restlessly above, and in the moonlight that came and went, three trees glowed white as Emma's grinning teeth. Not far away now. Not far at all.

Ian and Alicia would be all right. They weren't the prey here, not yet. As soon as Brigit reached the spinney, she'd make sure they never would be.

Every breath burned her lungs, her bruised body protesting at the pace. The air was colder than when she'd first broached the tree line, the fecund smell of mud and decay so strong now she could taste it. It wasn't quite the dirt that had haunted her for so long but it was close, so close Brigit spat more than once as she ran.

The forest stretched out in every direction, a sprawling beast with ten thousand limbs. She couldn't think of it, couldn't allow her brain to spread widely enough to encompass the Dell, or she would collapse midstride. *Although*, a small voice whispered, one that sounded not like Emma and not like Brigit but, horribly, like Ian, *how bad would that really be?* She'd seen the way he'd looked at her in Alicia's kitchen. While the others had been arguing and she'd been thinking of how best to incapacitate them once she slipped out the bathroom window. He hadn't been frustrated then, or scared, or even furious like that moment when he'd stopped her leaving the Super 8. He'd been tired. Resigned to whatever bullshit she might throw at him next.

Just give up, his not-voice suggested as another tiny branch cut a line across her neck. *Soon all this will be over. I'll probably make it out all right. We'll figure out what to do about James, and even if we don't, at least nobody else will ever get hurt because of your selfish tunnel vision again. Can you really make a better offer?*

Brigit slowed, then stopped. She couldn't make a better offer, no. But she didn't have to.

She was there.

It looked the same. No. It looked smaller. Haletown House's attic was twice the size of the spinney, and the birches were shorter than she remembered. More leaves had piled up in the center, and a few fallen branches now formed deltas and valleys she could barely make out.

Emma wasn't standing in that circle of trees. Nor was anything else. Tentatively, Brigit stepped up to the outer rim, a foot back from the closest birch.

"So cautious. You didn't used to be." That voice, the sibilant hush of leaves on bark, slithered around her like wind. This time she couldn't pinpoint where it came from. Brigit stiffened.

"When was that?" she asked, and if her voice was higher than usual, at least it was sharp.

"You don't remember."

The susurrus seemed to solidify as it spoke, threads of sound weaving into one another. Brigit tilted her head, listening, and narrowed its voice to the birch tree directly opposite the spinney from where she stood. Red gloves peeked out from behind the trunk, barely visible in the half-light, more like nubs of aborted branches than fingers on the other side.

"I remember," she said despite the sickness lurching in her belly, and closed the distance between herself and the edge of the grove. Her toes landed just outside where the circle would lie if you connected each birch by a thread. "I remember you hurt my friend. I remember you hurt my sister."

The red gloves disappeared. A cold breeze cut the dark, whistling through the leaves that clung to nearby treetops. "I harmed no one," the birches hissed, sounding almost betrayed. "If they harmed themselves because of choices they made, so be it."

Anger, she could understand. Anger made sense, as did the cruel amusement she had heard in Sam's armchair or Alicia's living room. This, though…this was *distress*. A raw vein of hurt Brigit refused to believe.

"I beg to fucking differ."

"You think you know why you're here. You think you know how this ends." The wind rose, snatching at her hair, at the hem of her jacket. That peaty smell was everywhere, deep mud, old earth. "All these years away have grown around your bones and you are not what you were. But you can be. We will be."

Brigit teetered at the edge of the spinney, something holding her back from that final step. In the distance, running footsteps crashed through the brush.

"What are you talking about?"

"Come closer," the thing behind the birch trees breathed, "and I'll show you."

"Only if you swear you'll let my friends go."

"We played the game. I hid and ran, you found but failed to catch. You win nothing now but the truth."

The red gloves appeared once more across the spinney.

Only this time, they slid across the bark until a small hand was visible, along with the sleeve of a bright blue jacket Brigit knew too well. She could still feel it after all these years, too poofy at the elbows. What her mom once called *rifle-proof chic*.

"After all," it continued, stepping out from behind the birch, "your sister's deal goes only so far."

There was no decision, no conscious choice left. Brigit walked into the spinney.

28: IAN

Ian reached her just as Brigit stepped into the trees. His camera flashlight caught the leather at her shoulders, adding a dull shine to the black of her jacket. Sticks and dead leaves littered her hair.

"Bridge," he said, coming to a halt before the first birch. Everything in him wanted to cross that threshold and go right up to her, reach out his hands and see if she'd take them, but his legs wouldn't move. The wound in his side pulsed steadily, pain flaring up and down with every beat of his heart.

The trunks. White bark striated with gray, like expensive cheese. That image struck him and suddenly he could feel it, the bark, could imagine his hand pushing into the core of a birch. How the wood might crumble, soft and moldering, and then so might his fingers. Alicia, Sam, and Max rushed up beside Ian, brushing his shoulders on either side. He tried not to let himself press closer.

"Hey," Sam said, his voice barely carrying through the trees. "Is she…"

That complex, earthy scent was strong enough here that Ian could taste it. When he said Brigit's name again, the flavor stuck at the back of his throat. "Brigit. Are you hurt? Just tell me that."

"Ian," she said without turning around. "You should leave."

"Not without you."

"I think if you turn around right now, it'll let you walk away." Brigit pivoted in place as she spoke. Dirt smeared her face. The blend of artificial lights illuminated several scratches on her cheeks and deep shadows underneath her eyes, but she was otherwise unharmed.

"That thing," Alicia said. "Where is it? Do you know?"

Brigit shrugged. It was such a careless gesture that for a moment, Ian couldn't speak. Then Max hoisted the drill and goosed the trigger. Screaming metal sheared the night.

"Fuck it. It's not here. Let's kill some demon trees while we can."

"No." Brigit stepped forward, close enough now that Ian could have grabbed her by the arm and hauled her out of the spinney. But she'd squared her shoulders too, and her fists were clenched. If he or anyone tried to touch her, she might swing.

"No?" Max stepped up to the spinney's edge, the drill at waist height. "You—"

"It was me," Brigit cut her off. "Not the trees. It was my fault."

She'd always been good at masking her emotions when she wanted to, but this toneless calm didn't read to Ian like a mask. "You didn't take Gabrielle and James," he said. "You didn't put that thing in my side."

Sudden nausea clenched his belly. White trees. White nub of life inside him. The seven birches reached upward, curving in long and sensuous ribbons toward the blackened sky. They breathed with him. Sam knelt and set down the bag of salt. He ripped the plastic at the top, and granules skittered over the leaves with a sound like popping candy. Ian inhaled through his mouth to keep the sickness down.

"True," Brigit said. "What I did was worse."

"Whatever you mean, we can figure it out. We'll get out of here and we'll go to a bar—" she was shaking her head now, pitying him "—and I'll buy you some cheap whiskey and we'll figure it out."

"Max." Alicia sounded as controlled as a certain kind of drunk. "Start drilling, please."

"Brigit, come on. Just—here. Take my hand." Ian reached out with his left arm, breaking the invisible barrier that seemed to connect one birch to another. His sleeve rode up. Tiny hairs on his wrist prickled with cold. The camera in his right hand trembled as Brigit shook her head. In the shivering beam of their flashlights, Ian saw her open her mouth. Before any words could escape, something large and loud crashed through the trees from his left. Ian dropped his hand and spun toward the noise. Max and Sam sprang upright at the same time, and Alicia backed away with her gun raised in both hands. There wasn't time for real panic to grab him, just the crash, the whirl, and then—

"Oh my god," Sam said hoarsely, and lunged forward in time to prevent a tall, loose-limbed figure from face-planting onto the leaves.

"Alicia Nguyen," said a raspy, sibilant voice from high above their heads. "Your bargain is fulfilled."

A boy who could only be James Mulroy sprawled half on Sam's lap, half on the ground. He wore a dark jacket of some outdoorsy make and jeans, and although his hair was a matted cap against his temples, he appeared surprisingly hale. Ian was pretty sure that, given a side-by-side comparison in good lighting, he'd come off looking worse for wear.

"Shit," Max breathed.

"Hey," Sam was saying, over and over, "James? Can you hear me?"

"Get him up." Alicia aimed her revolver upward, circling around behind them with her eyes on the birch canopy. "Someone needs to take him out of here."

Sam grunted, hauling at the boy's shoulders, but James had the build of an athlete and there was no way the shorter man could lift him without leverage. Max dropped the drill. Together she and Sam struggled James up between them. His head lolled down toward his chest, arms limp and dead around their shoulders.

"You'll let them go," Brigit said. Branches rustled. A gust of wind kicked leaf grit onto Ian's chapped lips. She made a cutting gesture away from herself and toward Sam and Max. "Go on. Get him out."

Something stirred below the surface of her voice. It reached into Ian's chest and twisted, telling him two things: Brigit was terrified, and she didn't plan on following them.

He'd crossed into the spinney before he knew he was walking.

Everything stilled. Not in Ian's head, but literally—an awful, airless clench. His feet sank into decomposing leaves, deeper than they had a moment ago, like the earth itself was eager to grip his ankles and pull. A low, insectoid hum rose in Ian's jaw, the roots of his teeth, the gum around the fake one. His skull seams vibrated as they had in Alicia's living room, and it didn't own him anymore, this place, what lived beneath and inside it, because Brigit had carved him open and torn it out with her bare, bloody fingers—but somewhere between *outside* the circle and *in*, Ian's body lost connection with itself. Vertigo rolled through him like a cold wind. Perhaps Brigit felt it too, because she lurched backward with none of her usual grace, and the world spun back into motion. Ian with it.

"No," she said.

"Yes."

"No."

Ian shifted his feet to break that sucking hold. It helped him say the next thing.

"Hey! Whatever you are—double or nothing. Let me play for us both."

Brigit scoffed. "Don't kid yourself."

From somewhere behind his back, Ian heard Sam hiss, "Detective. The salt."

"Get James out of here," Alicia said. "We'll be all right. Go."

Leaves crashed as they stumbled away, and regret stabbed Ian, painful, abrupt. He wanted to feel the weight of James's arm over his shoulders, and taste the open air outside the Dell. It was too late. The birches murmured, "They are free. Speak."

The hairs at his nape trembled. There was danger in that voice. Brigit stood with her shoulders set in a rigid line. She'd braced herself against Ian, the same way she'd braced herself in Alicia's living room as the thing in his body stalked closer, as if he—the real him—were the true threat here. The back corner of Ian's jaw popped.

He said, "I want to make a deal."

Brigit exhaled as though punched. Another rush of air skimmed Ian's ankles, like something low scurrying past. His hand spasmed on the camera. Behind him, Alicia moved around the spinney, scattering salt crystals over dry leaves. Ian concentrated on those small noises and set the camera down before he dropped it, half expecting cold, bony fingers to close around his wrist, but nothing touched him. The trees only creaked as he straightened. Waiting.

"How does it work?" he asked their shadows. "I tell you what I want and you tell me what it costs?"

"Shut your mouth," Brigit said. No more eerie calm. "What the hell were you thinking, coming in here? It spat you out once—what, you felt rejected?"

His father had taught him how to back down and be quiet, but Ian had taught himself how to keep the shaking to his insides, and he was not done talking. "I want us to walk all the way out of here," he continued. "Me and Brigit. What's the price tag on that?"

"Ian," Brigit said, "I'm serious. This is not a game you can win."

"And you can?" he asked. "You don't look like a winner right now." Leaves rustled above in eager susurration as Ian addressed the trees again. "What do you want with Brigit, anyway? You've taken other people in the last decade, why is this one so important? Is it about Emma?"

"Nope," Brigit said, lips stretching. The mud on her cheeks cracked like dried blood in the moonlight. "Emma was no fun. Guess that's why I left her in the dirt."

He couldn't help but look at her properly then, and it was a mistake because above that manic smile, Brigit's eyes were bright with tears.

"You didn't leave her," Ian said. "You were a kid. You couldn't have stopped her from doing whatever she was going to do."

"You don't fucking know that."

The spinney had gone quiet around them. Attentive. Part of Ian flagged that silence and picked at it—*What's different?* he'd asked—but the rest of him stepped toward her, again and always. "It's not your *fault*, Bridge."

"I know you have trouble with fault," she said. "Like re-membering what your dad did to you wasn't yours. But it wasn't, and you're nothing like him, or me, so congrats. You're a good person, Ian." All at once, her harshness crumpled. "You deserve better than this."

Ian almost laughed, fury and tenderness and deep, deep frustration briefly overwhelming the fear. "Right. I almost forgot. That's what I'm here for—making you feel however you want about yourself. Break out the big guns all you like, but you can't possibly think I'm that naive just because I don't use your messy bullshit against you. The whole time I've known you, I—"

His voice cut out. Something crunched behind Brigit, but Ian's brain was already whirring back through their years of friendship, everything they'd learned over these last few days, as an idea fought to make itself clear. Brigit stared at him. The air was thick and heavy as a layer of skin, but even as sweat ran down Ian's forehead, his own words played back to him: she'd been a kid. Playing out here in these trees alone for months, maybe years, until that final night. Then gone for so long, yet still haunted, still eaten away inside by Emma's death and other demons he could never wholly see. And when they came back to Ellis Creek, something had visited Brigit before they even set foot in the Dell. Had known when she was close to leaving, too, known to send Gabi stumbling into the road on that very first day. As if it only needed Brigit near the woods, not inside them, to exert its influence. As if—

As if it was already in her.

The drill whirred to life. Brigit spun toward where Alicia crouched at the base of one of the birches. "What are you doing?"

Ian caught her by the upper arm. "Wait."

"Let go. Now."

Before he could, the drill powered off. Alicia's headlamp

beam sawed across the spinney as she dropped to the ground. "Ah," she said. It came out like something pulled from her, and pulled bloody. "No. Please, Em, don't."

Ian couldn't help it: he searched for Brigit's gaze. She met his. He dropped her arm, and side by side they approached the edge of the trees.

"Detective?"

Alicia didn't reply. She stared up through Ian and Brigit, her eyes so wide they were like pools of ink on laminate. The drill slipped from her fingers and landed on its side with a muted thud.

"Alicia." Brigit slashed an arm between them. "It's not real."

Alicia's headlamp flared across the underside of Brigit's jaw. White light caught on a nasty scratch where a branch must have tagged her on the way in, red and taut across her tendon.

"I'm so sorry," Alicia said to someone Ian couldn't see. She lifted a hand to her mouth, touching her lower lip with two fingertips. "I didn't know…how it was."

Her fingers weren't static, now that Ian looked more closely. They were picking. Tugging chapped skin loose and dropping the tiny flakes onto her legs.

"I wouldn't have left you if I did," she went on, voice fading, confused. "I never… I would've…"

Alicia stopped to peel a corner of her lip. Ian was still staring, transfixed, when she dropped her hand to her flank and returned it with her revolver.

29: BRIGIT

Ian flung an arm in front of Brigit's waist and shoved her back toward the center of the grove. She stumbled and caught herself on his bicep as Alicia raised the gun, but the detective didn't level its small black mouth at Brigit. Instead she aimed the revolver directly at Ian's head.

Brigit uncurled her fingers from his sleeve. Part of her wanted to do the opposite, to grip him so tight she could pull them both through the earth and away. Instead she took his wrist, his cold skin warmer than her fingers, and moved his arm out of contact with her stomach. "What is this?" she asked.

"Your boy wants to make a deal." The spinney spoke from way down deep. Brigit felt its satisfaction on the inside of her skin. "We're giving him what he asked for."

"No," she said, just as Ian said, "Fine," and Brigit stepped forward just enough to jab her elbow into the wound beneath his ribs. He gasped, rendered voiceless. "You and he are not making any deals."

"Brigit," Alicia said. "G—" Her words cut off. Her mouth yawned open, back arcing up toward the charcoal sky, and the gun didn't waver but her face did. Alicia's cheeks rippled in the moonlight like a boot-stomped puddle. A low, hoarse moan filled the spinney, dragged raw from her chest.

Brigit realized only after she moved that she'd put her arm out as Ian had, blocking him from the edge of the grove as if her forearm could stop whatever was building now. Her heart pounded in her throat. Ian wheezed, still catching his breath. Nausea whirled higher and higher in her belly. Something churned inside Alicia's moan. The skin above her jugular throbbed in the cool, loveless light.

"You'll make this deal," said the birches, and Alicia started to scream. It didn't last. The saplings that burst from her mouth made sure of that.

"Oh, my god," Ian said before Brigit grabbed the back of his shirt and dragged him backward. Alicia shook at the edge of the trees, her right arm locked at the elbow, revolver barely trembling as the rest of her convulsed. Her throat pulsed, threads pushing up against her skin like tendons. Bone-white veins crawled out of her mouth and wormed upward, some drooping toward her buckling torso, others clinging to her jaw or wavering before her face like they were angling for a fight.

Ian was holding on to Brigit's wrist very tightly. She didn't know when he'd grabbed her. The meat of her lower wrist pinched in his grip, her bones grinding. "Brigit," he said, "we have to do something."

She couldn't move. This could have been her. This should have been her.

"Yes," said the thing behind the birch trees. "Stay. Play the game. You have until she suffocates."

"To do what?" Brigit asked. She wanted to vomit. She wanted a closer look. A faint metallic click jarred the spinney: Alicia's thumb, knocking back the safety. The roots erupting from her mouth had stopped reaching outward. Now they writhed along her temples, down along her collarbones. Her dark eyes found Brigit's, shiny with tears, the whites like old scars around each iris. Behind her, in the trees, something else flickered, pale and many-limbed.

"Not you," it crooned, worming through the dark. "Him."

Her nausea rose a little higher. Now Brigit felt it in her throat, pressing at her tonsils, and Ian spoke before she could.

"What do you want me to do?"

"Simple. Choose. One, or the other."

"Fuck that," Brigit said. "They're here because of me. All of this is because of me. Whatever you want, I'll do."

Her chest felt tight and hard, like the bones had warped together, formed seams where none should be. Whatever it asked of her, whatever it took to get Ian out of here—and Alicia, but god, please let her save Ian—she would give. Tension gripped her with such ferocity that when Ian released her wrist and took a half step to the side, Brigit nearly fell.

"You didn't make me do this," he said.

"Ian, now is not—"

"You didn't make Alicia do it either." Then he grabbed her hand and squeezed hard, his nails digging into her palm. "This may come as a shock, but you don't actually get to control how other people feel." Brigit couldn't name the look on his face, bright and vicious as her own pounding heart. "I'm here for all kinds of reasons, and only one of them is that I believe in you more than anything else in my life. Trust me, there are times I don't like it either. But it's true, and if you want to fight me on that, you're going to have to walk out of these goddamn woods with me. All right?"

Ian let go of her hand, and returning blood stabbed her fingers. He put more ground between them, staying in the spinney but angling his body like a shield. Panic slammed into her brain as Brigit realized what he was about to do. She went for the edge of the circle as though she could act before Ian, as though she could save Alicia through sheer force of—

"Let Alicia go."

Brigit stumbled to a halt a few feet from the invisible line, jarred to the bone by Alicia's name on Ian's tongue instead of her own. The spinney seemed to pause and settle, not so much a hesitation as savoring the moment. Then Ian's camera and Alicia's headlamp flickered out.

The darkness rose around them in a sweeping tide. Ian's elbow jostled hers as he reset his footing. From the blackness, Alicia sucked in a great, heaving breath. Birches rose out of the night like strips of glow-in-the-dark paint, the kind Emma had sometimes used on her nails. They curved upward, seven ribs, a cage in which she and Ian were the heart.

"Hey, Wild Child," Emma said as Brigit breathed, cold lips against her ear. "Do you remember our deal?"

Neither Ian nor Alicia reacted to the question. Because it wasn't Emma. It wasn't anything.

But now Brigit felt the cold of a toilet bowl beneath her thighs, heard the rasping weight of Emma's voice on the phone. *What I say goes. You promised.* Except that hadn't been her sister either. That had been whatever was now moving around the spinney in little padding steps almost too quiet to notice.

A branch snapped. Ian froze beside Brigit. The trees reflected faint moonlight where the bark clung to them, laced with darker ribbons where it didn't. Nothing visible moved past them, but Alicia gave a low, sharp exhale as undergrowth shifted near where she knelt.

"Done," said the spinney.

At first, only creaking trunks replied. The breeze smelled like dry leaves and distant smoke, a comforting smell, one

that made her think of winter as a child. Then something…
moved. In her. Unfurled itself.

Brigit was vaguely aware of her hand, the one Ian had
taken, drifting up toward her abdomen.

Dirt on her tongue and below it. She recalled her own
image reflected back at her in windows, in the lonely dark
of her motel room, in the half-heard giggle that had stalked
her and Ian and Sam on that first night in the Dell.

Her fingers made contact with her stomach as though
they belonged to someone else, dragged upward, caught at
the concave joining of her rib cage. Her hands were clean
and dry and she knew that, but suddenly she could feel it,
the warm blood, Ian's slippery layer of fat she'd slithered into
with her fingertips like she'd been gutting a fish, and then
her knees absorbed an impact. Cold pressed against her skin:
more wetness from the ground.

Brigit turned her head, feeling the muscles creak in her
neck, and the thing inside her exploded. Veins of pressure
uncurled from the deepest part of her chest, a hidden cache
between her lungs and her spine. White lines, thin as spider
silk, crept over her vision like frost.

"Bridge." Ian, somewhere to her left. Brigit couldn't see
him any longer, not even a silhouette, but his voice seared
into her brain. "Be the worst of you, okay? Be the one who
walks away."

His words dissolved in her ears, compressing the tiny hairs,
each delicate crystal crushed beneath a wave of white noise…
and then silence.

30: IAN

The spinney pulsed. Ian's arms prickled, fine hairs standing up against the lining of his coat. Brigit knelt on the ground with one hand curled against her chest and the other lax at her side, head lowered, like a robot powered down. Her filthy hair jabbed every which way. Just outside the ring of trees, Alicia had collapsed onto her back. Ian couldn't tell if her airways were clear. His ears were ringing. He couldn't look away from Brigit's slumped shoulders.

"Oh, fuck," someone said. It wasn't the spinney that pulsed, Ian realized, dragging his attention up with effort. It was his own heart pounding in his temples, aorta working overtime to keep him standing, keep him primed to fight or run (and run, and run). Near the detective, a blond head bobbed low to the ground. "Hey. Alicia. Get up."

Max grabbed the older woman by the shoulders and hauled her into a sitting position. Ian watched dumbly, frozen by his own gamble and its miraculous, horrible success. Alicia coughed, a sound like wet leaves being scraped from a gutter. Something black and tangled drooped from her mouth into her lap.

Behind him, Brigit grunted. Ian whipped back toward her.

The breeze kicked up. Everything smelled of compost and ice. Brigit knocked her head back, throat straining in the thin moonlight, her shoulders locking up as her right hand clawed at her thigh in vicious spasms. Ian wanted to grab her wrist again, but he was afraid to touch her in case it made things worse—and if he was honest, he was even more afraid that *she* might touch *him*. That whatever lived inside her would reach out and reclaim the ground Brigit had freed for him with metal and blood.

"Fight it," he told her instead, forcing the words through gritted teeth because Alicia and Max were there, and could hear him. Could see him stand at a safe distance and tell Brigit to fight the monster he'd thrown her to like a piece of meat.

But it was what Brigit would have done, if she'd fully understood. It was what she'd tried to do even without understanding. She had snuck out a window and sabotaged Alicia's car and flung her rage at him in order to give herself to the spinney instead of them, because she at least knew that it wanted her. And maybe the reason why was plainer than he'd thought. If he was right, and it sure as hell seemed that way, the spinney had been with Brigit most of her life, resting just under the skin. So maybe now it wanted what Ian did: simply for her to stay.

Except Brigit alone wasn't enough. Otherwise surely it would have taken her that night, not Ian, when they first blundered into the Dell with Sam. So the thing behind the birches—in, under, among—needed something else. The right circumstances in place. It hadn't forced Brigit to make a deal just now, after all. It had targeted him. Waited for Alicia to attack it, even, to seize her as leverage.

That quiet layer of Ian's subconscious tick-tick-ticked away while the rest of him watched in horror as Brigit convulsed— because something had kept her safe until now, the birches mostly dormant. Even here in Ellis Creek, the thing had been able to listen, to scare, but not fully take Brigit over. Whatever

this shield was had kicked in when Brigit was young enough
that she was able to rewrite her own memories before leaving
Ellis Creek, but not so young as to prevent infection in the first
place... *Emma.* Had to be. The beating heart of nearly every
lie Brigit told. Emma had done something to protect her sibling, and Ian had overwritten it? In some way Brigit couldn't?

Like a lens turned just so, another picture clicked into focus:
What's different? Of course. It was *him*. His anger, both planted
and nurtured. Those buried resentments tasting sunlight the
second Ian came out of the woods. Perhaps he wasn't only
insurance against Brigit leaving town. Perhaps he was a tool
the spinney thought it could use here too—by pitting him
against Brigit so he'd choose Alicia's life to save. But the detective had said it herself: *I wouldn't bet against her. Not in there.*
Neither would Ian.

"Fight it," he said again, willing his words to reach her. "I
know you both, remember? I know who's the better monster.
Don't you dare prove me wrong."

Brigit thrashed sideways, landing hard on her shoulder,
and someone screamed outside the grove. Ian turned to find
Alicia fumbling with the mass of shadows in her lap, both
hands scrabbling at the writhing pile that stretched toward
Max with long and jagged fingers. The other woman was
on her knees, fingers clawing at her collarbone. At the roots
that formed a noose.

"Get it off," Max choked out. "Get it off!"

Alicia threw Ian a desperate look. "Help me!"

Ian stood torn between leaving the spinney to drag the roots
away from Max, and staying as close to Brigit as possible. What
if leaving the birches dissolved his deal? What if it was a trick?
The wound in his side flared hot and angry, each ache in his
bruised body reminding him of everything these woods had
already taken. If he stepped outside the birches, time might

fold back on itself, enclosing Brigit like a straitjacket, pressing her smaller and smaller until there was no getting her back.

But the spinney wanted him paralyzed, and Brigit afraid. It wanted her to lose.

"*Ian,*" Alicia gritted out, and his body made the call. He lunged for Max.

Brigit clawed at his ankle, her nails scraping the skin between his sock and his jeans. Instinct sent his foot out in a sharp kick. Ian felt the side of his shoe connect with a snap, but he was already moving again, out of the spinney, and he fell on his knees where Max was writhing in a mass of shadows. Alicia knelt beside them, still fighting with the tendrils in her lap, but every time she gathered one up, more lashed out. It should have been impossible to make out these shadows from the darkness, not with all their lights failing and the moon half-dead from clouds, but the root mass caught that faint lunar glow like a thousand sentient slug trails.

Ian stared for a beat, mind blank except for the image of that cancerous web inside his own body. What Brigit had pulled out of him had been white, white and pale brown, roots like threads—still small and delicate. This was a twisting knot of cables, the thickest of them as wide around as his thumb. It must have been growing inside Alicia for weeks, ever since she made her deal. If they cut Brigit open now, how much of her would be the spinney?

Max slumped sideways, wheezing. Her fingers slackened at her throat. Ian ignored his churning stomach and plunged his hands into the coil of roots around her neck. They were cold, almost freezing, and slicked with some viscous liquid he didn't want to think about. Otherwise they felt like any roots—or almost. There was a softness underneath the bark, a cartilaginous give. They weren't inside him anymore but Ian *felt* those roots, working their way along his skeletal frame, winding toward his heart. He tightened his grip on the noose and focused as hard as he could on pulling it free.

Max's lips caught a slice of moonlight, newly red: she'd reapplied on her way back in. That sight struck him harder than the fear, clearing it away long enough for Ian to adjust his hold and work one coil out of the mess. It whipped at his wrist, trying to wrap around him instead; the movement filled his nostrils with the stench of rotting peat. He couldn't stop a grunt of disgust, but Max could have gotten the hell out of here. She could have walked away with nothing but nightmares, and instead she'd painted through the mud and leaves that smeared her face, and she'd come back for them. Ian ignored the clammy, stinking band around his wrist and fought another coil.

Behind him, leaves crunched and shifted in irregular bursts. Alicia raised one arm and stabbed it down, and Brigit cried out like she'd been punched. Everything in Ian wanted to turn back to her, but the roots underneath his fingers snapped up toward his face. He jerked away as they slipped from Max's throat, releasing his wrist at the same time.

Alicia heaved with both arms, and the whole black mess flew past him into the spinney and landed with a sound like a dozen snakes against a wall. She sat back on her haunches, breathing hard, her pocketknife open in her hand. Alicia looked down at the blade, which Ian could still feel in his side. "A gift from my wife. I never even used it before today." Her voice was raw, but the wonder was plain. Then Alicia looked at Max, and her face went still.

Heart pounding, Ian rolled her onto her back. Even in the dark, the bruising around her throat stood out as though someone had painted it on. Her red mouth was open slightly. So were her eyes. "Wait," Ian breathed. He leaned closer, holding his ear above her lips while searching for her jugular with two fingertips. The skin of her neck was warm, soft, and he hated to touch it, hated to think he might be hurting her by pressing down, but he had to find the pulse, he had to find a vein somewhere beneath those bruises.

"Ian." He ignored the detective. There was a pulse, would be one, just as soon as he could locate the right spot and apply the correct amount of pressure. "Ian," Alicia said again, and he became aware of warmth against his shoulder: her arm touching his. She was leaning over Max beside him, the knife gone somewhere, her voice horribly gentle.

Something clenched inside his chest. A fist around his lungs. And then rage, a flood of it, acidic enough that if any roots clung to his bones, it would melt them into steam. Ian was vaguely aware of himself sitting back. Cool night air replaced the lingering warmth of Max's skin. There was another noise in his ears. Not a buzz, more like cloth rasping, a hushed but building murmur.

"That's not enough," Brigit said, and her voice cut through the cloth with all the cold precision of a garrote. Ian and Alicia twisted on their knees.

She was on the ground too. Not thrashing anymore. Kneeling like them, knees planted for balance, one hand clenched at her side. The other, Brigit held beneath her muddy jaw. Something shone from that fist, dull but inorganic. For a second, Ian thought Alicia must have thrown the knife to her, that somehow she'd come out of her trance to catch it—but no, the blade was longer, and the wrong shape: an X-Acto knife with the razor pushed all the way out, its blackened tip pressed against the place where her throat met her jaw.

"You can't force me," Brigit went on. "Not even like that." Her eyes went to Ian, but she wasn't speaking to him. "Let them go or I'll end this right here."

INTERLUDE: 2003

Licia,

I don't know if I'll give this to you. It's been two months and four days since we broke up. Eight days and seven hours since I went crazy on you at the Ruritan. So I can't imagine walking up to you and handing you this note. I can't imagine you taking it. I can't imagine you not. I can't imagine you reading it and looking at me the way you do when you think I'm in a bad place and you don't know how to act.

I'm going to try something tonight. I'm out of ideas. If I tell the truth I'll go to some kind of psych ward, and maybe I will anyway. I said I hadn't slept for a couple days because of anxiety and stress and maybe they'll believe I just cracked for a night and drop the charges. Or maybe they won't. The cops said I'm old enough to go to jail for thirty days. My lawyer says there's no way that will happen. I don't really care about any of that, I'm just stalling. I don't think I'll give this to you after all. I just want to pretend I will so when I'm out there I can think about you and imagine you waiting for me to come back. I think that will help.

I don't know what it is, but I know it wants Brigit. I found out about some other kids who've died in the Dell, and they were all young. Most of them were girls (not all). It's hard to find out much, but I'm almost positive there was a boy in 1992 who knew the truth. There's an article about him you can read in the library. He tried to burn it too. He killed himself in jail. That won't be me.

I talked to it last week. It said it would bargain for her if I gave it something worthwhile. I don't know what would be worthwhile that isn't another kid, except for one thing. If I can trick it, I think I can get us both out of this. If Brigit does what I tell her and everything goes right, I think we'll be okay.

I know you won't read this. I know you think I've lost my shit and you feel more sorry for me than anything by now. But I am going to tell myself you think I'm a badass, and that when I get back, you'll be there.

Love,
E

31: BRIGIT

The knife smelled like blood. It couldn't possibly, not after all this time, but copper coated her tongue and filled the cracks between her teeth. Copper and the low, rich musk of the bog.

Once, that odor had bothered her. The way it traveled from her nose down the back of her throat like a living thing.

Maybe this was her own blood, though, and not Emma's, from the new slice in her palm. She'd flailed onto the open blade by accident as her body fought the thing inside her, cold steel biting through leaves and flesh and time, and *here*, here they were, here were all the splinters in her brain at fucking last. Freezing ground, pale trunks. The stillness, the cold dark night, no sound but metal on metal—that unnatural *SNICK*—

An X-Acto blade. Right where her sister had dropped it sixteen years ago.

Is it you? some desperate part of her asked as the knife fit to her palm. *Emma, are you here?*

Ian and Alicia watched from just outside the spinney. Their silhouettes wavered, fluttery around the edges. White threads wormed across her eyes in lazy, twining arcs. Black patches formed where they met and intersected, oscillating like static. But she didn't need to see the others to feel their panic radiating off them in thick, oppressive waves. She didn't need to see Max to understand that she was dead.

Inside Brigit, the birches moved. They were never still. Maybe they never had been. Maybe all the restlessness that had driven her from city to town to city, the queasy urge to run whenever she got too close to someone who might see what really lived inside her—maybe that had been the spinney all along. Dark things, growing. She could feel them now, how they twined around her ribs and held her organs in a fine and stubborn mesh. All those moments tasting earth beneath her tongue: a residual flavor, a memory that didn't belong to her.

Except that it did. She had chosen to carry it when she was eleven years old.

This knife belonged to Emma. The blade, now rusty and pitted with dried blood, once lived beneath her pillow. Brigit remembered sneaking into her sister's room while Emma was away and finding it there, retracted but still dangerous, a poisonous spider waiting to strike.

She thought of her mother—not for the first time since coming back to Ellis Creek, but the first time she allowed it purchase—and a moment that summer, when Emma got her license and started dating Alicia. Brigit knew about the X-Acto knife by then, and of course she'd seen Emma's legs in her swimsuit, shameless with marks. There had been a fight of some kind that day. She'd wanted to go to the reservoir, Emma wanted to be with her friends. It wasn't a screaming fight. Emma hadn't been a screamer, so neither had Brigit. Emma went cold when she was angry, and deliberate. Brigit had tried to keep up, hissing that at least she didn't hurt herself when things didn't go her way, but Emma just laughed with all her small, sharp teeth. That was the part that stuck with Brigit over the years, needling at her in various ways.

Now she recalled her mother at the kitchen table afterward, head in her hands, one of the last moments where they spoke the same language. *"Be patient with her, Idgy. Your sister loves you."*

And here, at last, the awful, damning truth: her sister had.

Cold wind blows in from the coast. It smells like snow and dead leaves. Emma stands in front of the Dell, her face floating pale above her white jacket. "How's this," she says over the rustle of branches. "Next week, I'll drive you to the movies after school."

This prize is good, but could be better. "You have to stay and watch with me. And buy the tickets."

Strands of fine blond hair drift around Emma's shoulders as she shakes her head at the Dollhouses that loom, silent and empty, behind Brigit. "Wow." Emma points one long finger at her and backs toward the trees. Her heel crunches down on a patch of bramble, a dozen tiny wood bones all snapping at once. "That's a hustle if I ever saw one."

"I play to win," Brigit says, high on her sister's smile, and Emma stops. Her face goes abruptly serious. Deep in Brigit's belly stirs a low and coiling fear.

"All right, baby sis," Emma says. "We have a deal." She holds out her hand. The name bracelet Brigit strung her in art class last year clacks against her wrist, plastic beads sliding on a blue nylon thread.

"Wait. You never said what you get if you win."

Emma frowns, just a little, and Brigit's stomach knots into a ball. "Clever," her sister says, except it doesn't sound like a compliment. "That used to work on you. If I win, you do what I say for twenty-four hours. No whining."

Emma hasn't dropped her hand. It hangs there, daring her not to agree. Brigit doesn't last fifteen seconds before smacking her bright red glove into Emma's black one. Emma rewards her with a grin, but it's not her normal smile. There's something living back there, behind her white teeth. Something bitter.

Then it disappears as Emma asks, "You want to be the wild child, Wild Child?"

Brigit yanks her hand free and steps back. "Don't call me a child."

This isn't a good night for the game. Emma isn't right. Sometimes when they play like this, no one else allowed, Brigit comes home crying. Sometimes Emma returns hours after Brigit. The worst is when she comes home long before and Brigit makes the lonely walk home to find Emma curled into the plush blue armchair in the living room with no mud on her face. Hi, sis, *Emma will say on those days.* Were you playing with someone else?

"I'll take that as a no," Emma says, bringing Brigit back to the Dell. "All right, then. I'll be Wild. But seeing as you're so very grown-up, maybe we skip the hiding part. Grown-ups don't hide, B. They take action. Timer starts…now!"

Brigit runs. Emma chases. Brigit is fast, but her sister is hungry. Brigit has no concept of how long it is before strong, narrow arms close around her waist and haul her off the ground in a squalling mess of limbs and fight, and it's over. But they do not go home.

"I won," Emma says, lacing their fingers so tightly their bones grind together at the knuckle. "Now you have to come with me."

"No!" Brigit tugs at her hand, angry and embarrassed that she's been caught, but it's too late. Her sister is already dragging her deeper into the Dell.

The canopy darkens further, branches tangling into one another, and the only sounds are their footsteps, the harsh and rhythmic panting of their breath. Brigit knows this path. She's never walked it with Emma, though. A branch snaps and Brigit cranes her neck to look behind them, and Emma stops so suddenly she slams against her back. They both go down hard. The fall breaks Emma's hold on her hand and Brigit scrambles backward on her butt, but Emma says, "Stop!" and all her muscles freeze.

Emma crouches where she fell. Pale ribbons of hair slip past her shoulders. They glow like the tree trunks at her back, to her left—all around them. The circle. Seven white trunks that break the darkness like elephant bones. Somehow, Emma has brought them to Brigit's secret spot.

Cold earth creeps through Brigit's jeans. Emma wraps her arm around Brigit's shoulders and pulls her tight against her side, and while part of Brigit wants to be angry, she leans into the embrace. "Do you know what a spinney is?" Emma's face is the color of mushroom caps. "I just learned it. A little grove of trees, just like this. Spinney. Isn't that a funny word?" Her grip on Brigit hurts. She isn't looking at her. "Hey!" Emma says harshly, which makes no sense because Brigit is quiet, Brigit is listening. "Come on. You know why I came here."

"I don't—" Brigit begins, but something low and fast scurries past their feet with a shuffle of dead leaves and Emma gasps, though Brigit does not. Brigit is used to this.

"Look," Emma whispers. "Look around."

Brigit doesn't need to look, but she remembers her promise. She does as she's told.

Seven pale trunks reaching for the sky, slender and skeletal, creaking gently in the breeze that lifted all the fine hairs on Brigit's arms beneath her jacket.

Flat, soft ground between the birches, covered in a dense layer of fallen leaves and moldering branches. A brackish smell, like pond water in the shallows.

Past the copse, darkness cut with blacker patches of oak trunks and the frothy pine trees that drag their needles on the ground like Victorian mourning gowns.

And Emma beside her, tense as a wild creature. Brigit can feel her sister's readiness thrumming in her teeth. Nothing else creeps through the trees now. Soon the silence becomes like Emma's arm around her shoulders, a physical weight that makes Brigit want to shrink, except the silence isn't just silence. Something in it screams at her not to tell Emma how well she knows this place—because fear is roped around

Emma's bones, pressed into Brigit through that violent grip. Her sister does not want to be here.

"Are you okay?" Brigit asks. Emma only squeezes tighter. Brigit looks up, and there are tears on Emma's cheeks like beads of glass. She stands at last, her feet crunching forest-skin to dust as she brushes off her jeans and reclaims Brigit's hand. It's more night now than it was when they first came into the woods. Clouds have moved across the moon so all that filters down is a kind of grayish haze.

"Do you want to go home?"

"Not just yet," Emma says, and her voice is grit and smoke and soft as ash. "I'm getting what I came for." She reaches into the pocket of her coat, not releasing Brigit's hand, and pulls out something small and oblong. "Do you remember our deal?"

"What is that? What are you doing?"

"What I say goes. Say you understand."

Emma presses her thumb against the sliding button on the object's side, and a loud SNICK cuts the air. A silver trapezoid emerges from the X-Acto handle, and Brigit is transfixed. Her answer will not come. The silence gapes before a new voice breaks it: Brigit's friend, rushing around them and through them and, finally, confirming it's okay to tell Emma the truth.

"She understands," it says, like loose bark in a breeze. "Why are you back?"

"I want to make a trade," Emma says, steel in her voice and in her hand. The X-Acto knife is stained at the edges. "For her."

Brigit winces as her sister tightens her grip on her hand. She can feel her bones grating. They've been out so long she isn't shivering anymore, and their mother has told her that cold is healthy. Cold is how you know you're alive.

The knife is a problem as well. The knife scares Brigit. It might scare her friend too.

"Emma," she whispers, "you're being rude." And then her sister does something she's never done before. She releases Brigit's fingers

and cuffs her on the back of the head. Brigit stumbles forward, shocked into silence. There isn't any pain, it's just the side of Emma's hand, but no one has ever struck her and she doesn't know how to react.

"What is it, anyway?" Emma asks loudly. "About her?" Outrage stirs beneath Brigit's confusion and fear, because Emma is talking as though she didn't just hit her, as if she isn't the one who dragged her out here in the first place. "Is it just that she's vulnerable? Easier to feed on? Or does she give you something the others didn't?"

"Asking means you wouldn't understand the answer."

There is laughter hiding underneath her friend's response. Brigit recognizes that strange humor, the slight disconnect between its words and its tone. It struggles, sometimes, to determine what's funny and what's not. It has asked her for help in the past.

Her sister clamps a hand on Brigit's shoulder and drags her back, X-Acto blade rising between them and the night. "You won't tell me, fine." Emma's fingers bite into her muscle. "I figured out enough on my own. You make deals with little kids who don't know any better. Now make one with me."

"What kind of deal?" Brigit's friend asks, and she knows this tone too: it's a calculating voice, the one it used when they first met. Mistrust is strong in the spinney. It even carries a scent, or maybe that's the mud.

"Leave Brigit alone. Whatever you're grooming her for—" and that word sticks in Brigit's mind because she doesn't understand what Emma means "—it stops now. Tonight."

You groom dogs. You groom horses. The birches seem to grasp what Brigit can't.

"And in exchange?"

"Me," Emma says, and suddenly Brigit is free. Emma holds out her left arm, palm up, and sets the X-Acto tip against her pale forearm. "This."

There is a breath outside time.

Brigit moves her mouth, but her lips stick together. A mottled leaf drifts past Emma's arm.

"You think that is valuable enough to buy my sacrifice?" Her friend no longer sounds calculating, or amused. It no longer sounds like any emotion Brigit can name. She wants to speak, to ask everyone to just calm down and take five, a peer mediation tactic she just learned in school, but Brigit can't look away from the knife and the skin beneath it.

"'Sacrifice,'" Emma scoffs. "I know how long you've been here. I know what kind of games you play. There will be other kids after her. I don't care about them. I care about now."

Brigit wants to ask her how she knows these things, or how she even knows her friend at all because it's never spoken of or to Emma as far as she's aware. At most it's led Brigit to the best and most secret of hiding spots while she and Emma play, or swirled the leaves around to mask her footsteps as she creeps from tree to tree in her bright coat and her red gloves, and even that's rare. It likes her best when she's alone.

Her friend doesn't seem to share Brigit's questions. It doesn't ask for details, or volunteer them. Instead it moves very close and whispers from the brush around their feet.

"Be precise with your terms."

In her defense, Emma had tried. She'd done a pretty good job of precision, actually, given what she thought she understood about the thing behind the birches.

I offer myself.

She'd known it wanted Brigit, and could be enticed that way.

I'll give you my lifeblood. On one condition. If she tries to do the same thing—if she tries to give herself back—you won't accept. You won't let her make that deal.

She'd also known how deep to cut to look convincing without going too far, assuming she got help quickly.

It was a brash and terrible plan. Of course it was. Emma was a precocious teenager who thought she was the only thing standing between her sister and a monster, and who believed the monster wanted what all fairy-tale monsters want. She'd been wrong about that. She'd also forgotten one key factor the monster had not, and that was Brigit herself. A frightened, angry kid.

One who might not try to make her own deal to save her protector. One who might not stay to help once Emma slit her wrists. One who might run instead, all the way out of the Dell, and leave her sister to drag herself toward safety tree by tree by tree. She'd made it pretty far before all that blood ran out.

The same blood Brigit smelled now.

"I'll do it," she said to the spinney. No wildness left in her voice, no coldness either. Only the hollow serenity of truth. "You're in here with me. You know I will. Then you'll have nothing. You'll be trapped all alone again, and this time you'll know for sure I'll never come back. Maybe you'll make another friend sometime in the next hundred years, but pickings are slim, aren't they? People do shy away from monsters, and the ones who don't keep dying on you. This can't be the end you had in mind."

"Bridge," Ian said. She could see him now. Kneeling just outside the birches, eyes wide and terrified. The sky had ripped itself clear of clouds and now his cheeks looked gutted.

Why? the branches whispered. Spindly fingers on her brain. *Why give up everything? Just for them?*

Brigit pressed Emma's knife a little harder, heart jouncing with fear and relief as the skin above her jugular began to give.

"Because I'm done hiding," she told it, and Ian, and Emma, and everyone else who might hear. "And I'm done running too. Make your choice."

A long, splintering pause. The faintest tickle as one drop of blood trailed toward her collarbones. The oldest, deepest ache inside her clawed into that tickle, some fevered voice that was altogether hers saying, *Do it, do it, cut your fucking throat.* Where her thumb braced against the triangular blade, she felt the dried bumps and calluses of Emma's arterial spray.

And then, slow and reluctant as spring, the spinney spoke again.

What are your terms?

32: IAN

He couldn't feel his fingers or his face. Not that it mattered. Not that anything mattered while Brigit held that blade against her throat. "Bridge," Ian said again, and Alicia clamped her hand on his shoulder.

The urge to shake her off and lunge across the spinney to knock that knife from Brigit's hand was almost too strong to fight. It rolled up from his stomach in a screaming wave but Brigit's eyes were open for the first time in what felt like a year, and her teeth were bared in her own mean snarl, and Ian held himself still. He could see Max's hand from the corner of his eye, pale fingers curling up toward the sky. He hadn't moved quickly enough to save her. Maybe he'd thrown away the chance to save Brigit.

"Ian, Alicia, and I walk out of here," Brigit said to nothing he could discern. "We don't salt your roots, and I don't cut you out of my head. You want me, you get me—I'll keep you close. I'll feed you as best I can. And that's all. As long as we're safe and well, you don't infect another person. You don't make a single deal."

Alicia's grip tightened. She was pinching a nerve that his camera had already left sore, but Ian didn't flinch. Brigit found his face, held his gaze for a moment, then closed her eyes. Her head tilted faintly to the right, listening to something he couldn't hear. A drop of blood crept out of sight beneath her collar. He tried to read her expression for the millionth time: the crease between her brows; faint pressure hollowing her cheeks. It could have been concentration, or worry, or neither. Without her hazel eyes on his, Ian couldn't force the pieces together. So he closed his as well.

"All right," Brigit said. "Done."

Ian opened his eyes to find her lowering the blackened X-Acto knife to her hip. Her thumb jerked. The blade shucked back into the hilt with a scrape of rust.

"Come on." Brigit stood and shoved the knife into her pocket. "Let's get the fuck out of the woods."

Nothing rose from the dark to grab her as she strode out of the spinney. The trees were silent save for a few clattering leaves that clung to their highest branches. Still he felt eyes on him, a low tingle of awareness at the back of his neck. The cut below his ribs throbbed relentlessly.

Brigit squatted beside Max. Licked her thumb and wiped a smudge of dirt from the bartender's lower lip in one sure, decisive movement. Then she raised her gaze to Alicia, who dipped her chin.

Foreboding sloshed in Ian's belly. He swallowed and it was a mistake. His own saliva tasted too thin, too sour, like bile. "We need to bring her out," he said. "She came back for us."

"We can't." Brigit wasn't looking at him.

"She came back for us," he said again. "She didn't have to do that. We can carry her."

"If we bring her out now," Alicia said, "no matter what we say, people will believe her death is connected to what happened to James and Gabrielle. They'll also believe you might be at fault. More people will come into the Dell. They'll find this place."

"I thought that was taken care of. No more deals." Ian looked from Alicia to Brigit, keeping his gaze high enough to avoid the woman on the ground. Sam would need to be told. He must have stayed with James. "She's dead either way. How are you going to explain the fact that she's never coming back?"

He thought he sounded rational enough despite the birdlike panic of his heartbeat, except Brigit was looking at him with an expression that made Ian want to rip his own eyes out. It wasn't pity, exactly, but it wasn't far off, and there was guilt there too. And regret. *It's still inside her,* he thought, reminding himself, and shuddered. Not least because he also wanted to grab her and pull her to him and never, ever let go.

"She thought Lacey killed herself because of Pete," Brigit said quietly. "She thought it was her fault Lacey stayed with him. And then Lacey did what she did *at* Max's bar."

"What? That's not..." And Ian stopped as understanding dawned.

"Ellis Creek is small," Alicia added. "People knew what was going on. When something bad happens here, the instinct isn't to look closer. They—" She grimaced. "*We* need to be forced. So. Max disappearing... It's a question with an obvious answer. If we make it easy to accept that answer, no one here will fight it."

Ian couldn't look at her or Brigit. He couldn't look at Max either. "She was making up for Lacey. She wanted to help." Sharp pain jabbed his fingernails and Ian realized he was digging his fingers into the earth. He'd gone through the undergrowth and reached the not-quite-frozen ground beneath. "It's not fair to leave her in the fucking dark."

"You wouldn't leave me." Brigit's voice sounded raw, but

there was a new, jagged note that he couldn't ignore. God, he wanted to. Now more than any other time in the world, he wanted to. But he looked up to find her lips seamed with blood, a dark splotch of it crusting the corner of her mouth. That hadn't been there before. He'd kicked her, Ian recalled now. Trying to get to Max. "Alicia wouldn't leave you," Brigit continued. "Max wouldn't leave us. I was going to leave everyone if it meant you would be okay, but you were right. I'm not the only one whose decisions matter."

That toxic anger rose in him again and Ian didn't know where it would land or how badly it would hurt, but she wasn't finished.

"Neither are you. Or Alicia. Or James or Gabrielle or Sam or Max or fucking Emma." She held his gaze like iron. "With James and Gabi alive and fine, there are ways to wrap this up for people who ask. There are answers that aren't great but make sense. People will remember one tragedy and one massive relief and it'll be clear in how they tell it, looking back, how it seemed like those two things might be connected but really they weren't. Really they just happened at the same time, to people who knew each other, because that is how it works in places like Ellis Creek. If we take Max out of this forest, all that falls apart. She turns into a body. We become responsible, all of us. And law aside, who the fuck knows what that does to this deal? I said 'safe and well,' and maybe I should have been more specific, but it's a little late for that. So unless you want to get arrested and risk undoing all of this, Max stays here."

She could have said it more gently, used words she knew might work on him more than they might on someone else. She could have moved into his space. But she didn't. The Brigit speaking to him now was not the Brigit of their scams or the evasive nights when he asked her something she didn't want to answer. She was someone sharper, uglier, and entirely real. And she was right.

It was a pain inside him, that knowledge. Huge and confusing at the back of his eyes and the place where his heart thumped behind his lungs. He didn't realize he was crying until the tears dripped off his face and landed coldly on the back of his wrist, the place where the root had grabbed him.

"So we are going to leave her," Brigit continued, "and we are going to remember every single thing about the way we did. We're going to write it down. We're going to talk about it. We're going to remember. Okay?" No one spoke. Brigit raised her voice slightly, and with more volume, Ian heard the way it shook. "I said, okay?"

"Okay," he said.

"Okay," Alicia agreed.

They stood. For a moment, all three of them hovered over Max. Maybe Alicia and Brigit were wondering what Ian was wondering: Should they bury her? At least drag some sticks or leaves over her face so she wouldn't be exposed? He didn't know what Max would want. Christ. He didn't know Max at all, not really, not the way you should know somebody you might or might not bury.

The movie posters in her office came back to him— science fiction classics, all brilliant colors and weird imagery. Other worlds. Other lives. It hurt, thinking that. And thinking it, Ian didn't want to put Max in the ground. Better to let her stay above the earth until she was made part of it by time and time alone.

Ian stepped around Max's legs to pick up his camera. As he passed back by Brigit, cold fingers brushed his wrist. In the space between breaths, he considered pulling away. Part of him wanted to. It would build a protective wall between him and what had happened to both of them in the spinney, this strange and formless grief. The things they had finally said.

Instead, Ian twisted his hand just a little. Brigit twitched her thumb. Then her palm was tight and close against his, and even as the muddy chill seeped from her skin to his, their hands began to warm. *All right*, Ian thought, to no one, as his heartbeat slowed. *All right.*

A bird chirped somewhere close. As another answered, Alicia fell in beside Brigit and the three of them started to walk. Ahead, the sky bloomed a soft and cautious gray.

33: BRIGIT

Three Weeks Later
Maine

"Getting anything?"

"Not yet." Brigit kept her expression open and searching as Ian filmed her profile. Snow pattered softly against the roof of the barn. Through the camera mic, it would sound like static. She moved toward the ladder that leaned up against the loft. Moonlight streamed through the pine slats of the walls, illuminating every bristle of hay in its path. Brigit reached out with her ungloved left hand, palm up so the light could play over the still-healing cut, then brushed the bare pads of her fingertips over a rung.

Anything in here? she thought as rough wood slid against her skin. Deep inside her something shifted, coiling tighter around itself, dozing and unperturbed by any rival presence in this barn. That was all right. There were other leads to check.

The man who owned the inn had promised them full access to the grounds, and to anyone they might want to interview (himself included, of course). He'd already wanted their services, but had been very impressed by the work they'd done in Virginia. Two young lives saved in a case with a tragic twist, but what a satisfying ending thanks to the shocking admission of domestic abuse caught on camera! Not everyone who reported on that story mentioned Brigit and Ian by name, but the inn owner knew which sources to trust. One post in particular, from a librarian who frequented the same message boards as he did, spoke highly of their dedication and sensitivity regarding matters that would not appear in mainstream reporting. The inn owner wouldn't be surprised if their show was syndicated soon, he said when they arrived, with just enough greed to it that Brigit had known then and there he would pay more than what they normally asked. He didn't care what they did or didn't find, as long as it went viral.

She and Ian had written up a new contract that night, printing it from the Fed-Ex store in town. The next few days were a blur of groundwork and research and the old back-and-forth: piecing together the background, storyboarding shots. Except it wasn't the old back-and-forth, not quite. Not with her new passenger along for the ride. Ian moved differently, too, with a faint, protective list toward his right.

Brigit slid her glove back on and started up the ladder, careful not to put too much weight on her healing palm. The loft would make for a good point of view shot, her first time putting their new tech to use. She'd worn the camera all day, but something turned in her gut at the thought of releasing an episode with Go-Pro footage. They'd bought it with the check Alicia gave them right before they left town. Nobody said it, but she knew they all thought it. Blood money.

Blood had bought other things too. Roots in her gut. Too early to tell how those seeds might grow.

"Hey," Ian called, and Brigit jolted. Her bad hand slipped. She caught herself with her elbow and swung around as if she'd meant the whole thing, some extremely minor stunt. Being cute for the viewers, which, it was true, were increasing steadily since the abridged Ellis Creek footage went live. Ian stood by the barn door, peering up at her with his Steadicam balanced neatly on one shoulder. "Where you going?"

"Up here." Brigit jerked her chin at the loft. "I've got the thing on, but don't lose me, okay?"

Ian stood in a pocket of shadow below the arching front door, but the slats allowed just enough light to catch his fleeting, crooked smile. "I don't plan to." Brigit waited a moment as he adjusted the lens, feeling the twist in her spine and the cold against her cheeks, until Ian realized she was still watching him and looked back up.

"Good," she said. Then Brigit turned her back on the camera and climbed.

★ ★ ★ ★ ★

ACKNOWLEDGMENTS

I put off writing my acknowledgments for as long as I could, and now that we're here, I keep changing my mind about where to begin and how to proceed...so, in one of many orders:

Thank you to my kick-ass agent, Erica Bauman, who not only fundamentally understood this book and what I'm about as an author—and managed to make me laugh through my outrageous nerves on that first phone call—but is the most thoughtful and savvy business partner I could ask for. To my editor, Leah Mol, whose enthusiasm for these characters rendered me literally speechless over Zoom (thanks for taking that in stride...), and whose keen, compassionate eye helped me deepen and hone this story without ever straying from its heart. I cannot believe I got this lucky. Thanks also to the rest of the team at MIRA, who took a chance on me and my weird, spooky book. In particular, props to managing editor Katie-Lynn Golakovich, copy editor Tracy Wilson-Burns, typesetter Bill Rowcliffe, and proofreaders Victoria Hulzinga and Joan Burkeitt—and to Sean Kapitain for designing such a bold and haunting cover.

But I wouldn't have gotten to say any of those thank-yous without the support, editorial guidance, and all-around cheerleading of my Pitch Wars mentors, Cole and Sequoia. They saw something in a very early version of *What Grows in the Dark* that spoke to them, for which I will be forever grateful. Pitch Wars also launched me into some pretty amazing online writer communities—here's to the Pitch Wars Class of 2020, and my incredibly kind and supportive Submission Slog Comrades.

And where would I be without the Cannibals, my Stonecoast crew of weirdos? This book began at Stonecoast—here I must shout out Elizabeth Hand, Robert Levy, Cara Hoffman, David Anthony Durham, and Nancy Holder, all of whom read early drafts in bits and pieces and provided invaluable feedback and encouragement—and in fact, I need to stop and specifically talk about Cara Hoffman for a second. The version she read did not include Ian's perspective, for one, and it was inert as hell. She told me as much and pushed me to dig into what felt raw and alive about these characters to me— their anxieties, their guilt, their ferocious desire to connect. Thanks for that, Cara. I needed the tough love. But back to the Cannibals: Jess Koch and Bess Brander, thank you for being my writerly rocks and partners in lite Irish crime, and I cannot wait to buy your books soon. Christopher Clark, Liz Moore, Delaney Saul, Amy Raina, Jacob Steponaitis— keeping a lookout for your words, too, and for the next opportunity to get snowed in for a writing session.

There are also so many people who've sat down to write with me or shown up for events, reached out to ask how it's going and celebrate the small milestones, been extremely patient when I cancel plans in order to work, and/or listened as I went through a publishing-induced meltdown. I started to list out names here, got stuck in the fear that I might forget someone, and decided to simply say: you know who you are, and I've probably (hopefully) reached out to you in real life already, and you are amazing. Thank you also to the people who've cared about me and my writing who are no longer in my life.

Thanks to my grandparents, Jackie and John Partin, to whom this book is dedicated. They clocked me as a writer when I was five years old and have encouraged me and my nonsense ever since. To my parents, Beth and Nick, who saw me barreling toward an English degree and said, "I mean, good luck!" then proceeded to support me and cheer for my creative aspirations at every turn, and to the rest of my family who've done the same.

Finally, thank you to my long-suffering rabbit, Russell, who kept me from spiraling on more than one occasion because he needed something like scritches or water or a raspberry; to Rusty the dog, who spent hours and hours of his life asleep on the couch beside me while I revised; and to Eric, who very publicly predicted that I would publish a novel before we even really knew each other, and has certainly regretted it at least once since then (just kidding). Here's hoping we get to do all this again—in which case, when I reach this part, I will try to learn from the greats and just list out several pages of names in alphabetical order…